THE SILENCE WAS HIDEOUS...

The bats were still there. They were a black mass on the body. But behind them stood a tall man, a pale, ghastly spectre, covered from head to foot in a black cloak.

He raised his white face to mine. His eyes were crimson and luminous. There was blood on his chin and his lips were curled back in a mocking smile.

I knew that face. It floated back from my childhood. It was now a hellish face, but its features were unmistakable; and I gazed out of terror and despair at the face of my father.

Indeed, it was Dracula!

BLOODRIGHT

Peter Tremayne

A DELL BOOK

Published by
Dell Publishing Co., Inc.
1 Dag Hammarskjold Plaza
New York, New York 10017

For Christos Pittas

First published in Great Britain as *Dracula Unborn* in 1977 simultaneously by Corgi Books and Bailey Brothers & Swinfen Ltd. First published in the United States of America in 1979 by the Walker Publishing Company, Inc.

Copyright © 1977 by Peter Tremayne
All rights reserved. No part of this book may be reproduced or transmitted in any form or by any means, electric or mechanical, including photocopying, recording, or by any information storage and retrieval system, without permission in writing from the Publisher.
For information address Walker and Company,
New York, New York.

Dell ® TM 681510, Dell Publishing Co., Inc.

ISBN: 0-440-10509-9

Reprinted by arrangement with Walker and Company
Printed in the United States of America
First Dell printing—June 1980

'. . . He must, indeed, have been that Voivode Dracula who won his name against the Turks, over the great river on the very frontier of Turkey-land. If it be so, then he was no common man; for in that time, and for centuries after, he was spoken of as the cleverest and the most cunning, as well as the bravest of the sons of the "land beyond the forest." That mighty brain and that iron resolution went with him to his grave, and are even now arrayed against us. The Draculas were, says Arminus, a great and noble race, though now and again were scions who were held by their coevals to have had dealings with the Evil One.'

'. . . As I learned from the researches of my friend Arminus of Buda-Pesth, he was in life a most wonderful man. Soldier, statesman and alchemist—which latter was the highest development of the science-knowledge of his time. He had a mighty brain, a learning beyond compare, and a heart that knew no fear and no remorse. He dared to attend the Scholomance, and there was no branch of knowledge of his time that he did not essay.'

—*Van Helsing*
From *Dracula* by Bram Stoker,
Constable, London, 1897

INTRODUCTION

I am not over fond of visiting street markets. I make this point merely in order to illustrate that it was quite by chance, and not by habit, that I found myself in Islington's Chapel Market, in North London, that hot June afternoon.

I was returning home, having spent a fruitless two hours with my publisher arguing about alterations to various passages he objected to in my latest book, when I decided to stop my car and look around the market. The reason for this step out of character was that the previous evening a friend, a little the worse for the major part of my last bottle of whisky, had collided with an old Victorian lamp bequeathed to me by my aunt. The glass had been smashed and it now occurred to me that perhaps a replacement might be found among the bric-a-brac of Chapel Market.

It was while I was searching among the stalls of the market that a large bundle of old papers caught my eyes, buried under a mound of musty Victorian morality books for children. When it comes to old papers, especially manuscripts, I am something of a squirrel, and so I pried the papers loose from the mound. They were tied with what had once been a red ribbon. A crumbling top sheet bore a sentence beautifully executed in copperplate script: *'Papers relating to the estate of the late John Seward, Medicinae Doctor.'* I skimmed briefly through the papers, which consisted of several unimportant letters, some bills and an obscure medical treatise. But it was the main part of the package, consisting of a manuscript dated 1898, that caused my throat to go dry with excitement.

I turned to the old woman in charge of the stall and asked, in a voice that must have been trembling, how much she wanted for the papers. She looked me up and down through narrowed eyes, cleared her throat, and said, 'One pound, mister.' She then thrust her jaw out aggressively, as if expecting me to challenge her, but I merely pressed two fifty-pence pieces into her hand and made for my car, gratefully clutching my prize.

All thoughts of my Victorian lamp were forgotten.

Once in the sanctuary of my home, I sat down to examine my acquisition. The manuscript was written in a fairly poor English, clearly by someone whose first language, judging by the sentence construction, was more severely Germanic. Indeed, the introductory note, attached to the manuscript, was signed by Professor Abraham Van Helsing of Amsterdam.

I caught my breath. I had always thought that Dr. John Seward and his colleague, Van Helsing, had been fictional characters, figments of the imagination of Bram Stoker, author of that classic tale of horror, *Dracula*, which was first published in 1897. In Stoker's book, Seward and Van Helsing were instrumental in tracking down the great vampire, Dracula, and eventually destroying him; now here I was holding a bundle of papers described as coming from the estate of the late John Seward, M.D. Not only that, but there was an entire manuscript written by Van Helsing himself. And such a manuscript!

I read the introductory note with growing excitement.

BLOODRIGHT

Explanatory note by Abraham Van Helsing, M.D., Ph.D., D.Litt., of Amsterdam

In the year 1898 I found myself travelling in Russia. I had gone there to listen to a great scientist, Konstantin Tsiolkovski, lecture on a new means of transportation, a method he called rocket reaction propulsion. While there I was privileged to be allowed research facilities in the Kirillov–Belozersky Monastery in northern Russia. It was thus, while looking for a tract by the monk Elfrosin on the infamous Dracula, who ruled Wallachia in the fifteenth century, that I discovered an ancient, crumbling manuscript dated A.D. 1480.

The manuscript, which was lengthy, was written in the Italian of the age, though the quality differed greatly by its poorness to Dante Alighieri's *La Divina Commedia*, which had its first printing at Foliguo a mere eight years before this date. I checked the catalogues of the Monastery Library but could find no reference to the manuscript. However, the reason why this poor Italian manuscript seized me with an almost unbearable excitement was its fading title:

'*A memoir of Mircea, son of Vlad Tepes, Prince of Wallachia, also known as Dracula, who was born on this earth in the year of Christ 1431, who died in 1476 but remained undead. God between us and all evil.*'

My hand trembled as I looked at the faded writing. Here was the very beginning, the Genesis if you like, of the undead monster that was to scourge the earth for centuries and whose end I had witnessed the sixth day of November in 1890.

That terrifying time when my English friends and I fought the powers of darkness was revealed to the public last year when a Dublin gentleman of Dr. Seward's acquaintance persuaded him to authorize that gentleman to edit some extracts from journals and papers relative to the affair. Only last year, 1897, did this volume appear under the title *Dracula*. Most people have dismissed it as a fantasy; others merely as a classic Gothic novel. Yet the English have a saying that truth is stranger than fiction . . .

That is why this manuscript excited me. I spent months, as the guest of the Abbot, painstakingly translating the manuscript, not into my native Dutch, which I warrant would have been easier for me, but into a passable English, the language by which Dracula has now become known to the world.

I am a man of science, of medicine, not of literature, and therefore I have neither edited nor altered the manuscript by so much as one iota. I have, however, taken liberties by the insertion of some footnotes whereby the reader may appreciate certain references rendered unclear by the passage of time. Thus do I give it to you to read and reflect upon.

I ask none to believe me. I do not wish to prove anything. All I ask you to do is consider the story of Mircea.

As Ambrosius Hüber of Nuremburg commented as early as 1499, it is 'a very cruel, frightening story about a wild, bloodthirsty man, Dracula the Voivode.'

This introductory note alone was enough to determine me to publish the work, leaving Van Helsing's manuscript almost as I found it, seeking only to correct his grammar and spelling, and deleting his more pedantic footnotes. Where I believe they aid the reader's understanding, I have left certain of the footnotes in.

I did make several attempts to verify points of the work, and in this I was helped by the Romanian Ministry of Tourism and the authorities of the U.S.S.R. For instance, Konstantin Tsiolkovski did start lecturing in Russia on the principles of rocket reaction propulsion in 1898. However, the library of the Kirillov–Belozersky Monastery no longer exists, though the manuscripts that were contained there when Van Helsing did his research are now housed in the Saltykov–Schredin Public Library in Leningrad under the title of the Kirillov–Belozersky Collection. Again, much as I tried, I could not find the fifteenth-century original manuscript from which Van Helsing made his translation, and was told that a large quantity of the papers went missing at the time of the October Revolution. I did, however, find the manuscript by the monk Elfrosin, referenced as MS. 11/1088, and written in 1488, which contained several tales on the evils of Dracula. And I did trace Ambrosius Hüber's pamphlet entitled *About the wild bloodthirsty berserker, Dracula Voevod*. Needless to say, the 'Dublin gentleman of Dr. Seward's acquaintance' was Bram Stoker, who was born Abraham Stoker in November 1847, at Clontarf, north of Dublin Bay.

Of the authenticity of the story that follows, I cannot make any statement. However, it is true that in 1431 there was born in present day Romania one called Vlad Tepes the Impaler, who was also called Dracula. This same Dracula (the name means 'The Devil' in Romanian) ruled in Wallachia in 1448, again in 1456–62, and briefly in 1476, at which time he died,

Peter Tremayne

horribly and as bloodily as he had lived. It is also true that Dracula had three sons—Vlad Tepelus, Mihail the Bad, who ruled Wallachia from 1508–10, and Mircea, of whom nothing is known save that Van Helsing claims he wrote the story which now follows.

Peter Tremayne

London, 1974

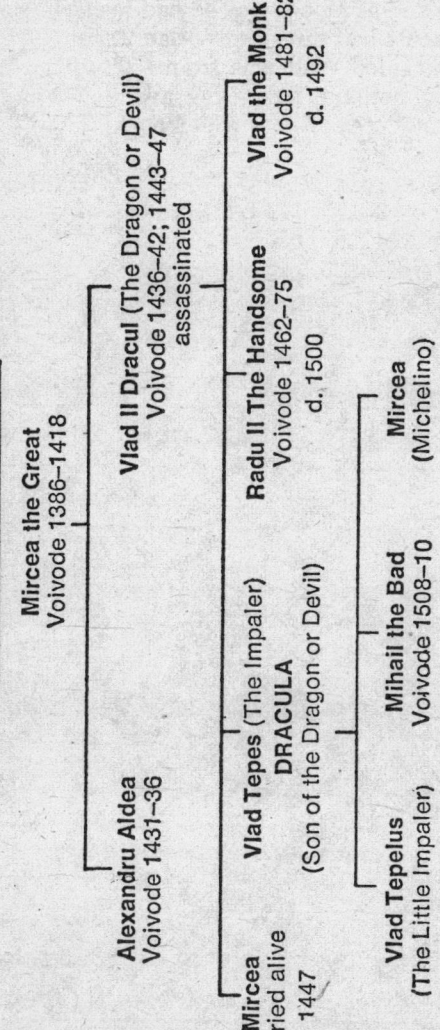

BLOODRIGHT

*A Memoir of Mircea
son of Vlad Tepes*

BOOK ONE

JOURNEY TO WALLACHIA

CHAPTER 1

Should I be called upon to apportion the blame to any singular incident which became the direct cause of the strange and terrifying adventure that I am about to narrate, I would say it lay directly with the indiscretion I committed with the Principessa Cinzia Lusignolo. Having decided to be scrupulously honest in my narrative, even though it now brings the blush of embarrassment to my cheeks, this fact I admit: it was my seduction of the fair princess and its consequences that drove me from the indolence of my life in Rome to the terrors of the principality of Wallachia and the evils of my ancestral home, Castle Dracula.

What made me embark on the amorous conquest of the princess, I know not; but I must hazard a guess that there were, perhaps, three reasons: boredom, infatuation and revenge—in that order.

My boredom was a prime cause. Indeed, a young man of twenty-two summers can still find himself bored, even in a city such as Rome.

Not long before my nineteenth birthday my mother, her name be blessed, had died and left me with an allowance with which I could indulge in a moderately comfortable way of life—a small palazzo near the Piazza Venezia and enough servants to care for my modest wants. Similarly, I had no need to worry about seeking a means of earning a livelihood, for the allowance, paid to me annually by a trustee, was enough to ensure I did not want for anything that reason dictated. Under such circumstances I became bored, as there seemed little that was not mine for the wanting. The only time I really enjoyed myself was the time spent in study at the University of Rome in the Palazzo della Sapienza, where I studied Latin, Greek, Hebrew and German, and was also tutored in art and mathematics. There, too, I dabbled in the sciences, learning a little of alchemy and natural philosophy.

But of what use was this learning to me? I was no scholar; nor had I any inclination to take to the cloisters where such learning would have stood me in good stead. I had recently decided that the martial arts were worth pursuing and therefore made the decision to travel to the Republic of Venice to join her armies. (Venice had been plunged into bitter warfare with the Turkish unbelievers of the Ottoman Empire since the year 1463 when the Venetians had refused to surrender to the Turks their trading colonies on the Aegean coasts.) Hardly had I made this resolve to become a soldier when I chanced to see the Princess Lusignolo—and all my resolutions crumbled.

I first saw her in the chapel of St. Constanza while attending mass, and even before I knew who she was, I was captivated by her beauty.

There, before me in the tiny church, was a figure of such elegance and loveliness that I moved nearer to examine more closely its owner. In spite of a black veil, her long fair hair spilled beneath it almost to her waist. I was transfixed by her beauty; and then her eyes, as she turned away from the altar rail, caught mine. At first I thought they were green, but even as I gazed unashamedly into them, they seemed to flash and change colour while, at the same time, her pale cheeks reddened. She stared fully into my own eyes for a few seconds before she passed out of the church. I watched her trim figure, which would have graced any visualization of Helen of Troy or Aphrodite herself, as she swept through the doors, leaving me trembling with a mixture of desires.

It is not directly part of my narrative to recount how I contrived to regularly attend mass at the chapel of St. Constanza nor how I finally drew into conversation with the princess, all of which took me nearly two weeks. Nor shall I recount how our friendship grew. However, what I must recount is that my amorous intent was strengthened when I learned that she was the wife of the Prince Guiliano Lusignolo, and that this strengthening came through a desire to revenge myself on the man.

I had known Lusignolo during my days at university when he was being tutored in the classics. I had known him and grown to hate him. What better revenge could I have than to show him to the people of Rome as a cuckold?*

Lusignolo was but a year or two older than me, well connected with particular contacts with the great anti-Medici families of the Pazzis and Salviatis who were now in the ascendent and, indeed, whom the Pope, Sixtus IV, favoured. The prince owned a large palazzo near the old Aurelian Wall behind the Piazza Navona and, I have heard it told, his estate was worth 200,000 *scudi*.

Lusignolo would always seek me out to make me the butt of his jokes, and he knew that inevitably my temper would rise to all his discourtesies. When a man loses his temper he always loses his argument, and

---

* Here, in Van Helsing's translation, he uses the phrase 'to put the horns on him', obviously translating literally the fifteenth-century *cornuto*.

countless times I was reduced to impotent rage at the cleverness of his tongue and wit. Sometimes he was merely content in calling me a foreigner; other times he called me 'the Slav'; but more often than not he would mockingly call me 'Slavato', playing on the word that means colourless or drab. He would mock at my title of baron, for when my mother brought me to Rome as a child we sought to hide our real identities and somehow Lusignolo had learnt of it.

(It was not true that I was a Slav, although I came from the Slavic provinces. In Rome I was styled the Barone Michelino, but my real name was Mircea and my ancestors were rulers of the principality of Wallachia, a small country bordered on its north and east by the great mountains of Transylvania and to the west and south by the river Danube. The country was named from the Volokh or Vlachs who are descendents of the ancient Romans who founded the province of Dacia just to the north of the country many years ago. So in my veins, I warrant, flowed purer Roman blood than in Lusignolo. Indeed, in honour of their ancestors, the Wallachians called themselves Romanians. Now, however, Wallachia had become a vassal state of the Turks, a wasted Ottoman province called Iflak, because of the curse of the house of Dracula which ruled it from the time of my illustrious ancestor Mircea the Great. Therefore, in my veins ran the noble blood of princes, though my mother had taught me never to speak of such things.)

Lusignolo was typical of his breed. A vain man who strutted like a turkey-cock down the *corso* in his fine clothes, appraising the young ladies as they took the air with their families. I have heard it said that he kept two mistresses. Ah, but he was a fine *Romano di Roma*. He was also a man determined to bribe and befriend his way into high office. It was even rumoured in certain quarters that this was the only reason he had married the Princess Cinzia, for she had been Cinzia della Rovere and related to Francesco della Rovere who now bore the august title of Pope Sixtus IV.

I confess that I know not exactly what her relationship was, for I heard it said that Sixtus was but a Franciscan of humble origin—though the noble bearing of the princess belied any notion that noble blood did not run in her veins. However, as all Rome noted, the Prince and Princess Lusignolo were wont to dine three or four times a year with the Pope.

Whatever the origin of the princess, I was now enamoured with her, both as an object of my own amorous desires and as a person through whom I might humiliate the hated Lusignolo.

I did not immediately press my amours upon the girl, but instead acted the sympathetic friend with her over her confessed loneliness, enforced while her husband played politics against the Medicis. Indeed, several times she hinted at the unhappiness of her life, and once she even admitted that the prince subscribed to the Italian proverb that a woman is like an egg: the more she is beaten the better she becomes.

Such confessions increased my ardour, not only because they placed emphasis upon the frailty of the princess's relationship with Lusignolo—and thus strengthened my own position—but because they also filled me with genuine pity and touched my cold calculations with the warmth of a genuine friendship. Nevertheless, I could not let myself forget the real purpose of my seductions, and thus the need for vengeance, rather than pure love, shadowed my every thought and deed.

While the prince was away, I twice attended dinner parties at the Palazzo Lusignolo. These affairs took place with at least thirty other guests and so I had to bide my time, watching and waiting until the princess would be alone and receptive to my advances. I knew that soon, like the grape, she would be ready to fall into my hands, and I did not want to miss any opportunity. The moment had to come—and come it did when the Palazzo Lusignolo was given over to a great party in honour of the prince's name day.

The Palazzo stands off the Piazza Navona. You make your way there through the squalid narrow streets of the *rioni*, the districts of the peasants which, thanks to the dictums of Pope Sixtus, are now being pulled down, the streets widened and paved, and new buildings put up to replace the original crumbling structures. The Palazzo itself lies close to the Aurelian Wall on the flat plain in a bend of the Tiber which was Campus Martius of classical times and where, until some twenty years ago, stood Domitian's great circus. (I tell you this to show you what a fine, great edifice the Prince Lusignolo lived in.) It is surrounded with great gardens, carefully laid out and tended by the best husbandmen that the prince could pay for.

There were some three hundred guests present that night, so it was without difficulty that I avoided being formally introduced to the prince and managed to stay in the background for much of the evening, chatting superficially on this and that to my fellow guests.

All the while I hovered near to the princess and her group, until, having played the dutiful wife, she drifted towards her own circle of friends, leaving the prince to rage against Lorenzo de' Medici and the brigands of Florence. Then, when I saw Lusignolo swallowed up by his faithful admirers, I moved towards the princess and bathed in her radiant smile of welcome.

As the wine flowed and the guests grew more interested in one another, we slipped away into the garden. It was such a night that Rome alone knows, the blue-black sky lit by a multitude of brilliant white pin-points and the great orb of the moon lighting the garden almost as if it were day. The air was warm and the fragrance of rosemary almost overpowering. We walked to the summer-house, entered, and sat for awhile looking at the sky without speaking. After a time I felt her hand find mine and grasp it lightly.

'Ah, Michelino, Michelino,' she murmured, her voice like a soft caress.

'You are unhappy, Cinzia?' I asked, bringing a tone of sympathy into my voice, hoping she would not hear the excitement that must surely be edging it.

'It is Guiliano,' she replied, holding my hand tighter, sitting up and letting fire flash in her eyes. 'He is a pig! He angers me more with each passing day.'

'Poor Cinzia,' I said, reaching forward and letting my fingers trace the delicate outline of her cheekbone. 'I wish I could do something. Believe me, I would do anything to make you happy.'

She reached one hand up and held mine and pressed it to her cheek. I felt her warmth at my fingertips.

'I am always happy with you, Michelino,' she whispered.

Indeed it was the time. No man can blame me for taking what was freely offered. And who could deny that as much as I took from her, she, in her turn, took from me?

Ah, but she was beautiful! I had known only two women before Cinzia, but their love-making had consisted of lying back passively, resigned and still, whereas Cinzia was a veritable goddess of the art. I unveiled her pale skin. Her body gleamed in the moonlight. The shadows fell around her face and I saw her moist lips and my need made me blind to all else. The memory is too vivid. My hand trembles as I write. She was lovely and she flowed all around me and our bodies were joined. How much she seemed to know! How much I was to learn! My desire was like a furnace and my lips found her throat and I felt the pain of sorrow and rage, of pure need and vengeance. The experience was confusing. I felt grief and triumph. I felt sorrow and the cold thrill of victory and my nerves were on fire. And yet she was insatiable. She would not let me go. There, in the silence of the moonlit summer-house, we struggled fiercely with one another, mouth to mouth, flesh to flesh, until we had satiated our desire and fell apart, gasping torturedly.

The moonlight fell upon the summer-house. The fragrance of rosemary was overpowering. We were silent and our shame and satisfaction had the stillness of dread. Finally, as if in a dream, she whispered my name.

'Ah, Michelino,' she whispered, 'what do we do this night?'

I had no words to offer in return and my silence condemned our love. Indeed, she, too, must have understood this truth, for she sighed and turned her head to look away.

No more need to be recounted of this matter beyond the fact that what had been freely offered had been gladly accepted and both of us now knew what we had wanted: she, escape from the brutalities of her husband; and myself, the cauterizing of old wounds.

Nevertheless, through the chill of this truth, our desire for one another was undiminished. After a while she began to tug me towards her, and I, beyond resistance, reached out for her.

'*Bastardo!*' a voice suddenly hissed.

I turned quickly, but not quickly enough. Prince Lusignolo had already launched himself at me, his two hands outstretched to grasp my throat, spittle forming around his mouth as he screamed abuse at me. The princess shrieked. The prince's body bowled me backwards. We rolled across the floor while the princess sprang back into a corner, her two hands in front of her mouth, her eyes wide with horror. How long the prince and I grappled on the floor I know not. It seemed an eternity, but it could only have occupied the passing of a few seconds. The princess shrieked again.

Voices were now raised in response to the prince's cries of rage. Soon all would be lost. With a sudden surge of strength I pulled Lusignolo's hands apart and threw him back across the floor of the summer-house. Then, leaving him no time to recover, I reached down and drew my sword, springing across the floor after him.

'*No!*'

The plaintive wail of the princess stayed my upraised hand. The prince lay before me, breathing heavily, watching the point of my sword with venom in his eyes.

'*Bastardo!*' he hissed again.

I brought down the pommel of the sword, smashing it against the side of Lusignolo's head. He groaned and collapsed unconscious to the floor.

The princess, white-faced, looked silently for a moment at the inert body of her husband; then she raised her wide eyes to mine.

'Mother of God!' she cried, distraught. 'He will kill you for this!'

We both quickly dressed and then I raised her hands to my lips. I kissed her wrists and then I kissed her palms, but before I could offer some reassurance, I heard the guests calling out.

'Lusignolo! Where are you? What is it?'

Cinzia gasped. There was fear in her eyes. 'Quick!' she said. 'You must leave here!' She pointed to the garden wall. I saw the moonlight washing over it. 'Over there!' she exclaimed. 'It's the only way! Hurry! *Hurry!*'

I nodded, bent my lips to hers once more, and then very quickly left the summer-house. I swung myself at the creepers, was over the wall in a trice, and within moments had put distance between myself and the despised Palazzo Lusignolo.

I walked home that night with a sense of achievement. In one act I had relieved my boredom, satisfied my lust and revenged myself on a worthless poltroon.

Yet little did I know that my trials were just beginning; that my flight from Lusignolo would lead me to an adventure whose dark culmination would haunt me for the rest of my days.

CHAPTER 2

On my return to my house my *maggiordomo* informed me that some hours before a messenger had delivered a letter for me. I did not send for it until I had bathed and taken a glass of wine, because I presumed that it was merely a package I had been expecting from Naples, a first copy of Masuccio's *Novelino* straight from the new printing press. The buying of the new printed books was becoming a great fad in Rome and I had decided to follow the example of my friends by purchasing the book of Masuccio's whose short stories were being printed in Naples that year.

When my *maggiordomo* brought me the letter, I found it was not the expected book but a thin piece of paper—a paper of rich texture such as only the brothers of holy orders use in their endeavours to record learning for posterity. On it hung a large wax seal with a symbol and motto—a seal that had haunted me from childhood and which had caused both my mother and me much suffering.

I recall that my heart began to quicken and my face flush with a surge of blood as I broke open that dread seal.

The seal was round, the size of a large coin. In the centre was a tree and on one side of the tree was the bust of a king. On the other side of the tree was the bust of a queen. The inscription that encircled it was

in an old Slavonic language, the language of my ancestors which my mother had forbade me to learn.*
The letter contained therein, addressed to me in my real name of Mircea, was written in an exceedingly good Latin hand.

> *Written at Castle Dracula, Poenari, on the second day of the month of January, in the year 1477.*
>
> *Brother—it is with much sadness in our hearts that we write this, our first letter to you, bearing the news that our father, Dracula, Prince of Wallachia, is dead. He died as he lived, spilling the blood of the enemies of our house. Brother Mircea, now that this is so and your mother no longer lives, and the quarrel they had lies in the tomb with them, we entreat you to return to Castle Dracula and your home.*
>
> *For sixteen long years you have been a stranger to your brothers. This castle, its estates and revenues, aye, even the principality of Wallachia itself, are your birthright to share with us. So return to your family and claim that inheritance.*
>
> *Prosper, brother Mircea, until we meet at Castle Dracula.*
>
> *Your loving brothers, Vlad and Mihail.*

I sat a long time meditating on this letter from the brothers I could scarce remember. What strange thoughts and half forgotten memories that message from Castle Dracula evoked!

It is now incumbent on me to recount a little of my

---

* I have seen this seal in the Monastery Library of St. Gall, Switzerland. The inscription is, indeed, in Old Slavonic, though not the language of Wallachia, and reads thus: 'Vlad the warlord, Prince of Wallachia, by God's grace.' Van Helsing.

history and that of my unfortunate country, Wallachia, in order that you may attest to the feelings that this communication aroused in me. Did I not believe in the vagaries of history I would merely record that I am a Dracula and that my father, who but lately ruled Wallachia, was the fifth prince to bear the name of Vlad and is known throughout Europe as Vlad Tepes, the Impaler. But knowing full well the caprices of history, where memories grow dim or events become distorted or confused, I feel I must explain more of the history of the family of Dracula.

The house of Dracula is an ancient one springing, it is said, from the loins of the great Genghis Khan. Their blood had run in the veins of the voivodes, or princes, of Wallachia since the prince Radu Negru crossed the Transylvania Alps to carve out the principality in 1290.

My father, Dracula, was born in the old German fortified town of Schassburg,* in the country of Transylvania because his father, my grandsire, Vlad II, was in exile there while his half brother, Alexandru Aldea, ruled Wallachia. It was in that year that Vlad II went to Nuremburg to be invested with the Order of the Dragon by the Holy Roman Emperor Sigismund. (It was this Order of the Dragon from which we now take our family name Dracula, for in the language of Wallachia the name *dracul* means dragon and thus Vlad II adopted as his escutcheon a dragon on a cross.) When he returned to Wallachia as ruler in 1436 he became known as Vlad Dracul—Vlad the Dragon. But the name had another meaning for the people. Dracul can also mean the devil. Therefore my father became known as Vlad Dracula: Vlad, the son

---

* Now Sighisoara. Van Helsing.

of the dragon or the son of the devil. It was the latter meaning that most people adopted.

History, as I have cause to know, can be boring, but I must ask you for patience while I explain the history of my father's life in order that a better understanding of my subsequent narrative can be achieved.

When my grandfather, Vlad Dracula, became ruler of Wallachia he showed great friendship to the Turks who, many years before, had expanded their empire north of the Danube and claimed Wallachia under their suzereinty. In return for tribute, however, the Ottomans allowed Wallachia to retain its own dynasty, territory and religion. And to ensure that Vlad Dracul paid his tribute, the Turks took my father, Vlad Dracula, and his young brother, Radu, as hostages. Old Vlad Dracul's enforced friendship for the Turks displeased the rulers of the neighbouring states, such as Transylvania and Moldavia, who were fighting to drive the Turks away. Iancu de Hunedoara, the voivode of Transylvania and Regent of Hungary, who had often been victorious in battle against the Turks, had Vlad Dracul and his eldest son Mircea assassinated and an anti-Turkish ruler, Vladislav, placed upon the Wallachian throne. As a consequence, the Turkish Sultan, Murad II, freed my father, Dracula, and, after defeating Vladislav at the battle of Kossovo Plains in 1448, placed him upon the throne.

Three months of puppet kingship were enough for my father who fled to Moldavia where he became a friend of the prince Stefan cel Mare. In 1451 the new Turkish Sultan, Muhammed II, unleashed the Ottoman hordes on the citadels of Christendom and his victorious armies entered Constantinople, defeating and killing the emperor Constantine XII Dragases. With this act of infamy the great Byzantine Empire fell into a dark age.

My father, Dracula, now swore to drive out the Turkish horde and he went to Transylvania where he threw himself on the mercy of Iancu de Hunedoara and his son Mathias Corvinus, King of Hungary, the assassins of his father and brother.

In the year 1456, supported by a Transylvanian army, Dracula entered Wallachia and defeated the Turkish puppet prince at Tirgsor and seized the throne. To the Wallachians he promised that nobody would be poor, that all would be rich in the country. He was stern, authoritarian and completely merciless to his enemies.

He was particularly merciless with the Saxon merchants who had settled in many parts of the country and who tried to organize an insurrection against him because he had destroyed their trading monopoly. At the same time he had to protect Wallachia from Turkish invasions. In May of the year 1458 my father, Dracula, defeated an army led by Mohammad Pasha and set free all the slaves taken by the Turks. But in the following year he had to suppress the plottings of the Saxons who tried to overthrow him and placed a puppet ruler called Dan upon the throne. In Christendom Dracula's reputation for his fight against the Turkish unbelievers was known far and wide. Yet another Turkish army, led by Hamza Beg of Nicopolis, was destroyed by him at Tirgo-viste, and Dracula even marched his victorious Wallachians south of the Danube, putting many Turks to the sword.

In April 1462, Sultan Mohammed began a great campaign to reconquer Wallachia. His aim was to replace Dracula with Dracula's younger brother Radu who had grown to manhood in Turkish captivity as a lover of all things Turkish.

At first my father, Dracula, was successful in defeating the vanguard of the great Turkish army which was commanded by the Grand Vizier Mohmud Pasha. Soon, however, he was forced to retreat northwards, and by November he had to cross into Transylvania thinking, once again, to seek aid from the King of Hungary, Mathias Corvinus. But Mathias had been listening to the stories of the Saxon merchants who held great economic power over his empire. On their advice, Mathias seized Dracula at Piatra Craiului and incarcerated him in the great prison of Vishegrad, which stands in the city of Pest, opposite the Hungarian capital of Buda, which cities straddle the Danube. There Dracula was imprisoned for twelve years.

It was early in that year of 1462, a few months before that great Turkish invasion, that my mother took me to Rome. I was then six years of age and would have been celebrating my seventh birthday, on 2nd March. My mother was Dracula's second wife. The first wife had borne him two sons, Vlad and Mihail, and had died bearing the second child. In 1454, while Dracula was living in Hungary, he married my mother who was of the Catholic religion. There was some conflict for, of course, Dracula subscribed to the Orthodox faith, but my mother ensured that my devotions were made to Rome.

Since his imprisonment by Mathias Corvinus the evil deeds of Dracula have become the subject for many a chronicler; indeed, they have been more than emphasized. It should now suffice to say that he was a cruel and merciless man and that his cruelty was aimed at my mother on more than one occasion.

Again, not trusting to the vagaries of history, I must record that my father, Dracula, was a most wild, profane and godless man (though in truth, saints have never flourished in these mountain lairs of Wallachia). It was said that in him, particularly, there dwelt a certain wanton and cruel humour which had made his name a by-word in Christendom. He was a man of dark passions. In his godlessness he often persecuted the church, and it is well documented that in Brasov he burnt the church of holy St. Bartholomew and stole its vestments and chalices. There are many stories that I have heard and, indeed, which have been recorded, concerning his evil humours.

It was said that once my father met a peasant who was wearing ill fitting and tattered clothes. Dracula inquired if the man was married. On receiving an affirmative answer, the voivode told the peasant: 'Your wife is assuredly of the kind who remains idle. How is it possible that she allows her husband to go forth in such rags? She is not worthy to live in my realm. She must perish.' The peasant begged for mercy for his wife. 'My Lord, I am satisfied with her,' said the poor man. 'You will be more satisfied with another since you are a decent and hard-working man,' answered Dracula. The wretched wife was brought before Dracula and executed on a stake and a new wife was given to the peasant.

There was another time when Dracula was witnessing the execution of his enemies and a certain boyar stood by him. This boyar could not stand the stench of the rotting corpses and politely suggested to Dracula that the royal party move away a little. 'Over there the air is pure,' explained the boyar, 'whereas here it is impure. The bad smell might affect your health.' Dracula asked: 'Does the stench worry you?' The boyar answered that it did and that it would be well to remove to a place which was not so detrimental to the health of the party. Then Dracula ordered his servants to bring a stake three times as long as those his enemies were being impaled upon. 'Make it up for me immediately in order that you impale the boyar so that he may no longer be able to smell the stench from below.'

Ambassadors and papal emissaries to Wallachia never tired of telling of the evils of the prince of that country; of how he would bury a man up to the navel and use him for target practice or how he had gypsies and others boiled alive. But always there were stories of his hideous executions by impaling people on great wooden stakes. Thus did Dracula become known as Vlad the Impaler.

Such was the husband of my mother.

As the years passed my mother grew lonely and desolate at Dracula's court and it was when she was in such an unhappy state of mind that a boyar of Dracula's ruling council of nobles sought her out and proclaimed his friendship and devotion for her. The man was Dracula's *stolnic*, or high steward. My mother and the boyar grew together in friendship and soon the friendship had deepened into something more.

Early in 1462 Dracula discovered the affair and sent for the unsuspecting boyar. He had the unfortunate man impaled on a high wooden stake before the walls of Castle Dracula, but before he could send for my mother, she seized me and fled from the castle.

I dimly recall the flight, days and nights, sometimes on foot, sometimes on horseback, and sometimes perched precariously in a boat on some river. How long the journey lasted I do not know, but eventually we arrived at the eternal city of Rome where, with the aid of relatives, we received sufficient funds to live in a degree of comfort. My mother changed our names and tried to expunge the very memory of Wallachia and Dracula from her thoughts and mine.

(It was later discovered that a servant woman, who remained loyal to my mother on the night of our flight, tried to prevent Dracula's soldiers from entering my mother's chambers to delay the discovery of our escape. She was promptly thrown to her death from the battlements of the castle* and my mother was officially proclaimed dead throughout Wallachia.)

I have already recounted how I grew to a somewhat indolent manhood while my father was languishing in the dungeons of King Mathias Corvinus of Hungary. How did I discover all this when my mother refused to talk of it to me?

Well, but a few years ago, when I studied at the great university at the Palazzo della Sapienza, I chanced to meet and become friends with an aged scholar named Antonio Bonfini, who was chronicler to King Mathias himself and knew Dracula and, indeed, wrote a history of the unhappy ruler of Wallachia. I did not acquaint the kindly old man of my relationship to the voivode, but I pressed him eagerly for stories of my father. Thus did I learn what knowledge I have of my true country and family.

Moreover, I learned that about the year 1467 my father's friend, Stefan cel Mare, had become voivode of Moldavia and allied himself with King Mathias. He took it upon himself to plead for my father's release and his pleas were reinforced by the fact that Dracula had secretly married King Mathias's sister, a Catholic, and had given up the Orthodox religion. This marriage greatly displeased Mathias, but forced him to release Dracula in 1475.

No sooner was Dracula released than he joined with Stefan cel Mare and Stefan Bathory of Transylvania to invade Wallachia and throw out the Turkish puppet

---

* It is historically reported, erroneously it would seem, that Dracula's wife was thrown or leapt to her death from the castle tower. Van Helsing.

Basarab cel Batrin, who had succeeded Dracula's brother, Radu the Handsome. In November 1476, Dracula was reinstated as ruler of Wallachia; but in December came the news of his mysterious death and the return of Basarab cel Batrin . . .

Thus is my history concluded, and I assure you that your patience in following this chronicle will be rewarded by a better understanding of subsequent events.

Now, after such a history, I had received a letter from my half-brother, inviting me to return to Wallachia, to Castle Dracula, in order to claim an inheritance.

Inheritance of what? I wondered as I sat sipping wine and musing before the fire. Basarab was ruler now, albeit on behalf of the Sultan Mohammed, and I would hazard that Wallachia was still torn by bloody war and conflict. Yet had I not a few weeks ago thought to join the Venetian army to fight the Ottoman unbelievers? War and conflict would certainly offer me adventure enough. And yet . . . yet there were in my mind grave doubts and misgivings concerning the advisability of an expedition to the lands that the Turks held sway over.

I know not how long I sat there musing before the clatter of a carriage in the courtyard of my palazzo heralded the arrival of the news which would take the decision from my hands.

Ah, how unkind fate can sometimes be, and in what disguises she comes!

CHAPTER
3

A few seconds passed before my *maggiordomo* ushered the Princess Cinzia Lusignolo into the room and then discreetly withdrew. I rose from my chair as she impulsively moved across the room and grasped both my hands in hers. She stood for a moment, gathering her breath, the candlelight flickering over her face and shadowing her eyes. There was a pink hue to her cheeks and her bosom rose and fell rapidly under the flimsy material of a light satin cloak.

'It's Giuliano,' she breathed at last. 'He's going to kill you.'

'I would not have expected less,' I said.

She shook her fair hair and began to say something, but I interrupted her by calling back my *maggiordomo*. When he arrived, I removed the princess's cloak, handed it to him, and ordered wine to be brought for the both of us.

'You don't understand, Michelino,' Cinzia said as I seated her on a couch before the blazing hearth. 'Giuliano is arranging a duel.'

'I had expected as much,' I said casually, 'but your prince is not renowned for his swordsmanship whereas I have practised the art with many masters. I would have no fear on my account, Cinzia, nor indeed for your prince. I can handle Lusignolo with ease and

I will but prick him a few times in the arm to satisfy honour and there will be an end to it.'

'You still do not understand,' Cinzia said, shaking her head almost impatiently. 'Do you really think that Giuliano will risk his position by fighting you himself?'

I was frankly puzzled. 'What then?' I asked as my *maggiordomo* returned with the wine.

She did not immediately reply. The *maggiordomo* poured two glasses of wine, left the bottle on the tray, bowed low and respectfully withdrew. Cinzia waited in silence until the door had closed behind him.

'What then?' I repeated.

She reached forward and placed a hand on mine. The flames from the blazing fire illuminated her face and I felt her beating warmth at my fingertips. The room wrapped us in silence.

'I overheard Giuliano speaking to someone in his room,' she said finally. 'He was asking them to seek you out and challenge you to a duel in such a way that you would be forced to fight. I waited and I heard the man agree. Only then did I recognize the voice . . . It was Francesco Gullo!'

Had the princess said it was the Holy Father himself I could not have been more shocked. Francesco Gullo di Panerea was the most feared *spadaccino* in all Rome. His sword had accounted for the deaths of forty-seven men in duels, and who knows how many others had fallen before him. Yes, I was shocked. Against Francesco Gullo I would be but a babe in swaddling clothes.

'You must leave Rome,' Cinzia said, articulating my very thoughts. 'You must leave Rome before he discovers you.'

I took a long swallow at the rough red wine and nodded slowly.

'You must go somewhere far away from here until the affair . . . is forgotten.'

She blushed and lowered her eyes. Perhaps she was waiting for me to avow eternal memory of her, but more important thoughts tumbled through my mind. Indeed, at that moment I was as far removed from her as the sky is from the earth; I could scarcely recall the exciting lures of her body, the radiance of her smile, the beating of her heart against mine. Rather, as with all young men who have a large love for life, I was thinking only of my immediate survival. It shames me now to record this, but such was the truth, and the truth is itself like the plague. My love was a lie. My passion was selfish. And she, with that fierce light in her eyes, was obviously aware of this.

'Yes,' I said. 'I must leave.'

I called my *maggiordomo* and ordered him to have my best horse saddled and to pack a *bisaccia de ella*, a large saddle bag, with the items I would need for a long journey, as well as a money belt containing all the available money in the palazzo.

'The baron is going to be away long?' the old man inquired.

'That depends,' I said. 'However, in my absence you will see to the running of the palazzo and the wellbeing of the servants. I shall send you instructions from time to time until I return.'

'Very good, baron,' the old man said imperturbably, as if my hurried departure were in no way an unusual occurrence. He then bowed and left.

I went immediately to my bed chamber where I changed into clothing more suitable for travelling and where I also picked up my sword—a sword I prized highly as it had been the property of a Roman soldier-priest who had carried it on a crusade after it had been blessed by the Pope. In my turmoil I had all but forgotten the princess, and it was not until she had entered my bed chamber that I actually remembered her presence.

She closed the door behind her and leant against it and looked at me with smiling eyes. She was breathing heavily. Her smooth breasts rose and fell. I was aware of her attractions, and of the desire that grew within me, and I realized at that moment that she, too, had won, that in giving herself to me she had humiliated Lusignolo and released herself from her fears. In her eyes there was wickedness.

'Sir,' she said mockingly, 'you have surely forgotten your duties as a host.'

I stood uncertainly in the middle of the room, my feet still bare, my shirt open at the front, the belt on my breeches hanging loose.

'Madam,' I said, 'you have me at a disadvantage.'

'Then, sir,' she said, advancing smilingly upon me, 'we must balance up the affair, if you would demean yourself to act as ladies' maid.'

And so for the second time within hours, but this time with more honesty, the princess and I satiated our desires with one another to such a degree that all thoughts of a hasty departure were driven from my mind and I had to sleep to recover from the exhaustion of my endeavors. Indeed, it was some hours later that I left the princess asleep in my bed and the sun, peering over the distant hills, found me outside the walls of the city and urging my horse southward down the ancient Via Praenestina, travelling towards an adventure more hideous than my wildest imaginings.

CHAPTER 4

At that time I had no clear idea where I was making for and it was not until noon, when I stopped to eat, that I contemplated my future prospects. It was then that I pulled from my purse the letter from Castle Dracula and it was then that my destination was settled.

The details of my journey are perhaps of little importance. I rode across the mountains to Barletta and there sold my horse and took a ship across the Adriatic to the city state of Dubrovnik.

The city, with its narrow coastal belt, had become an independent republic when the rest of Bosnia fell to the Turks fourteen years ago. I was extremely curious on my arrival in the city, but things were not as strange as I thought they would be, this being due, in part, to the close contacts Dubrovnik has with Italy and the fact that Dubrovnik passed from a Byzantine dependency in 1205 to Venetian suzereinty and then became part of Bosnia in 1358. It is a part Latin city, but with a strong Slavic background. Its institutions are all autonomous and its merchants own extensive inland areas. The Turks interfere little with them, for they also own a world wide maritime trade. They are also the principal entrepreneurs in mining, in which mines a great number of Saxons, known locally as *Sasi*, work.

When I left Dubrovnik I noticed almost immediately a drop in temperature. The short cool summer was ending and I was now entering a region where one could look forward to long cold winters with heavy snowfalls which I gather are typical of the area. The countryside through which I rode was greatly wooded; indeed, the whole country seemed covered with forest which was inhabited by a diverse number of animals such as brown bears, wild boar, wolves, foxes, martens, chamoise, red deer, rose deer, eagles and falcons. The wild life was rich and abundant and I was amazed at its profusion.

From Dubrovnik I travelled northwards to the cathedral city of Mileseva. From time to time I saw detachments of Turkish soldiers, but they did not stop me or bother me in any way. However, several times I was stopped by large bands of armed Bosnians who still determine to drive the Turks from their country. Hearing my Italian accent, these good people were convinced I was a Venetian and therefore an ally in their battle against the Ottomans. I prayed that no Turk would stop me and reach a similar conclusion.

From Mileseva I went on to Studenica and up to Kalenic; by this way I came to the city of Vidin on the western side of the Danube, on the borders of Wallachia itself.

Vidin is a medium sized independent city which was once a great trading centre of the Bulgars within sight of the towering Transylvania Alps to the north and the Balkans in the south. The area has recently become known as the Balkans, as more people adopt Turkish usage; for Balkan is, I believe, the Turkish word for 'mountain chains.' These southern Balkan mountains gleam white in the sun due to the rocky limestone ridges they form, but by the standards of the Italian Alps, they are not really high.

BLOODRIGHT

The city of Vidin is dominated by a great Orthodox monastery which has a claim to great piety since three centuries ago Prince Ajtony, whose domains then stretched from the Korcos to the Danube and from Tisza to Transylvania, was baptized a Christian in the city. Soon after, the Byzantine Empress Basil II captured the city. Vidin was strong, however, and in 1281 it broke away from the empire and constituted a semi-independent principality until 1322 when the Serbs conquered its Bulgar inhabitants.

I found that in spite of the political eclipse of the area and the domination everywhere of the Turks, the native nobility seemed to regard themselves as the spiritual heirs to Byzantium. They still maintain an essential identity with what they consider their religious, artistic and cultural centre: Constantinople.

The capture of Constantinople by the Turks in 1453 has indeed changed the face of this country. Byzantium is now no more, and I believe that history will not prove me a liar when I say that there is little hope of it being raised again. Those who supported the Orthodox Church believed that it was not possible for Christians to have a church and not to have an empire, but I believe they will now resolve their differences with the universal church of Rome.

Some years ago the Orthodox Metropolitan of Moscow declared that the fall of Constantinople was God's punishment for the Greek betrayal of the Orthodox Church at the Council of Florence, when a union between the Greek Orthodox and Catholic churches was tentatively agreed upon. That union, which I understand was never popular with the citizens of Byzantium, collapsed with Constantinople and the remnants of the Greek Church reverted to Orthodoxy. Vidin, it would seem, has now become a stronghold of that Orthodoxy.

The inn at Vidin where I stayed was run by a Saxon named Herder and therefore my knowledge of German, albeit a knowledge of the Minnesänger of the court romances and heroic epics, was enough to let me understand and converse in the rolling southern Germanic tongue. The horse I had bought in Dubrovnik was exhausted and before continuing my journey across the Danube into Wallachia I asked Herr Herder whether he could purchase a fresh mount for me. At this he shrugged his broad shoulders.

'It would be useless to even inquire, young Herr,' he said. 'Across the river in Wallachia there still rages a war, even though most of the country is desolate and devastated. Three times in the past month, soldiers, either Turks or Christian, have raided Vidin and carried off practically all the horses. And, young Herr, that is the least of the things they have taken from us . . .'

His voice trailed off and he was silent awhile. Then, finally, he drew himself up and spat into the fire.

'Ah,' he said despairingly, 'Turk or Christian, both are equally as bad. No, young Herr, there are no fresh horses in Vidin.'

There would be nothing for it, I realized, but to delay my journey for several days in order that my mount might recover. This did not please me. At this stage of my journey I detested the idea of delay and the knowledge that I would have to quell the feeling of excitement that was growing in me as I neared the land of my birth.

CHAPTER 5

'Excuse me.' A short, plumpish man pushed himself from a chair, in which he had been relishing the inn's fire, and bowed ungracefully in my direction. 'The Freiherr will permit? My name is Strasser, Erhard Strasser. I am a merchant on my way to Tirgoviste and I would be delighted for the Freiherr to join me on the journey, if he so wishes.'

Tirgoviste is the capital of Wallachia and was on my route to Castle Dracula at Poenari. The Saxon merchant looked ill-bred and boring, but it would be even more boring to delay my journey for several days.

'I would be delighted to join you, Herr Strasser,' I said.

Herr Strasser nearly glowed with obvious pleasure. (I was to learn later that he had sought my company for two reasons: firstly, he was a snob and to travel with a Freiherr, as the Saxon title for baron is, marked him as a man of distinction and influence; secondly, undisciplined hordes of Turks and Christians still roamed Wallachia and a young man was a welcome addition to the cortege of a fat merchant.) Herr Strasser then called for wine and, out of civility, I drank with him.

Early the next morning, having breakfasted very simply with ale and a loaf of Herr Herder's freshly baked bread and some local cheese, Herr Strasser and I set off for the ferry which would take us across the Danube, which the natives called Dunarea.

Herr Strasser's coach was drawn by four sturdy cobs, but in spite of the size and the large numbers of boxes that Herr Strasser was carrying, the Saxon merchant was attended only by one dour-faced Wallachian called Amza whose only language was Wallachian, called the Valakian.

Although, as I was to find later, my faulty German was enough to get me by in most areas of the country, it was a sadness that my mother had steadfastly refused to let me learn the language of my ancestors. From Amza I did, however, learn certain words that caught my attention because of their similarity to the tongue of the Valakian genesis, Latin, and this engaged me for some part of the journey.

The ferry across the Danube from Vidin was merely a large raft upon which only our four horses could go first and then our uncoupled coach. The whole business of our crossing was a lengthy process and took upwards of an hour and a half. The leader of the four swarthy men who piloted the raft from bank to bank asked Herr Strasser for the payment of two *aspi*, which I understood to be a Wallachian coin of silver. There was some argument, for Herr Strasser had none of the local coinage, but he eventually managed to pay them in German *groschen*. I resolved that at the next town I would endeavour to change a few of my gold *ducats* and *perpers* for *aspi*.

Safely on the Wallachian side of the Danube, the raftmen helped Amza to recouple the horses to our coach and we were soon heading at a brisk trot towards the distant mountains.

It was near noon, a bright, hot day with scarce a cloud in the sky. I had cause to praise the new concepts of fashionable clothes that were becoming popular in the Italian city states. Fashion was now abandoning the ostentatious effects of fantasy and abstraction in clothing and moving towards simplicity in everything. My doublet fell to the natural waist, open at the front to show the soft gathers of a low necked shirt; my sleeves were fastened loosely on the arms, allowing easy movement; while the shirt puffed through the openings. Had I been wearing the old style pleated Gothic gowns, so much the fashion a mere five years ago, I would have stifled in the heat.

It was while I meditated on such things, bathing in the fierce golden rays of the sun, that a sudden cold shiver shook me. At once the sky began to turn dark.

Amza brought the coach to an abrupt halt, the horses rearing and whinnying in confusion. Herr Strasser cursed and peered out of the door.

'What is it, Amza?' he demanded in German before repeating the question in the man's native tongue.

I was now leaning out of the coach to observe this peculiar phenomenon. Amza pointed a shaking finger at the sky. I peered up. It was very strange indeed. There was still not a cloud to be seen in the sky and yet, slowly, ominously, the sun was being blotted out from our vision as if a black cloud was being drawn across it. Inexorably, bit by bit, the sun was disappearing, shadows swooped across the land, and the countryside was growing cold and dark. I felt myself shiver.

Suddenly, Amza leapt from the coach and fell to his knees, one hand describing the sign of the cross and the other fingering a rosary. All the while he mumbled in his own language, of which I regret I knew not a word. *One* word, however, I heard him repeat several times with vehemence: *varcolac*.

Then, as I looked, I saw a very strange occurrence.

The blackness suddenly left the sun and the dark shadows began to grow bright, growing into a large white light that moved gracefully towards the heavens and descended towards the horizon, forming a glowing curve that spread out and disappeared until, within minutes, the day sky was normal once more.

Herr Strasser and I glanced at each other. Amza was still on his knees, staring fearfully at the sky, still fingering his rosary and mumbling. Herr Strasser slowly shook his head.

'There is no cause for alarm, young Freiherr,' he said to me. 'This is a natural phenomenon that I have witnessed once before, some years ago. When was it now? Five years ago. It is called a comet, Freiherr. The one I saw was in 1472, but more brilliant than this one. It had a vast tail. Do not fear, Freiherr, it is only a comet.'

I found myself bristling at the condescension in his voice. I had heard of such things from the learned astrologers of Rome. In fact, I recall being told of a great comet appearing in 1456 which astrologers said would cause a grievous pestilence or some great calamity. It appeared at a time when Christian was fighting Turk and it is said the common saying was 'God save us from the Devil, the Turk and the Comet.' Irreverent men say that Pope Calixtus III even excommunicated it, though when Christian beat Turk it was felt that it had portended good. This was, however, the first time I had seen one, and although I was bristling at Herr Strasser's condescension, I still felt a little uneasy and glanced up at the sky. The comet had gone.

It was Amza who seemed most affected by the partial eclipse made when the comet passed across the face of the sun, so I asked Herr Strasser what the man was mumbling about.

'Ah, young Freiherr,' smiled the merchant, 'it is only a local superstition.'

'What does the word *varcolac* mean?' I insisted.

At the very mention of the word, Amza feverishly crossed himself and began jabbering once more at an alarming rate. The merchant merely shrugged cynically.

'These superstitions, Freiherr, are as common as berries in a pail. A *varcolac* is a vampire who climbs to the heavens to eat the sun or moon. Amza is merely saying that the sun was being eaten by the *varcolac*. The Wallachians are a very superstitious people, Freiherr.'

Amza was now quieter, watching intently as Herr Strasser was speaking, nodding each time the word *varcolac* was uttered.

Suddenly, as I stood looking upwards towards the sun, half expecting some new phenomenon to materialize, Amza screamed.

It was a strange sound from an old man. He had been kneeling before us, his face turned towards us as we conversed, and Herr Strasser and I now stared at him in bewilderment as, trembling, he rose to his feet, his outstretched hand pointing directly at me, his mouth working frantically but in seeming incoherence until, eventually, I caught the word '*Moroii!*' which he repeated several times as in a dream.

Herr Strasser moved forward and spoke sharply to the man, but Amza ignored him and continued to stare wild-eyed at me, all the while repeating the word *moroii* as if it were some magical incantation. Herr Strasser then raised his walking cane and struck the man violently across the shoulders, shouting at him as he did so, but still the man did not flinch. At this point I moved forward and laid a hand on Herr Strasser's arm to prevent him inflicting further injury on the poor man, but as I did so Amza gasped, threw one arm over his eyes, and backed away like one scalded by hot water.

'*Moroii!*' he hissed, and then, quite clearly: 'Moroii! Moroii! *Dracula!*'

I froze where I stood. I could not believe what I had heard. I was amazed that the old man had suddenly discovered my identity, and even more amazed by the depth of his fear of me.

'Amza!' I said.

On the instant he turned and, before Herr Strasser or I could recover from our surprise, darted away through the trees and was gone, leaving silence behind him. Herr Strasser finally spoke.

'Well, Freiherr,' he said, pulling himself together, 'it is twelve miles to the next village where we may obtain the services of another coachman who, mercifully, may not be as mad as this one. Alas, I have little knowledge of coaches.'

'Do not worry, Herr Strasser,' I replied, trying to act as natural as possible, 'I believe I can drive such a coach as this.'

He seemed relieved and even offered to ride postillion with me. We climbed aboard the coach and set off, moving at a brisk pace, and I soon learnt the knack of controlling the horses. Again the sun was bright and the day very hot as if nothing unusual had happened . . . yet I still felt uneasy.

'It is incredible, Freiherr,' Herr Strasser eventually said. 'Amza has been a good servant to me five years now. What could be the cause of his sudden dementia? He has long been a superstitious old fool and often claimed he had the gift of second sight.'

'What was that word he kept repeating?'

'*Moroii* is a word I do not understand, though I do

know the other word he spoke—Dracula. However, *why* he spoke it, I know not.'

'Dracula?' I asked innocently.

'Yes, Freiherr.' Herr Strasser turned and spat. 'Dracula! God's curse on the name.'

'Why so?'

'Dracula is the name of the voivodes of Wallachia, but when one speaks the name they refer only to Vlad Tepes who was a scourge to all God fearing men—a *wütrich*, a blood-thirsty monster. The evil that this Dracula did before his own death, which occurred last December, would cause the strongest stomach to turn.'

'You intrigue me, Herr Strasser,' I said.

'Do I? Well, let me tell you. My home town was called Berkendorf in Wuetzerland. Should you go there you will not find it, though you may find a few houses settled by Wallachian swine called Benesti. But it is not Berkendorf. Vlad Dracula had that town burnt to the ground; the men, women and children that inhabited it he had burnt or impaled. And why? Because they were Saxons.'

'But isn't it the truth,' I said, 'that Dracula was popular with the Wallachians and simply punished the Saxons because they attempted to overthrow him and place Vlad Dan on the throne?'

'The truth?' Herr Strasser said with obvious agitation. 'The truth is that the man was a bloodthirsty tyrant. True we Saxons supported Vladislav Dan in an attempt to overthrow a bloodthirsty maniac. And Dracula tracked him down . . . tracked him down to Fagaras Castle where the Saxons tried to defend him. Alas, Dracula's hordes overwhelmed the Saxons and Dracula ordered Vladislav Dan to dig his own grave and read his own funeral service before he cut off his head. Then began Dracula's persecution of all the Saxons in Wallachia.'

Herr Strasser reached a hand into his pocket and brought forth a collection of printed pamphlets which he waved in my face.

'Do you read German? No? Well, over the years I have collected many pamphlets concerning the evils of this Dracula. It is the intention of us Saxons that Europe will know of his misdeeds. Good Saxon merchants in several cities have paid for the printing of these pamphlets by which Dracula's evil deeds have become known.'

Herr Strasser was obviously very agitated. He put the pamphlets back into his pocket and gazed straight ahead with his eyes narrowed.

'Let me tell you more,' he said. 'Once he killed almost the entire merchant population of Wuetzerland. Then there was the great Wallachian boyar Albu who sided with our plight: Dracula executed him and his entire family. I recall meeting a man from Hermannstadt, or Sibiu as it is now called, and he said that the dead were impaled on great wooden stakes like a huge forest.

'This Dracula persecuted us because of his blood lust, and rightly was he called Vlad Tepes, the Impaler.

'Once, I recall, the Turkish Sultan sent some ambassadors to speak with Dracula. They entered the castle and, as is the custom of the Turk, paid tribute to him by not removing their *fezzes*. Dracula asked them why they did not show him respect by removing their hats. They answered that it was the custom of their country to show respect by not removing their *fezzes*. Dracula said: "I, too, would like to strengthen your customs so that you may adhere to them more rigidly." He then ordered some nails and a hammer to be brought, and he hammered each *fez* to the head of its owner. He then told them: "Go tell the Sultan that he may be accustomed to suffer such indignity, but I am not so accustomed. Let him not send ambassadors to me exporting his customs." Ach, such a terrible, uncivilized man!'

I believe that Herr Strasser, like most of the Saxon merchants who had lost their property and position during Dracula's rule, was more motivated by personal feelings than by abhorrence at the blood shed by Dracula—for such blood letting was not so uncommon in those parts—and I should have carried on the discussion, reminding Herr Strasser of the blood thirst of his forefathers, the Teutonic Knights, had not the little merchant suddenly caught his breath.

'Ach, mein Gott!' he exclaimed.

He had raised a hand to shade his eyes and now he pointed to a distant mountain slope. Following his pointing finger I saw a band of horsemen galloping towards the roadway to intercept us.

'Bandits?' I asked the white-faced Saxon.

'Worse,' he whispered. 'Turks!'

I looked upon the approaching horsemen with a shiver of apprehension. At last, after the tales of horror that were circulating in the cities of Christendom, I was to come face to face with the hordes of the unbelievers, those who fought the knights of civilization for countless generations. Tales of Turkish murder, atrocity and rape made the alleged evils of the house of Dracula pale into insignificance.

'Will they harm us?' I asked, observing that the horsemen were drawing close and thinking it might be better to attempt to flee.

Herr Strasser shrugged resignedly.

'It depends, Freiherr. Firstly, they might think you are a Venetian with whom they are at war. Secondly, these may not be regular troops of the Sultan but *akinois*—irregulars who are little more than bandits, in which case they will murder anyone if they have a mind to do so.' He shuddered. 'I have seen too many victims of the Turks. 'Twould be best if we humoured them.'

The body of the horsemen had formed a scythe-like formation, the extreme points of the scythe extending and closing around to encircle us in a well disciplined manoeuvre.

Herr Strasser nudged me. 'God be praised, Freiherr,' he said. 'These are not irregulars, but *sipahis*, the cavalry of *der Grösse Heide*.' I was puzzled by his reference to "the great pagan," but I learnt later that most of the German speakers were wont to call the Sultan Mohammed by this title.

The leader of the cavalry had brought his men to a halt in a circle around our coach. He was a young man with heavy black moustaches, dressed in a most outlandish and colourful costume with a back and breast armour plate. He wore a conical helmet with a single spike surmounting it and carried loosely across his saddle bow a short, curved sword with a thick blade which was broadest at the point end, the like of which I had not seen before. Apparently, as I was later told, this sword is a favourite weapon of the Turk who took it from the Persians. It is called a scimitar.*

The Turkish officer studied us in silence for a moment, as well as in obvious puzzlement, since it is not often that those of the higher orders are seen driving their own coaches. The officer then addressed us in his own language. We shook our heads and the officer

---

* The word used in the original manuscript was the Italian *scimitarra* from which philologists claim the English word derives and that it is but a corruption of the Persian *shamsir*. Van Helsing.

frowned in annoyance before speaking hesitantly in German.

'I am Murad Bey,' he said, 'servant of the great Sultan Mohammed, blessings on his name. What seek you in Iflak?'

I noted immediately that the officer had used the Turkish name for Wallachia. Meanwhile, Herr Strasser bowed awkwardly.

'Great Bey, I am but a humble merchant of Bosnia seeking to trade my wares in Tirgoviste.'

'And you?' The officer eyed me sharply.

'I am Barone Michelino,' I said. 'A citizen of Rome, travelling also to Tirgoviste in the course of my studies.'

'An Italian, eh? A Venetian spy, perhaps?'

'No, great Bey,' I said, adopting the attitude of Herr Strasser. 'I am merely travelling to Tirgoviste to study the local art of wine making, for in Italy I own great vineyards and I would now like to study how the Wallachians prepare their wines. You see, great Bey, I am trying to perfect a blend of wine . . .'

The lies came easily to my tongue, though it is true that I have more than a passing interest in the juices of the grape. The Turk regarded me with an expression of disgust.

'Pah!' he said. 'Merchants! A man such as you should wear a sword for more than ornamentation. You have the heart of a woman.'

I could see that the Turk addressed me thus, with what for a Moslem is a great insult, in the hope that I would take offence, his reasoning being that if I were a fighting man I could not let such a slight go unanswered. However, instead of rising to his bait, I merely smiled and said:

'Better to live as a coward than to die a brave man.'

The Turk spat in disgust.

'You are typical of the Italians I have fought with,' he said. 'You all like life too much.'

'Why not?' I replied. 'Is death then so enjoyable?'

He opened his mouth to speak, but before he could do so one of his men urged his horse forward, shouting and waving his scimitar towards the distant hills. We all followed his gaze and saw a large force of horsemen galloping towards us. The Turkish officer bit his lips and turned back to us.

'You may thank the Prophet Mohammed for your safety,' he said. 'We must go. Remember, though, you have no Kazikly Bey to protect you now, and, by the beard of the Prophet, we shall return.'

With that he urged his mount forward and sped away up the valley, followed by his men.

'What did he mean by Kazikly Bey?' I inquired of Strasser.

'It means Impaler—the name the Turks gave to Dracula.'

A few moments later we were surrounded by the second group of horsemen. They wore very simple costume. For the most part they were merely mounted peasants with heavy sheepskin coats belted over rough shirts and trousers. Few wore anything on their feet, but most carried a round metal target shield and a long sword. Their leader was better dressed and equipped. He was a good looking individual with a stern face but smiling eyes. He exchanged a rapid conversation with Herr Strasser in the Wallachian tongue and then he and his men wheeled their mounts in pursuit of the Turks.

'Who were they?' I asked.

'They call themselves soldiers of the new Voivode Basarab cel Tinara, Basarab the Younger, who is now acclaimed ruler of Wallachia. It seems that last week Stefan cel Mare entered Wallachia again with an army to avenge the death of Dracula, who was his friend. Laiota Basarab, the Turkish puppet, and his supporters were driven from Tirgoviste. Stefan then installed Basarab the Younger as the new ruler and the Turks have since been driven south of the Danube.'

'It is good news for the Wallachians.'

Herr Strasser sighed.

'The Wallachians are sheep. Always they are doomed for conquest. One day the Turks, the next the Hungarians. What matters, providing we merchants can continue to buy and sell out goods in peace? One conquerer is as good as another, and one man's money smells just the same as another's.'

He paused and looked up at the sky. I followed his gaze and saw that the darkness was gathering. Black clouds were forming, shadows crept across the land, and the air had turned grey and quite cold. I know not the reason, but this land now seemed strange and somehow threatening. Again I felt uneasy.

'We must hurry, Freiherr,' Herr Strasser said. 'It will soon be dark and it is some way to the next village. There are wolves and bears and other scavengers abroad at night who present danger to travellers such as we. Let us push on quickly."

We whipped the horses forward through the gathering dusk.

CHAPTER 6

It was evening when we arrived at the next village, though to call it a village was to do it an honour it little deserved. Even though they were shrouded in darkness I could only make out half a dozen rude cottages clustered around a squat building which was a church, one of those ugly edifices erected by the Teutonic Knights crusaders some two centuries ago. To one side of the village lay a sprawling cluster of buildings which Herr Strasser, having passed that way before, informed me was a tolerably good inn.

The first strange thing I noticed was that no light lit our passage into the courtyard, and despite the clatter of our coach as I reined in the horses before the inn doors, no shutter was removed, no door was thrown open in welcome, and no ostler came running out to relieve me of my burden. The inn remained dark, silent and inhospitable.

Herr Strasser gave an impatient sigh and aired his oft stated view that all Wallachians were lazy swine. He dismounted, not without difficulty as his portly frame was much given to being pampered through the perplexities of life by a host of servants. He strode to the inn door and gave three resounding knocks on the heavy timbers with the head of his cane. There was a faint stirring from within, and then silence again. I climbed down from the coach and joined Herr Strasser at the door.

'A strange welcome from an inn,' I observed.

'Ah,' Herr Strasser shrugged, 'you will find, Freiherr, that these lazy Wallachian swine are totally inefficient. You have to stir them into activity.'

And suiting the action to the word, he again beat a resounding tattoo upon the door.

A voice called out in Wallachian. It was obviously a query and Herr Strasser replied curtly. There was some mumbling behind the door and I heard the sound of heavy bolts being drawn. Only then did I notice that there were garlands of flowers hanging around the door.

Although I am not a scholar on botanical matters, I observed that the garlands were made up from thistles and garlic. I drew Herr Strasser's attention to the flowers, suggesting they were a strange choice for decoration and wondering what they symbolized, thinking that perhaps it was some religious festival that had taken place that day, for the flowers were fresh. However, Herr Strasser shook his head and mumbled something about the peculiar superstitions of the peasants.

The door finally swung inwards to where a tall, elderly man stood. He wore simple homespun clothes and a soft leather apron, the universal uniform of the innkeeper. His shirt was open and I could not help but observe the delicately wrought metal crucifix that hung on a chain around his neck.

The man scrutinized us for what seemed a longer time than usual, then he bowed, a half bow, deferential but not subservient. He spoke in German, having correctly guessed Herr Strasser to be of that nationality and having observed me to be a foreigner and therefore probably without knowledge of his native tongue. He waved his hand towards the brightly lit room behind him.

'You are welcome, mein Herren. You will forgive my delay in opening to welcome you.'

Herr Strasser snorted and strode in, ignoring the man. For my part, I informed him that our coach stood outside and we had no coachman to uncouple it or put the animals in the stables. The innkeeper looked puzzled for a moment and then politely said he would attend to the matter. He bid me enter while he called another man to take charge of the horses.

I now noticed that there were several people in the inn, which was brightly lit. I also noticed that everywhere, but especially around the doors and windows, hung the strange garlands of flowers.

I could only conclude from this that we had interrupted some village festivities which were not normally opened to strangers. Certainly the atmosphere was quiet and strained, and it seemed to me that the dozen or so villagers had removed themselves to the farthest side of the room from us. Only one or two cast glances in our direction, and these from the corners of their eyes.

But there were no complaints about the efficiency with which the innkeeper's wife moved forward with a smile of greeting and helped us off with our travelling cloaks; nor with the prompt insistence of her husband that we have a glass of local mulled wine to warm us. It was exceedingly rich red wine into which he inserted a red hot poker and which tasted pleasantly warm and sweet. In fact, I suggested another glass, but the innkeeper smilingly warned me of its unusual potency, adding that it would be unwise to drink further on an empty stomach. It was advice well taken and much in keeping with Herr Strasser's philosophy.

'We keep but simple fare here, mein Herren,' the innkeeper told us, 'but you are welcome to all we have.'

A table was soon cleared for us in a corner of the large room, a little to the side of the large, roaring fire. A pretty, buxom girl called Maria, whom I later learnt was the daughter of the house, laid the platters and pewter mugs before us. I suppose she was the first Wallachian maiden I had encountered, well built with indications that as middle age approached so would stoutness; but now, in maidenhood, her buxomness quickened the blood. Her skin was bronze, a healthy outdoor quality, never seen among the grand ladies of Rome, and her cheeks had natural dashes of red upon them. Her hair was almost the colour of pitch, and her eyes were a bright, penetrating blue. She smiled often as she bustled about the table, showing her ivory-white, perfect teeth.

The food was in fact far from simple, for to start with we had a sort of caviar which, I was told, was made from aubergines, with onions, cloves, tomatoes and garlic, and which was served to us on lettuce leaves. (It appeared to be a speciality of the area.) This was followed by a roast of pork, and to finish came sweet cakes. All of this was washed down with a white wine, for it is in white wine that the Wallachian usually excells.

As we thus enjoyed the 'simple' fare offered by our hosts, a man detached himself from the villagers and joined us at our table. No word was spoken, but our host placed a glass of wine before him and acted with a marked respect. Certainly the man could be differentiated from the rest of the company by the superior quality of his clothes, an authoritative bearing and a full black patriarchal beard.

As he reached forward to raise his glass, his coat

parted and I noticed a crucifix hung around his neck; it was similar in design to that worn by our host, but there the comparison ended. I caught only a fleeting glimpse, but observed the gold encrusted with flashing stones and superb workmanship. Was this man a boyar? It was only when the man smiled and inclined his head that I realized, with a blush, that my curiosity had caused me to stare at him for several moments.

'God be with you, mein Herren,' he said in German. 'You have come far?'

Herr Strasser nodded, his jowls not ceasing their rhythmic motion around a large portion of meat.

'I have come from Rome,' I replied. 'And this gentleman has kindly given me the use of his carriage as I could not find a fresh mount in Vidin. There are no horses here that I could purchase?'

The bearded man shook his head.

'The Turks have taken everything,' he said. 'There was little enough before, but now . . .'

He held out his hands, palms upwards, and shrugged.

'Where are you travelling to?'

'I am going to Tirgoviste,' I replied.

'What does a man of Rome seek there?'

'You ask a lot of questions of a stranger,' I said, frowning a little.

'We are a curious people,' he replied with a half smile. 'We peasant folk have questioning natures and strangers are a rarity among us—especially on nights such as this.'

The emphasis did not escape me, though the meaning behind it did, and his smile was as enigmatic as his words.

'You, a *peasant*?' I said in disbelief.

'You know who I am?' he asked.

'No,' I said. 'But not a peasant. Perhaps you are a

boyar, as I understand the nobles of this country are called.'

'No, my young Herr, not a boyar.'

Suddenly, from somewhere outside the inn, came a distant howl. I have often heard wolves howl among the hills near Frascati, outside Rome, and such a howl was it that I heard now. In all truth it made my blood turn cold.

Immediately I became aware of a change in the people in the room. It was as if they had all been turned to stone, for they now seemed fixed in the one position, with only their eyes, wide open and fearful, darting here and there yet not seeing. Then a coldness descended.

Again came the long, drawn-out howl. Someone gasped. Several people crossed themselves. And the innkeeper, Grigore, hastened to the side of the bearded man.

'It must be time, Father,' he said.

I stared. 'Father?' The question sprang involuntarily to my lips.

The bearded man rose and laid a hand on Grigore's shoulder, ignoring me.

'The people are ready?' he asked. 'They know what to do?'

'Yes, Father.'

'Then it is time. Have them light the torches. We will start this end of the village and work our way towards the church.'

Grigore turned and motioned the villagers to follow him. I noticed that each one wore a crucifix of some description outside his shirt. Grigore, standing by the door, handed each man a bundle of twigs and, as each man went out through the door into the night, these were lit to make torches. Grigore himself then did the same.

The bearded man had watched in silence, but now he also strode towards the door. Halfway there he paused, turned back, and looked directly at me.

'Young Herr,' he said, 'this can be a strange country to a foreigner. My advice is that you conduct your business in Wallachia as quickly as possible and that you return to your homeland with all speed. As for now, I should go and rest . . . follow the wise example of your companion.'

He smiled and pointed. Herr Strasser had fallen forward into the empty platters of his feast and was snoring the gentle sleep of the replete.

'He has had a good night,' I said.

There was no reply. When I turned back to face the priest, he was gone. The door of the inn was shut . . . and only the blood-chilling howl of the wolf could be heard in the stillness of the night.

I glanced across the room to see Grigore's wife bustling about, clearing away the remnants of the meal. At first she appeared to be quite normal, but then I noticed that she occasionally betrayed her true nervousness by darting wide eyes towards the shuttered windows of the door, festooned in their strange garlands of flowers. I also noticed that the room still seemed cold and, more important, that I myself felt uneasy.

'Where are the men gone?' I asked the woman.

Immediately her nervousness increased.

'Hunting, mein Herr,' she whispered.

'Hunting?'

'Ja, mein Herr.'

'But what is there to hunt at this hour?'

Her eyes blinked and grew larger. She glanced at me and away from me. Then she turned perceptibly pale and made the sign of the cross.

'Come, my dear Frau,' I said. 'You said they had gone hunting. For *what*?'

Her lips opened and closed, and she looked at me desperately, and then, with the greatest reluctance, she hissed a familiar word:

'*Moroii!*'

I started. It was the same word that Amza, the coachman, had coupled with Dracula before rushing away into the trees. My uneasiness increased.

'*Moroii?*' I asked. 'What is *moroii?*'

'No, mein Herr, no . . .'

She was now trembling like a leaf in a storm and, dropping a plate in fright, she suddenly turned and rushed from the room.

'Who are *you* to ask what is *moroii?*'

I became aware of a blast of icy air and turned to see Grigore standing in the doorway. His face was troubled and his eyes watched me in suspicion. He shut the door behind him and then walked slowly into the room, stopping before me.

'What do *you* know of *moroii?*' he said.

I confess I was a little perplexed. Grigore seemed the same, and yet different. He was uncommonly aggressive, but behind the aggression lurked a fear that I could not define. My confusion was deepening.

'I merely asked your wife what men hunted at this time of night,' I said. 'She answered *moroii* and I wondered what manner of beast was it that kept such strange nocturnal hours.'

At this Grigore sat down heavily on a bench and buried his face in his hands. Anguished sobs wracked his body for a minute or two before he managed to regain his senses.

'No beast, mein Herr! No beast! Ah, gruss Gott, if only it was a mere beast that it could be killed as such. But no! It is a curse, mein Herr, an evil, a stealer of souls, a stealer of young children . . . my own daughter, only twelve years old, mein Herr, *my own daughter!*'

Suddenly the eerie howl of the wolf pierced the air, and Grigore, his eyes blazing with fury and hate, immediately sprang to his feet.

'There it is!' he exclaimed. 'The *moroii!* Ah, but we shall be more than a match for it this night!'

He started for the door, but I held him back, saying, 'Grigore, do you mean you are wolf hunting? A wolf that has attacked children in the village?'

He laughed almost hysterically.

'No, mein Herr. We hunt a beast that dons many disguises . . . a man who has sold his soul to *der Teufel*—the Prince of Evil himself!'

Then before I could properly digest these words, he had turned and rushed out into the night.

For a moment, as the full implication of his words sank into my brain, I was rooted to the spot. I have heard several times of the superstitions that were prevalent among the village communities (and Herr Strasser had not been loath to remind me of them), but this was my first encounter with a superstition that could lead to tragedy. I have heard of some rural communities outside Rome in which old women with deformities of the body are singled out, denounced as practitioners of the black arts, and stoned to death; in some countries they are even burnt. Now, here in this Wallachian village, it would seem that some poor demented man was being singled out for death because of the fear and superstition of the villagers.

If he had, indeed, been responsible for the death of the innkeeper's daughter, then he should be given a hearing. I shook myself angrily. It was my duty as a civilized man to put a stop to such primitive practices.

It was my duty to save the poor man who was about to suffer at their hands.

I pulled on my travelling cloak and leaving Herr Strasser snoring by the fire, went out into the damp chill of the night. A ground mist had risen from the warmth of the day and the entire village was shrouded in it. Here and there I caught a glimpse of a burning torch, held aloft by a villager as he hunted the poor unfortunate. From time to time I heard a shouting, but it seemed that the man they called a *moroii*—which I now presumed to mean murderer—had thus far eluded the searchers.

Pulling my cloak tightly around me, I walked towards the squat, square-towered church. On reflection I know not what drew me there, for the line of searching villagers was still composed of mere shadows at the very far end of the village.

The church was surrounded by a small cluster of graves, and this graveyard was separated from the rest of the village by a low stone wall with wrought iron gates. It was untypical of the kind of church that is usually associated with the Orthodox religion and this was due, as I have previously stated, to its builders being crusaders on their way to the wars in the Holy Land.

The mist swirled about me. I heard faint cries in the distance. The gates swung open on their rusty hinges with a protesting squeal as I pushed through them and made my way up the path. As I stumbled on a stone, half blind in the darkness, I cursed myself for not bringing a torch to light my way.

It seems strange to me now that I should have thought that the poor unfortunate would hide out in such a place as that, yet at the time my footsteps were slow and sure, as if some uncanny power was guiding me to where I would find him.

I did not even go into the church itself; instead, my steps swung away alongside the church walls, towards a patch of land where nothing reposed save a large mound of earth. It was very dark here. There was not the slightest sound. I peered intently through the mist and discerned a freshly dug grave. I suddenly felt fearful.

'Dracula!'

I started. It was a sigh, a breath, long drawn out. A shiver ran down my spine and my head jerked around. First I saw nothing. Then the darkness seemed to shift. I heard a soft, mocking laugh and I shivered and the night fell about me.

'Who's there?' I demanded.

'Dracula!'

'Why do you call me Dracula?'

Again the scornful laugh. It seemed to echo all around me, to fill me and dissolve me, and I found myself shuddering with dread.

'Who is it?' I cried out.

Again I heard the laughter, sneering, macabre, echoing all around me and dissolving me and leaving me helpless. I tried to step backwards. I was unable to move. The mist hung in chill, white tatters about me and the darkness seemed total.

'Dracula!'

Suddenly a figure loomed forward. It was tall and dark as the night. I held my breath. It seemed almost to glide towards me. I wanted to reach for my sword, but I couldn't make a move and the fear only heightened my paralysis. I was shivering and sweating. I could feel my heart pounding. The figure moved through the gloom and then stopped a few feet from where I stood. There was the sound of harsh breathing.

Then, through the darkness and the swirling clouds

of mist, I saw two piercing eyes, hellish, hypnotic, luring me, blazing like hot coals from the deepest and most scorching fires of Hell.

'*Dracula!*'

I found myself walking forward. I had no will of my own. The hair was matted across the face, obscuring all other features, and the creature's long cloak, which was dark as pitch, hid him effectively from my gaze. I walked forward in terror.

'*Come, Dracula . . .*'

The piercing eyes burned into me, the obscured face moved nearer, and I suddenly felt drowsy, removed from myself, forgot the night and the cold and the fear and seemed to drift into sleep . . .

'Stop!'

The voice hurled me back to reality, and a hand, holding a crucifix, appeared miraculously before my eyes.

I almost fell backwards into the hands of two village men. The graveyard was now athrong with villagers, all holding their blazing torches and surrounding the dark becloaked figure. The man was twisting furiously this way and that, apparently trying to find some opening through the heaving, unrelenting wall of villagers. Everyone was shouting, and I thought I heard the struggling man screaming.

Finally, the villagers managed to pull the man to his feet and I saw him straining for release. I had now recovered my senses enough to wonder why the man, who was certainly very big, could not simply tear himself free and run. Then I saw that the priest (for it was he who had held up the crucifix) was standing in front of the man, his crucifix in one hand, intoning rhythmically in his native tongue. This succeeded in making the man cringe as if terrified. I know not what the priest said, save that he mentioned the names of

God and Jesus Christ several times and, each time he did so, the unfortunate man within the circle flinched as if he had been physically struck.

My previous fear was now fled and I felt sorry for the suffering of this unfortunate creature. I went to move forward, but the hands of the villagers who held me served not only to stay me in a moment of faintness, but to restrain me also. Then, as I watched the priest intoning before the cowering man, his face pale and ravaged and demented in the light of torches, I suddenly saw something that made me cry out in horror and beg the priest to desist.

The circle had opened to allow in a burly villager who carried a pitchfork. He immediately raised it, pointing the iron spikes towards the face of the captured man, who then let out such a pitiful howl of terror that it drained the very blood from my heart.

The man looked desperately around him, vainly seeking some escape, and then he raised his eyes to mine. No longer did his eyes burn with malevolent, seductive fury; now they were glazed and despairing and filled with strange grief.

'Help me!' he sobbed. 'Help me! In the name of your great sire, in the name of the blood that flows in your veins, in the name of Dra . . .'

Yet before he could finish what I did not want to hear, the burly villager had stepped forward and, with his entire weight behind him, thrust the iron spikes of the pitchfork straight through his eyes, and the man, thus impaled, fell backwards to the ground, writhing and shrieking horribly, his legs kicking as the villager leaned forward even further, pressing down on the pitchfork, finally impaling the man's head to the ground while, to my horror, the blood that spurted from the sockets shot upwards like a geyser, saturating those who stood nearby. Then, not content with this outrage, a sullen-faced villager moved forward, holding in his hands a heavy wooden mallet and an iron stake, and without further ado, and with the acquiescence of the priest, placed the stake above the heart of the dead body and drove it in with the brutal force of his mallet, until, to my shocked disbelief, the black blood rose like a fountain and, from the lips of what I had already considered a corpse, came a scream such as I had never heard before.

My heart pounded furiously, my head started to spin, and I sank down into merciful blackness.

CHAPTER 7

'Fühlen sie sich besser?'

I opened my eyes and gazed into Grigore's face. I blinked and looked around. I was lying on a bench in the main room of the inn. Grigore and the priest were bending over me while Grigore's wife and daughter stood silently in the background.

'Are you feeling better?' Grigore asked again in his thickly accented German.

I licked my lips and tried to speak, but only a croak would emerge from my dry throat.

Grigore placed a glass into my hands.

'Drink this, mein Herr, but slowly,' he said as I raised the glass to my lips. 'It is a spirit we distill here from the residue of the grapes, and it is strong.'

I took a swallow of the water-coloured liquid and felt a fire-like sensation burn its way down my gullet to the pit of my stomach. I coughed and handed the glass back.

'I'm all right now,' I said, struggling to a sitting position.

'The young Herr has had a bad experience,' Grigore said.

Suddenly the memory of those moments in the churchyard came flooding back. I shuddered and reached for Grigore's glass.

'A man has been murdered,' I said, looking at the priest.

The priest returned my gaze steadily.

'A beast has been destroyed,' he said softly.

'Beast! Man!' I cried hotly. 'I saw a man done to death in a most vile manner by a pack of superstitious brutes!'

Grigore went white.

'How dare you speak to the Father in that way! Do you not know that you owe him your immortal soul? Had he not arrived in time and shielded you with his crucifix from the *moroii* . . .'

The priest placed a restraining hand on Grigore's arm, and Grigore, white-faced and ghost-like in the flickering candlelight, seemed to float out of my vision. I glanced up at the priest.

'Immortal soul?' I cried. 'And what of the immortal soul of him that lies in the churchyard?'

'He had none, young Herr,' the priest said sorrowfully. 'He was a *moroii*.'

'Since coming to this God-forsaken country,' I said, unable to conceal my agitation, 'all I have heard about is *moroii*, beasts without souls. I demand an explanation!'

Grigore's face floated through the ever-shifting shadows, the candlelight illuminating his eyes and revealing his outrage. The priest motioned him away with an imperceptible nod of his head, then he leaned closer to me.

'I told you before, young Herr, that this is a strange country of shadows where blood is cheap and flows like water, where the mountains and plains have for centuries been drenched in the blood of many races. Death is no stranger to the men and women of Wallachia. And, in whatever form it comes, we have no fear of it. No, that which we *do* fear is undeath, eternal suffering and torture, and we know and fear those who have succumbed to live as immortals in the cursed guise of the Undead.'

I raised a protesting hand, to question him, to tell him that I knew not what he talked about, but he spoke like one in a dream, seeing images in the blazing fire before us.

'You ask me, young Herr, what a *moroii* is,' he continued. 'I shall answer, and I pray to God that you may never have to utilize such knowledge. It is the belief in Wallachia that when a man dies his soul does not pass into Paradise until forty days have gone by. Thus, three years after all burials, we exhume the bodies to make sure that the spirit has ascended and the body become putrified. For unless we are vigilant, the spirit of a dead person can reanimate his corpse to suck at the life of the living.

'When I was a young priest here, there was a young woman who died and was buried. Yet several weeks later there came reports that the same woman had been seen at night playing with children in the village. At that time, living here, was an old man, wise even beyond his years, but whom I, in my youth, called superstitious and ungodly. This old man came to me and told me that the village was in turmoil, that the spirit of the dead woman had not departed and therefore she had become Undead. He asked that the ancient remedy be invoked. Naturally I laughed. I thought I knew better. Then, one day, the old man came to me and said that the villagers had taken matters into their own hands since I would not act for them.

'A young boy who had not yet committed a sexual act was mounted on a jet black stallion which had never mated with a mare. The villagers led the pair across the churchyard until the horse stopped at the grave of the woman who had died and was reported to have been seen. In spite of whippings, the horse stood at the grave and refused to go on. Two men of the village then dug down and eventually exhumed the body. The old man brought me to the graveside and I looked down at the body, eight months buried, and it lay as fleshy and fair as if the girl were but sleeping. The old man then sat down and honed a spade, sharpening its edge, and then, deeming it sufficiently sharp, he stepped forward, raised it high above his head, and brought it down into that fair white neck, severing the head from the body. The blood spurted forth, florid and fresh, so that I would have sworn that he had cut the throat of a woman in full health and vigour. Then the old man turned away, crying . . . for the woman had been his own daughter.

'The body was reburied, face downwards, with a thorn bush on the grave to stop the corpse from rising. And no more was the woman seen and no more were the strange illnesses that had afflicted the children of the village. This, young Herr, was my first encounter with a *stigoi* . . .'

The priest was leaning over me. His eyes were bright and intense. There was the movement of people behind him, and the candlelight flickered. I felt suffocated. My heart was still pounding. I offered a brief, nervous smile and felt my reasoning falter.

'Are you asking me to believe that the man killed tonight was a . . . *stigoi*? A corpse?'

'No, young Herr. He was a *moroii*, a vampire, but not yet one of the Undead. A *stigoi* is an Undead vampire.'

'Ridiculous!' I snapped, though my uneasiness tormented me. 'I would not have thought that a priest would give credence to such childish, peasant superstitions.'

The priest merely smiled.

'You think that I fall prey to an unreasoning awe or fear of something unknown, something imaginary which creates a fear founded on ignorance? Does it not occur to you, my young Herr, that fear can also be founded on knowledge—a fear and respect for the evil that the unknown can do? To each person, the belief of a fellow which is at variance with his own belief is a superstition. I know the *stigoi* and the *moroii* to be a reality, and I warn you, young Herr, to be on your guard, especially at this time of the year.'

'What do you mean?' I asked.

'Why, we are in the last days of November. It will soon be the Eve of St. Andrew's Day when the evil forces are at their strongest. There are three times in the year when our defences reach an ebb and when the evil forces ride rampant through the world. In the month of April, on the Eve of St. George's feastday, and later that month, on the Eve of St. Walpurgis' feastday, and on the penultimate day of November, the Eve of the feastday of St. Andrew. Beware, young Herr, for our superstitions in Wallachia are not taken lightly.'

I did not reply. I felt tired and truly shaken. The priest rose and smiled, and I saw that he, too, was exhausted.

'I see you are tired from the exertions of the day,' he said. 'I will therefore leave you in the hands of Grigore. May you pass the night in peace and safety, and, should you be receptive to advice on the morrow, I would return to your own country.'

I was, thanks to the drink given to me by Grigore, already asleep before he left the inn. It was a strange, troubled sleep in which I saw a great concourse of people rising from their tombs, rising above the mist and the obscene, shifting darkness, clad only in their burial clothes, crying out in one mighty voice: 'Dracula! Dracula! Save us, Master!' Then, once again, I saw the man in the churchyard, black eyes glistening, wrapped protectively in the cloak, and, in my dream, I suddenly recognized him as my own father, Dracula . . .

I awoke, cold and sweating, and was thankful to see the grim, grey light of dawn seeping in between the cracks in the shutters. I stayed awake, unable to return to sleep, until I heard the noises of people in the kitchen. The smell of freshly baked bread caused me to wash and then rouse Herr Strasser, who still lay oblivious to the hideous events of the previous night.

As we breakfasted, I let Herr Strasser negotiate with Grigore to hire a man from the village to drive our coach to the capital, Tirgoviste. The arrangement was concluded and it was not long before we climbed into the coach.

It was a cold, bright morning. The sun shone, but without any degree of warmth, and a frost still lay thick on the ground. A few groups of silent villagers stood around us, watching our coach suspiciously, but it was inconceivable to me that the event of the previous night could actually have taken place. A man murdered by superstitious villagers, the act condoned by their priest. Indeed, at that moment I felt a rage against them. Had I been in Rome I would have gone to the authorities, but here, in this strange and unfriendly country, who were the authorities? Yes, I raged against them, their ignorance and their stupidity, but even as I did so I was haunted by the memory of the priest's quiet and unwavering conviction . . .

The coach started off through the village, the villagers staring unblinkingly after us, saying nothing, just watching.

'A strange people,' said Herr Strasser, arranging a travelling rug over our legs. 'Eh, mein Freiherr?'

My eyes caught sight of the freshly dug grave in the churchyard. It had since been filled in and had a thorn bush planted on top of it. I saw the sun blazing down upon it, and it all seemed quite natural.

'Yes,' I said quietly. 'Strange indeed.'

Then, as we drove out of the cluster of buildings, I looked back along the road to Tirgoviste. By the graveyard wall I caught sight of the bearded priest. As I watched him, the sun suddenly shone on his figure, flashing all around him, illuminating him in the greatest detail. Slowly, he made the sign of the cross and pointed two fingers at me. Then the coach rounded a bend in the road and, first the priest and then the village disappeared from my gaze.

CHAPTER 8

By midafternoon our coach had rumbled into the narrow streets of the Wallachian capital. We had crossed two great rivers in our journey, the Arges and the Dimbovita, both tributaries to the Danube yet as broad as any river I have seen. The Dimbovita especially was memorable, flowing through a valley of steep mountain walls, with wild gorges and spectacular grottoes.

Although but a village compared with Rome, nevertheless Tirgoviste is a fair sized city and stands on the banks of another river called the Ialomita. The town is built around the court of the Grand Voivode, now Basarab cel Tinar, that is Basarab the Younger who, but a few short weeks before our arrival, had overthrown Basarab cel Batrin, the man who had defeated Dracula with the aid of the Turks. Early in November the famous Stefan cel Mare of Moldavia had once again defeated the Turks and placed Basarab the Younger on the throne of Wallachia in place of the Turkish puppet. Now Basarab cel Tinar was in the process of rebuilding the despoiled city with its many churches and monuments. Already work had started on the restoration of a sumptuous looking building which I understood was the metropolitan church of Basarab.

Indeed, the city seems a very pious place, and

houses not only monasteries within its walls, but outside as well. One of the most beautiful churches I have ever seen is not far from the city, in an area of vineyards up in the hills. I am told that some of the Voivodes of Wallachia are buried here, including my grandfather, Vlad Dracul.*

The strangeness of the previous night was soon forgotten as I looked eagerly about the city that had once been the capital of Vlad Dracula, my father. Herr Strasser directed our coach to an inn that he praised highly, called Hanul cu Petru, which means Peter's Inn. The inn, like most of the houses that are not churches or palaces, was built mostly of wood—oak, I believe. Hardly had we settled in then I embarked upon a journey through the city, intent upon learning as much as possible during my stay, but no sooner had I stepped forth than it grew dark, and I had to return to the inn.

The next day I was abroad early and found the day passed exceeding quick. Tirgoviste is essentially a city of churches, though much desolated now with the wars that have taken place in recent years. The monasteries, with cloisters, chapels and decorative courtyards, add to the colour of the city and are rewarding to the students of architecture. Apparently, so I have heard, a traveller from Venice thought it 'a vast, gaudy flower house.' But apart from churches and monasteries, I discovered a surprisingly large number of boyars' palaces, each one a small fortress.

I remarked later to Petru, the innkeeper, on this, and he explained that Tirgoviste was a city of anarchy where people did not know from one day to another

---

* It would seem that this church was rebuilt by Dracula's cousin, Radu the Great (1495–1508) as part of the Monastery of St. Nicholas.

who would be ruler and who would be victim to political assassination. The lower orders tried to ignore the changes in order that they might survive, but the boyars sought to fortify themselves.

The main churches were of the Orthodox faith, and in the city lay a grand palace of the primate of the church, called the Metropolitan. But there was also a Franciscan monastery. Here I made myself known to the abbot, a Florentine who had come on a mission to Wallachia and stayed in spite of the troubles. He was generous with his wine and bid me stay for the midday meal.

The abbot was a verbose man and soon he had fallen to reminiscences of Dracula's reign, which appears a favourite topic with Wallachians. I leant forward eagerly, for it was my wish to know more of this supposedly gruesome father whose reputation seemed to stink in the nostrils of Christendom.

'What was this Dracula really like?' I asked the abbot. 'We have heard so many tales of his evil acts . . . but surely they are somewhat exaggerated?'

The abbot shook his head.

'Rather, my son,' he said, 'they are understatements, for truly he was an evil man. Why,' the abbot rose and went to a window, 'down there is a narrow street, and halfway along is an old, dirty house where once dwelt one of Dracula's mistresses. Dracula had merely lusted after her body, but she, poor child, loved him. One day he went to visit her when a mood of despair was upon him, and she, wishing to arouse a spark of happiness in him, told him that she was with child by him. The innocent girl thought this news would bring cheer to Dracula. Ah, the poor creature. Dracula took out his sword and cut open her womb, exclaiming that he wanted to see where the fruit of his loins was.

There was no child, and he left her there to die in terrible torment. Such was the evil of his mind.'

The abbot paused to replenish his glass.

'He was an austere man whose austerity for others begat such evil,' he continued. 'If a woman consorted with a man who was not her husband, this Dracula had her skinned alive and her skin tied to a pole in the middle of Tirgoviste . . . right in the market place. This same act he performed against widows and young girls who lost their virginity.'

A feeling of nausea arose in me, and I began to wonder whether such tales were really true or whether they were invented against an enemy to discredit him. I had known that Dracula had won the enmity of the Saxon merchants who had done their utmost to spread such stories, and I knew also that he had sometimes displayed intolerance against the Catholic church. But even so, I began to believe that there must exist some truth in such tales of horror.

Later that day, my uneasiness increasing, I bade farewell to the abbot and returned to the inn.

Early that evening, just after the descent of dusk, Petru, the innkeeper, knocked on my door and told me that there was a man waiting for me downstairs.

To describe the man as ugly would be an understatement. His stockiness belied his height, which must have exceeded six foot, and such was his width that he seemed to block out all the light from the room. His head was set well down on his shoulders as if he had no neck; it was a square-shaped head with an exceptionally low forehead, surmounted by a matted mass of dirty hair that must have once been black but was now streaked with grey. Across one cheek a scar traced a livid red line from ear to mouth, drawing the lips up at one end in a permanent sneer. There was a second scar across the eyebrow which caused the right eyelid to appear semi-closed. From this travesty of a face the eyes that stared out were dark and dead; there seemed little hint of life in them as the man watched me descend the stairs into the room. Then, as I reached the foot of the stairs, the man bowed.

'I am Tirgsor,' he said in a thick accent which made me strain to hear the meaning of the German. 'Tirgsor, the *stolnic* of Castle Dracula.'

'You are the steward of Castle Dracula?' I asked, surprised.

For reply he held out a paper. I took it and broke open the familiar seal.

> *Written at Castle Dracula, Poenari, on the twenty-ninth day of the month of November, in the year 1477.*
> *Brother—Welcome to our home, your home. We are awaiting your arrival with impatience. We pray you have rested well. Tirgsor, our steward, has a carriage which will take you on the last part of your journey to the home of your ancestors. Be well, come safely.*
> *Your loving brothers—Vlad and Mihail*

I raised my eyebrows in surprise.

'How did you know I was here?' I demanded of Tirgsor. 'I only arrived last night and have sent no word to Castle Dracula of my coming.'

The big man shrugged.

'I was sent here to escort the young Herr to Schloss Dracula,' he replied simply.

'But who told you I was here?'

'I was sent here, mein Herr.'

I dismissed the matter for the moment. The solution

of this intriguing riddle would have to wait until I saw my brothers and questioned them. And doubtless Tirgsor was possessed of a simple mind.

'Very well, Tirgsor, I will be ready to leave tomorrow morning. You will find yourself quarters for the night.'

The man shuffled his feet.

'I was sent here to escort the young Herr to Schloss Dracula,' he repeated stubbornly. 'The carriage is outside.'

'Tirgsor,' I said firmly, 'I have just arrived in this capital of Wallachia and I counted on several days' rest here. But in deference to my brothers' invitation, I shall continue my journey tomorrow.'

The huge man frowned and bit his lip.

'I was ordered to bring you at once,' he said slowly. 'The carriage is outside.'

So saying, he took a step towards me, almost as if he would seize me and throw me into the carriage whether I wished to go or not. But at that moment there was a footfall on the stair behind me, and I turned to see Petru, the innkeeper, who was watching us both with frightened eyes.

'Forgive me, mein Herr,' he said. 'I could not help but overhear you. The young Herr does not plan to continue his journey tonight?'

'Why?' I asked.

'Oh, young Herr, know you not what day it is? It is the eve of the feast of St. Andrew. Please do not travel tonight for there is much danger abroad.' I must have smiled broadly at this, for Petru suddenly grasped my hand and, almost whimpering in fright, said: 'Please, please, young Herr! You cannot imagine what can happen on such a day! Should you be travelling at nightfall, then you will become prey to all the vile and evil things that hold sway.'

Now laughing, I disengaged myself from his clutching hands.

'Have no fear, old man,' I said. 'I do not intend continuing my journey until tomorrow, for I wish to rest this night, not travel in some uncomfortable coach.'

An expression of relief crossed old Petru's face.

'God save the young Herr,' he said, 'for a long, full and vigorous life.'

He crossed himself and extended two fingers towards me, even as the bearded priest had done. I have since learnt that, among the Wallachians, it is considered to be a charm against evil.

Then a sound, remarkably like a snarl, broke from the lips of Tirgsor. I swung around to face him. His eyes were resting on old Petru and now, for the first time, I saw some animation in them. And what I saw was black hatred.

'Tirgsor!' I spoke sharply, 'you will find quarters and will then meet me outside the inn tomorrow morning, after I have breakfasted. Only then will we continue our journey. Do you understand?'

The steward's eyes, now lustreless again, looked deeply into mine, and I became aware of something strange in their blackness . . . it was almost as if they had no pupils. Then I became aware of a blue flickering in those vitreous depths, blue and black, black and blue, and I watched, fascinated, as the eyes seemed to dissolve, luring me in, my own eyelids growing heavy, a drowsiness descending, wanting to sleep, to close my eyes and drift away, thinking how simple it would be, how much more rewarding, to let Tirgsor drive me immediately to Castle Dracula, where I could sleep, sleep for a long time, sleep in a large bed with snow white linen sheets, sleep, just sleep . . .

Suddenly I jerked awake, almost falling over myself, as if I were being held by some unseen force and now had to jerk myself free.

I blinked and glanced around me. Old Petru was gazing at me in some alarm. Tirgsor was no longer staring at me, but instead was standing quietly with his eyes downcast.

Then I noticed that two others had entered the inn, and I saw from their apparel that they were priests of the Orthodox Church, for they were resplendently dressed and had large gold crucifixes hanging around their necks.

Tirgsor studiously ignored the crucifixes and he seemed almost frightened.

'You have your orders, Tirgsor!' I snapped in a loud and firm tone of voice.

He bit his lips together and refused to meet my gaze; then he shuffled his feet and looked away.

'Very well, mein Herr,' he said. 'I shall be here with the coach first thing in the morning.'

With that he turned on his heel and strode out of the inn, while old Petru stepped closer and laid a tentative hand on my arm.

'The young Herr is all right?' Petru asked.

'Yes,' I said, 'but a little travel weary. I will go and rest awhile in my room.'

Alone in my room, I know not what made me rummage in my bags and take out the small velvet-covered box that my mother had given me on her death bed. Inside was a short gold chain to which hung a gold crucifix with a figure of Christ executed in loving and intricate workmanship. I took it from its box and hung it around my neck, under my shirt. This done, and feeling strangely happier, I lay down and closed my weary eyes.

* * *

I could not sleep. Strangely, after my extraordinary moment of tiredness downstairs, I felt wide awake when in the bed. Indeed, there was no hint of sleepiness in my mind at all and so, after a while, I rose impatiently from bed and went out.

There were signs of great activity in the streets. Benches and tables laden with food and wine were appearing, while various musicians stood about in groups, playing fascinating airs on their peculiar instruments.

On asking Petru the cause of the festivities, he explained that the people of the city were holding a *hora*. It would appear that this custom arose from the superstition of St. Andrew's Eve when, it was felt, great merrymaking and entertainment kept the evil spirits at bay, for, so they reasoned, the evil spirits only prey on the unhappy and fearful.

It was a custom I heartily endorsed and, perhaps to throw off my own inexplicable fears, I threw myself eagerly into the activities. One particular dance I insisted on joining in was called a *perinita*, the literal translation being 'little cushion,' and the dance itself being known as the 'kissing dance.' The Wallachian girls took this in great spirit and, in my honour, the dance was performed three times with much gusto and much drinking and laughter.

Later that evening I found myself seated next to an old man whose name, I seem to recall, was Costel. He was a veteran of the army of Iancu de Hunedoara and told me that he fought at the battle of Belgrade when Iancu defeated the troops of Mohammed II, a month before he took sick and died of the plague. The old man spoke a voluble German, so voluble that I had difficulty in understanding all he had to say. He gestured at the lines of dancing men and women, whirling down the streets in the flickering light of thousands of torches, and then turned to me.

'I knew a *hora* once,' he said, 'here in this city of ours, but one which was not so joyful.'

'When was that, old man?' I asked.

'Dracula's father, the old Vlad Dracul,' he said, 'was assassinated by certain rich and powerful boyars, encouraged by Iancu de Hunedoara, because he had made terms with the Turks. And Dracula's brother, Mircea, whom, God believe me, I knew well and served with in battle, became the Voivode of Wallachia. This Mircea also treated with the Turks, for Wallachia was almost a desert because of their victorious troops, so the great boyars, by guile and cunning, seized Mircea and brought him in chains to Tirgoviste and had him slain.'

The old man sighed and nodded to himself.

'It was in the year 1456 that Dracula returned to Tirgoviste as Voivode,' he continued. 'The first thing he did was order that his brother's coffin be exhumed from the public burying plot of Tirgoviste to be reburied among the voivodes of Wallachia up in the *podgorie*, the hilly region outside the city. When the coffin was opened, it was found that Mircea's head was twisted and showed that he had been buried alive and died struggling for breath. Dracula ordered him to be reburied with the ceremony befitting a voivode.

'It was not long after this that Dracula formulated his plans to punish the boyars who had slain his father and buried his brother alive.

'In the spring of the same year there was a great feast and dance in Tirgoviste, then as now, and Dracula had all the boyars of the city go to the great hall of the palace—and there was the Metropolitan himself, five bishops and all the abbots of the monasteries. As the feasting went on, Dracula asked them how many reigns they had experienced in their lifetimes. One of them came forward and said: "Since your grandfather, there have been no less than twenty voivodes, and I have survived them all." Even the youngest boyar said he had known seven voivodes. Now Dracula knew that the boyars had scant regard for a voivode and that they believed they would survive him because they were more powerful—but Dracula was cleverer than the boyars.

'His soldiers surrounded the hall and, at an order from Dracula, seized five-hundred boyars who had experienced more than seven reigns, for among them, so Dracula reasoned, would be the assassins of his father and brother. These unfortunates he had impaled on wooden stakes in the vicinity of the palace, until the flesh rotted and blackbirds grew fat on their feeding.'

The old man sighed. He scratched at an eyebrow. I glanced down at the floor because I did not dare gaze at his eyes.

'Aye,' he said slowly, 'that was some feast day . . . just over twenty-one years ago. A strange, terrible man was Dracula, but, by my sword, at least he drove the Turks out. Perhaps he was the best of all our voivodes: you have to be harsh and ruthless to rule a country constantly at war.'

I left him to his musings. I will admit that the more I heard of the bloodthirsty acts of my father, Dracula, the more I began to feel that an injustice was being done. Indeed, were not the stories being enlarged out of all proportion to the real events? I well recall, a few years ago, the Papal Nuncio, the Bishop of Erlau, reporting to the Pope that Dracula had personally ordered the killing of 100,000 people—an entire fifth of the population of Wallachia. Yet who accused Dracula of atrocities? Always his enemies.

'Tis true that the man was cruel—the experience of my mother told me that—but was he really the devil incarnate as they made out?

Old Costel had said that to rule a country constantly at war one had to be ruthless. Wallachia was being squeezed by both Turk and Saxon, while there also reigned internal anarchy, intrigues by the boyars or aristocracy, aided by political plots from Hungary. Dracula's virtual destruction of the boyars had given Wallachia an immediate, albeit horrible, lesson: that the voivode's title, and all that it implied, was not to be taken lightly. A nation should unite behind its prince and be obedient to his commands, his resolution and discipline, in order to defeat its constant enemies. In this light, then, Dracula's actions were no more ruthless or tyrannical than those of Louis XI of France, or Sigismondo Malatesta, the Lord of Rimini. Indeed, even so far west as the kingdom of England, it is reported that my lord the Earl of Worcester, during the current civil wars between the houses of Lancaster and York, impales his enemies to such a degree as to make Dracula seem a saint. Given this, why the reputation of Dracula above all the others?

Thus meditating, I turned in early to be refreshed for the journey I would undertake the next day to Castle Dracula.

CHAPTER 9

We started our journey early in the morning. Tirgsor, as he had promised, presented himself before the inn at first light and I, after a breakfast of good local ale and warm, freshly baked bread, climbed into the coach. It was an open coach, entirely coloured in black, and even drawn by two black horses. The only relief was the escutcheon—a white dragon's head— painted on the coach door. Although the coach was open, there were plenty of furs, the skins of bears which I gathered were numerous in the mountain regions, and these I tucked about me while Petru handed me a large basket of food and drink which his wife had prepared for the journey.

Tirgsor, who had exchanged but two syllables that morning, climbed on to the raised box at the front of the coach, raised his whip and cracked it, and the horses lunged forward, the coach seeming to fly along the road and out of the city.

I caught a last quick glimpse of Petru, crossing himself and holding the inevitable two fingers in my direction. At this I smiled, and hoped that his charm against the evil eye was successful.

The day was pleasant. A clear blue sky, with a bright if warmless sun, followed us for most of the journey. It was a clear autumn day holding the promise of a cold winter to come; however, I was wrapped up warmly and excited by the thought that this was the last lap of my journey.

We swung northwards along the Dimbovita valley, following parallel to the river. From fairly flat land, which I understand is called the Wallachian Plain, small hills soon began to rise and give way to more sharply rising ground. The area here was quite populated, and there were many fortified large houses which are called *cula*. The people of this area are mainly free men or *mosneni*, as they are called. They work small areas of land which belong to them. There are few boyars in the area and few slaves, a sign that feudalism seems to be declining here.

The journey was very pleasant until we reached Catateni din Vale, a small cluster of houses standing by a river and overshadowed by a grim castle on a mountain. I demanded that Tirgsor stop here while I refreshed myself, otherwise I am sure the surly brute would have continued driving the animals all day until they dropped.

Actually, I had twice asked the sullen steward whether he was ill, for he appeared so pale and weak for a man of his girth, and I noticed that he seemed almost blind in the light. He wore a heavy black cloak which completely encased him, and a hat which he had drawn down so far little of his face could be seen. The previous night he had given the impression of enormous strength (in spite of his pale face and lustreless eyes), but now I perceived that it was almost as much as he could do to control the horses. Nevertheless, he dismissed my solicitous inquiries with a grunt, and so I gave up trying to communicate with him. Instead, I told him to see to the horses' refreshment and then I set off to explore the place a little.

There were few people about, but one man told me

that if I climbed the mountain towards the castle I would find a church built inside the rock of the mountain where three monks hold vigil and say mass each day. Time precluded this interlude, but I was led to understand that there is not a mountain gorge, torrent or river in the area that does not evoke some stormy history or deed of war, and, had I the time available, I would have found willing narrators among the peasants.

Tirgsor was impatient and so I climbed into the coach and again we set off at a fast pace, swinging suddenly away from the river Dimbovita and following a smaller tributary which was called the Arges. The steep hills had now given way entirely to precipitous mountains pushing skywards, which seemed to grow higher and higher as we made our way further into the ranges. These were the formidable Transylvanian Alps that separated Wallachia from Transylvania.

I noticed that we were travelling constantly uphill, and several times the horses stumbled. Every time I offered to alight and assist Tirgsor in leading the horses to surer ground, the monosyllabic steward grunted his displeasure and told me to stay in the coach.

Perhaps it was merely caused by the mountains blotting it out, but it seemed that the sun had already set, so cold and dark it now was. Storm clouds were hurrying across the sky, brushing the mountain tops. Unlike the *mosneni* areas we had passed through, this area seemed sparsely populated. The few villages we encountered were smaller and poorer in appearance, and the houses had less decoration. There were one or two people about, and these wore very simple and dirty clothes. I had grown accustomed to seeing villagers with gaily embroidered jackets, but these people wore no such trappings, which is most unusual in mountain districts.

Once or twice Tirgsor had to draw rein because of cattle in our path. At such times I leant out to greet the drover or ask a question, but the only reply I received was a furtive look and the sign of the cross, before the peasant scuttled away like a rabbit. At this, Tirgsor would laugh and crack his whip after the man. I rebuked him more than once, but to no avail.

It may have been my imagination, but with the growing dusk it seemed to me that Tirgsor began to shake aside the vapours he had displayed throughout the day and instead to show a strength I have seldom seen in his handling of the horses.

We now skirted a place called Curtea de Arges, the citadel of Arges, a group of dwellings and a few large houses surrounding an ancient cathedral. This was once the capital of Wallachia, many generations ago, and in that cathedral many of the line of Dracula were anointed before the assembled boyars. But here we hardly paused, for darkness was descending rapidly.

Tirgsor, all signs of weakness gone, forced the horses on at a pace that made me cry out in alarm, for I felt that he would overturn the coach if he were not more careful.

Suddenly my prophecy almost came true, for both horses reared and whinnied without warning, rearing and straining in opposite directions. The coach slewed around and wound up half in a ditch. I would have been thrown into the roadway had not the plunging of the horses jerked the coach up out of the ditch almost before it had toppled in. Tirgsor, shouting curses, tried to calm the horses, but still they reared and plunged, their terrified whinnies echoing in the silence of the mountains.

The breath had been knocked from me and I lay back, gasping and wondering what was amiss. Then I saw the cause of the incident.

A man in the dress of a priest, his face white, his eyes blazing, stood in front of the horses, his arms held up as if in benediction. It would seem that he must have leapt out into the road, almost under the hooves of the horses, and frightened them. As I watched, I saw this startling figure of a priest, his face distorted with hatred, run towards the carriage. He held some kind of bottle in one hand, and, as I sat there stunned, he ran towards me, uncorked the bottle, and cried out in a loud voice: *'In nomine patria et fili et spiritu sancti!'* Then, without further ado, he flung its contents in my face.

Naturally I recoiled, and saw a triumphant smile on the priest's face—a triumph that swiftly gave way to disbelief, and then puzzlement. I, too, must have shown my own puzzlement as I sat there with water dripping down my face.

What strange manner of man was this, dressed in the guise of a priest, to run out on unsuspecting travellers and throw water in their faces? Was he mad?

As I was thus contemplating, too stunned to do anything else, the man leaned heavily against the side of the carriage, gasping spasmodically, and peered intently into my face.

'You are not he!' he exclaimed.

He turned away a little, shaking his head in perplexity; then he quickly turned back to face me, his eyes blazing angrily.

'What are you doing in that coach?' he demanded. 'Do you not realize to whose house it belongs?'

I started to reply, but Tirgsor, who had now quieted the horses, suddenly turned around and struck out with his whip. The lash caught the priest full in the face, making him cry out with pain before falling down to the roadside.

'Out of the way, Christian pig!' Tirgsor snarled.

The priest raised himself on one elbow, his face once more distorted with hatred, his eyes fierce and staring directly at Tirgsor.

'Spawn of Satan!' he cried out. 'I know you well, Tirgsor! Tirgsor is well known, as is the evil thing he serves, and God will not forget him!'

Tirgsor snarled. It was a sound that chilled my blood. The gloom was descending and the shadows filled my gaze, and then I saw Tirgsor step forward with the whip and bring it down on the priest again.

'Stop it!' I shouted, suddenly regaining my senses. 'The man is a priest, mad or not!'

Tirgsor paused. He glanced at me and at the priest. He snorted and stepped back, and the priest, still on the ground, peered sharply at me.

'Young Herr, young Herr,' he said, 'you are not one of them. What do you do in that coach? Know you not that it belongs to the house of Dracula? Yes! Evil spawned them, evil nurtures them, and by evil they live in half-death. I beg you, young Herr, listen to me! Do not go to Castle Dracula if you value your immortal soul!'

With this the priest started to crawl towards the coach, and again Tirgsor brought his whip down upon him. I heard the priest cry out, and then Tirgsor had urged the horses forward, so sharply that I was thrown back into my seat. By the time I had regained my balance, and had managed to glance back, the priest was but a blur in the gloom. I watched the darkness devour him.

I made up my mind to report the conduct of Tirgsor as soon as we arrived at the castle. I might be a stranger to the customs of this land of Wallachia, which still labours under feudalism, but no man has a right to whip another as one would a dog. I determined that Tirgsor should be punished for his sullen malice.

Night had fallen with incredible swiftness. One moment there had been an eerie twilight, a quickly gathering dusk, and the next there was a blackness in which not even the surrounding woods could be discerned. Tirgsor halted the coach and lit two torches which were hung on either side, but even with this assistance the journey became slower and more difficult, the horses being forced down to a trot. And then, in white brilliance, the moon came racing over the distant peaks, lighting our road almost as if it were day.

We left the wooded area and went across a small plain. The air had become intensely cold and I was glad of the heavy furs which I had heaped about me. Even so, I could not help shivering. As we emerged on to the plain a sudden cold wind began to blow, causing the trees in the area to bend this way and that, whispering and forming strange patterns. I fancied that I saw several dark shapes slinking across the moonlit expanse, and I was just beginning to wonder what they were when I heard the macabre baying of wolves which, I understand, thickly populate the area.

To my surprise, as I looked across the plain, I caught sight of a faint, flickering blue light and then several more beyond it. I blinked and looked again. Across the plain were some half dozen ghostly columns of blue, dancing and flickering in eerie silence.

Even as I saw them, Tirgsor pulled up the horses and leapt from the coach without a word. I saw him make his way towards the flames and bend over one. Then there was a strange optical effect that somewhat startled me, for although he stood between me and the flame, I could still see its faint blue light as though it shone right through him. He went to each blue light and I could see him doing something at each—bending close to the ground as if searching for something—then he returned without a word of explanation and we drove on.

Strange as it seems, I was glad of this sullen brute's return, for I could see the low, long black shapes drawing closer and closer to the coach, while the horses stamped, tossed their black manes, and rolled their eyes in growing nervousness. Indeed, I could not but wonder how Tirgsor had managed to wander so far from the coach and not be attacked by the grim, carnivorous beasts.

As we moved on, I fell to wondering what the blue lights portended, and then, almost in relief, because I was beginning to think that I, too, was falling a victim to the superstitions of the Wallachians, I recalled attending a lecture in the Palazzo Della Sapienza given by a learned Florentine alchemist who called such lights *fuoco fatuo*, or will-o'-the-wisp. His theory was that such lights were caused by a marsh gas, formed by decayed vegetation in swampy land during a drying out process. When this vegetation dried out, it formed a material that could be used as a fuel for fire instead of wood. The light was therefore a natural phenomenon and there was nothing magical or supernatural about it.*

---

* Friend Jonathan Harker, on his journey to Castle Dracula, encountered a similar phenomenon; see his journal entry for 5th May. The old alchemist explanation for the blue light is substantially correct. To be accurate, the genesis of our fuel coal is well understood today: some millions of years ago the environment on our earth was warm and humid; swamps and bogs proliferated and as vegetation died and decayed it formed vast compost heaps in which oxygen was consumed by putrefactive bacteria. An anaerobic fermentation took place and a marsh

We soon left this plain and began to climb rapidly along a narrow track through steep gorges. Then we suddenly encountered a group of miserable dwellings. There was not a soul about, but uncannily, as our coach rounded the bend into what was sadly a village, a church bell began to peal vigorously, to which Tirgsor threw back his head and laughed a horrible choking laugh. He did not pause to find out what the cause of the bells could be, but merely whipped the poor horses to further exertion, so that we passed through the village almost before we realized it. I did see, by the bright light of the moon, that each poor house was shuttered and each door was shut, and at each shuttered window and each closed door I saw garlands of flowers, the thistles and garlic I had witnessed several times on my journey. In addition, each house had a dark cross painted on the door.

One building, which looked like an inn, had a sign above it which read: ΑΡΕΦΩ. The cyrillic letters, I realized, stood for Arefu, which village, I recalled, was the nearest to Castle Dracula.

The coach was now climbing the mountain track at an alarming angle. On one side of the narrow path lay a sheer drop into the valley, and I shuddered lest we tip over, for all would be dashed to pieces on the rocks that showed so clearly in the moonlight. And even if we were lucky enough to miss the rocks and fall into the silver strip of river, the impact from this

---

gas—methane—was formed while plant debris was converted to humic acid. The process still occurs in swamps and bogs which give off this will-o'-the-wisp light while the residue forms peat which is used in many areas of Europe for fuel. Dracula told Jonathan Harker that the local belief was that gold could be found where the flames shone, but few peasants had the courage to mark the spot. Van Helsing.

height would have meant at least broken necks. I hung on to the side of the coach grimly, while Tirgsor, not even a tremor in his voice, cursed at each of the horses and urged them on to greater speeds. Thus we went on for nearly an hour, and I was beginning to think that the terrible journey would have no end.

Then, all at once, the coach reached a small level patch of ground and we rumbled over a wooden bridge into a stone courtyard. The abrupt entrance into the castle left me speechless, for there had been no indication of an approach. We had simply swung around a sharp bend in the pathway and were now inside a courtyard with grey-black walls towering on all sides of us.

As I sat there trying to adjust my thoughts to my sudden arrival, a tall man, with long black moustaches such as the Wallachian boyars wear, long and almost drooping, emerged from the shadows.

I discerned no hint of welcome on his face. It was a thin, bloodless face; and the eyes, like those of Tirgsor, were large, black and lustreless in the flickering light of the coach's torches. He made no effort to stretch out his hand in greeting, but instead stood a little way off.

'Welcome, brother Mircea,' he said, in a voice that lacked all emotion. 'Welcome to Castle Dracula.'

BOOK TWO

CASTLE DRACULA

CHAPTER 10

I must confess that as I stared at the pale anaemic face and black lustreless eyes of my brother Vlad, I felt no fraternal feelings such as I had imagined would course through my veins at our first meeting. I experienced only a strange curiosity. In no way did this Vlad Dracula resemble me, though, of course, it must be pointed out that while we shared the same father we did not have the same mother and therein must lie the explanation. Even so, I had assumed that I would feel some brotherly warmth, and in this I was now proven wrong. In many ways—and this is indeed a curiosity—it was as if I were staring into Tirgsor's face all over again, for the pale, dry skin, the cold, corpse-like temperature of the extended hand, and the blackness of the eyes that revealed no emotion all seemed to be more the attributes of Tirgsor than of our common blood.

As I stared at the dead face of my brother Vlad, wondering what manner of greeting to make, a second man appeared at his side to welcome me and to introduce himself as my brother Mihail. So alike were the two that they could almost have been hatched from the same egg, though I knew that there were several years distance between them, and that they were both my elders.

Both were tall, a good head taller than I, and I am

not considered to be below the average height. Both wore their hair long, with large black moustaches that threw their pale faces into sharp relief as did the dull black eyes. The clothes they wore were simple: an embroidered shirt, trousers held by a wide leather belt, woollen-lined sleeveless jacket, called locally a *cojoc*, which was also embroidered, and a pair of *opinci*, which are soft pigskin sandals. This was the typical 'Darcian' costume much worn by the peasants.

'Welcome, brother Mircea,' said Mihail. 'Welcome. Come freely. Go safely. And leave something of the happiness you bring.'

I understood this strange speech was but a typical Wallachian greeting. My two brothers gathered what few belongings I carried and escorted me to the main door into a great hall whose chilly atmosphere made me gasp for breath. I was led up a vast winding staircase to a landing where they threw open two large wooden doors. I felt relieved at the sight of a well-lit room with a great roaring fire crackling in the hearth and a table spread for a meal.

'We have prepared a small supper for you after your most fatiguing journey,' said my brother Vlad, as he closed the doors behind us. I had in fact noticed that they both spoke excellent German, and on querying this I was led to understand that all members of the nobility used the language as their mother tongue, though not the tongue of their mothers. Vlad continued: 'I suggest you sup first and then retire to rest, for you must be very weary. On the morrow we shall talk and seal our friendship as brothers, as we should have done many years ago had it not been for the ill starred fate of our ancestors.'

I did indeed feel a tremendous weariness and could not find any words to answer him. I merely nodded and allowed Mihail, who is some three years younger than Vlad, to draw me to the table where there was a simple meal of cold meats and bread. I could only pick at the food and take a glass of wine which, with the roaring of the fire and the change from chill to warmth, caused my eyelids to prick and droop until Mihail raised me from the chair, on an arm that gave lie to his weak appearance by its considerable strength, and conducted me from the room, along a small gallery to a tower.

We ascended a curving stairway and went through a door which led into a large bed chamber. Again, it was well lit and had a roaring fire which was throwing sparks merrily into the hearth. A large bed had been turned down and a warming-pan inserted between the crisp white sheets. Mihail himself removed the warming-pan and asked me if I needed anything further for my night's repose. I shook my head, noting that my belongings had already been placed in the room, and, with a sense of strangeness, realizing that I had not yet spoken a word to them.

Yawning, I threw off my clothes and fell into the large, warm bed and, before I knew it, I had succumbed to a deep sleep.

Tired as I was, however, the effects of my excitement at meeting my brothers, the arduous journey, and the peculiarities of my brothers' appearance must have influenced the workings of my mind, for I had one of those strange waking dreams.

I came awake in the darkened bed chamber. The spluttering fire had lapsed into a dull glow which threw grotesque shadows over the walls. And, in this strange half-sleep, I thought three people stood at the foot of my bed, my two brothers and a third man, a stranger much darker than the others, a phantom, who seemed to tower above his companions and yet seemed unreal.

'. . . he is no Dracula,' my brother Vlad was whispering.

'I agree,' came the voice of Mihail, edged with a sneer. 'I feel he has no kinship with our house. He is but a stupid Italian ladies' man.'

'Nevertheless,' imposed the sonorous tones of the stranger, 'he is a Dracula. In his veins runs a noble blood. His sires were your sires and he has the right to join us in making our house immortal. Let him rest now. His blood is young and will keep awhile.'

Bewildered, fearful, I sank back into the sleep of the exhausted.

When I came awake a small shaft of sunlight had entered through a crack in the shutters and was shining on to my face. I felt as if I had been asleep for a long time and, indeed, when I arose from the bed and threw open the shutters, I found the sun already stood at its zenith.

While I appreciated the courtesy of my brothers in letting me sleep late, I was nevertheless somewhat annoyed that I had missed a goodly portion of the day. However, this was but a passing annoyance, so overcome was I by the breathtaking beauty of the scene that unfolded before my window.

Gone were the shadows of the previous night. Castle Dracula stands on top of a mountain and, as I looked down from my window, I saw that this side of the castle stood right on top of a precipice, falling vertically nearly one thousand feet into a valley through which ran the river Arges, beginning its tremulous descent to join the greater river of Dimbovita. The steep gorge was breathtaking. I could see the tiny houses that made up the village, away beneath me like so many tiny dolls' houses. In all directions were mountains covered in woods which seemed to contain every conceivable shade of green, and I could also see a tremendous amount of blossoms. Also, from my window, I could peer southwards and view the hills sinking away to the sun-scorched Wallachian plains. In the other direction were impenetrable mountain ranges, many snow-capped peaks, which separated Wallachia from Transylvania.

I do not know how long I stood there, breathing in the beauties of the scenery. It was not until the sun reminded me of the lateness of the hour that I turned back into my room and found that I had been so engrossed that someone, without my hearing, had already placed a jug of hot water on a stand beside the bed.

I had washed and was about to commence shaving when I observed that there were no mirrors in the room—an oversight that surprised me as most Wallachians, while they sport large moustaches, clean shave their beards. I had also noticed that this seemed to be the custom with my brothers.

Once dressed in shirt and trousers, I thought I would try to find a servant and ask for a glass. As if in answer to my thoughts, I heard at that moment a noise outside my door, which was confirmed when I heard a woman's laugh. It was deep, almost velvety in its quality.

Immediately I crossed the room, swung open the door, and peered up and down the stairs of the tower. Surprisingly, there was no one there, and I stood still awhile, quite perplexed. Then I heard the sound of rustling skirts from below and I quickly started down the stairs.

The castle seemed shrouded in gloom, there being little or no light penetrating from the glorious day outside, and, as I made my way down the dark stairs, I found myself puzzling over the fact that, in spite of the lateness of the hour, no servant had opened the shutters. This mystery, combined with the rustling of the unseen lady, made me feel even more confused.

Stumbling a little in the gloom, holding on to the cold walls for guidance, I eventually reached the doorway to the gallery which led to the room where I had supped the night before. As I opened the door I glimpsed, at the far end of the gallery, a figure in a white, billowing skirt disappearing into a room beyond.

I called out, but no one answered. Now slightly annoyed, and just a little uneasy, I followed along the gallery and found myself in the supper room. To my surprise, I found a cold breakfast had been laid and a single place set as if in wait for me. Then, from a door beyond, I again heard the throaty laughter of a woman. I strode immediately to the door and threw it open.

There was nobody in the passage . . . but again I heard the rustle of skirts fading down a stairway.

I was now convinced that one of the servants was leading me a merry dance, and I resolved to follow her and seek an explanation for this unwarranted baiting of a guest. I started down the stairway, which was a small, circular way, as if built inside a very small tower. It led deeper and deeper until it grew so dark that I could scarce see. By the dampness of the walls I could ascertain that the stone steps had led me underground, and I was on the point of giving up my quest and climbing back to the warm room I had just quit when the narrow stairs suddenly opened out.

Spread out before me was a large, cellar-like room, lit by some strange phosphorescent light which seemed to glow from the stone walls. By this light I could see the cellar spreading into an infinity of low arches and stone columns, and could also make out the shape of large wine vats. The place was very chilly and damp, and caused me to cough several times as the musty atmosphere seeped into my lungs. It was very quiet. I could hear dripping water. The sound echoed and it made me uneasy and I felt I should call out.

'Is anyone there?' I called.

My words echoed and came back at me, hollow, disembodied, and the shadows of the vaults stained the floor and the silence was vibrant.

Then, again, came the deep-throated laughter, accompanied by the rustling of the skirts.

It came from the far end of the vault.

'Is anyone there?' I called out again, advancing a step or two and staring into the gloom, stricken by a strange, formless fear and not admiring myself for it. 'I know you are there,' I cried. 'Cease this play-acting at once and tell me why you behave thus to a guest.'

The chuckling ceased. The rustling skirts ceased their movement. The silence seemed to be breathing and I heard the dripping water and the gloom swooped around and was stifling. I stepped forward again.

'*Mircea!*' a voice hissed. '*Son of Dracula!*'

I confess, I was startled, but I swung around to face the voice, peering intently through the gloom and seeing nothing . . . nothing but darkness.

'Do not start so,' said the voice, low, voluptuous, almost whispering in my ear and yet unseen. 'I seek only to welcome you home to your rightful place.'

I was bewildered. Whereas before the voice had been to my right, now it seemed to come from my left. I swung around again to confront the ghostly speaker, but once more, amazingly, there was nothing.

Then, again, I heard the low laughter.

'*Mirceal Son of Dracula!*' The voice was obscene,

voluptuous. '*Soon you shall know what we know! Soon all will be shown to you! Come, Mircea! Come now . . .*'

The whispering was receding to the dark depths of the cellar, and at that moment, I am certain, I caught a glimpse of the woman in white.

'Who are you?' I cried out, feeling ashamed of my own fears, peering forward into the darkness and instantly noticing that the walls seemed to be losing their phosphorescent quality.

'*Come, Mircea! Come!*'

At that instant a door suddenly crashed open, and there stood the raging Tirgsor, holding aloft a blazing torch. Then, though I cannot swear to it because the sound of the crashing door was echoing and re-echoing around the cellar, I thought I heard from the gloom at the far end of the cellar a woman's most hideous scream of rage. Silence swooped in before I could confirm this.

'What are you doing here in the *pivnit?*'

Tirgsor's voice resounded like thunder.

'Pardon?' I asked, surprised that he should dare to address me in such a tone of voice.

'What are you doing in this cellar?'

Coldly, contemptuously, I told him about the girl, at which he seemed unusually troubled. When I had completed my tale, he stepped quickly forward, holding the torch above my head and peering intently at me. Then, before I could resist, he reached out and seized my jaw, twisting my head first one way and then the other, staring with blazing eyes at my neck.

'*Che diavolo!*' I exclaimed, forgetting my German. 'What in . . . ?'

Tirgsor took no notice of my outburst. Deep in thought, he heaved a sigh and mumbled: '*Der Hals . . . der Hals draussen blutet.*'

His German was poor, but to me it sounded like 'The throat without bleeding.' However, before I could ask him what he meant and how he dared treat me in such an impertinent fashion, the sulky brute seized me by the arm and propelled me from the cellar, slamming the door behind us and shooting home two heavy iron bolts.

'What of the woman in there?' I demanded, trying to shake loose from his iron grip.

'Woman?' he said, as if he had not heard the question properly. 'Ah, do not worry, mein Herr. It is my daughter. She loves to joke. Sometimes she does not realize her jokes are in poor taste. I will punish her, have no fear, mein Herr.'

With that he ushered me up the stairs and into the room where my cold breakfast still awaited me. Pointing at it, he said, unnecessarily, *'Frühstück.'* Then he turned and left without another word.

In spite of the merry dance she had led me, I was horrified that Tirgsor had left the girl locked in the cellar. Then I realized that the door from this room led down the spiral stairway to the cellar, and that this would provide an exit for the girl. I went to the door and tried to open it, but, to my surprise, I found it locked. Somewhat mystified by these events, I sat down to a light breakfast.

I was still puzzling over the events of the day when my two brothers entered the room and, after an exchange of meaningless pleasantries, I told them of the morning's adventure. They exchanged a glance which I interpreted as something akin to annoyance.

'Do not worry, brother,' Vlad said. 'Tirgsor's daughter, Malvina, sometimes is taken with devilment and executes all manner of tricks upon us. She is a simple girl. Tirgsor will punish her.'

'He has no need to on my account,' I said. 'On the contrary, to be locked in that dank cellar will be enough punishment for her, so please tell him not to take the matter further.'

Vlad nodded and then dismissed the subject by informing me of the dangers I could encounter in the castle.

'This is an old, old building, brother Mircea, and beneath it are many caverns leading into the hollow of the mountain. Indeed, a man may travel from one cellar right through the mountain into the valley of Arges, beside the river, if he but knows the way; however, the routes are many and the same man may become lost for eternity in the vaults. Therefore, we pray you, do not wander the castle either in the day or at night, especially, for then the greatest dangers are abroad.'

'What dangers?' I asked.

'As a man might travel to the caves in the Arges valley, so it has been known that wild animals, the wolves and bears, seeking a home in the caves, can enter into the vaults at night for warmth. It would be wise to keep to the confines of our room and those rooms we will show you today. All other doors you will find locked, and those you will naturally have no wish to enter.'

I looked at Vlad closely. His tone of voice was strange. I had the feeling that he was hiding something from me, though I could not imagine what. Nevertheless, it seemed a sensible arrangement if, as he had said, wild beasts had been known to enter various parts of the castle.

'Very well,' I said.

Mihail smiled thinly.

'Good,' he said. 'And now we will show you your

home . . . our home. And we will talk of the past and of the future.'

Vlad and Mihail led me through another door which led on to a balcony, part of which was still bathed in the rays of the westward journeying sun. Vlad and Mihail preferred to remain in the shadows of the doorway, while I tried to gather warmth from the dying rays.

In daylight I could observe no change in my brothers' complexions, still pale as if the very blood had been drained from their bodies. It struck me as odd, however, how weak and anaemic they seemed in daylight whereas the night before, though pale, they had seemed a trifle more animated. Then, with a start, I recalled Tirgsor, and decided to observe if they, too, gathered strength and vigour with the setting of the sun.

I wondered if they might be suffering from some malady, for I recall a learned doctor lecturing students in Rome on the case of a man who suffered from a morbid acuteness of the senses. This man was tortured by light, by odours, by noises and by textures of certain substances, even clothes. But such a morbid acuteness of sense was a condition of the mind and not the body, so how could both my brothers, as well as their steward, share this strange condition?

These thoughts passed through my mind as I observed my brothers. I felt ill at ease with them: they seemed like total strangers instead of the blood of my blood.

My attention was drawn back to the square stone balcony on which I stood. It protruded from what I observed to be the main tower of the castle and which overhung the castle courtyard, which was some thirty feet below.

'Here, brother,' said Vlad, waving a thin hand around the ramparts of the castle. 'Here is the home of your ancestors, where you were born and from where you were cruelly parted from us as a young child. This, dear brother, is Castle Dracula!'

CHAPTER
11

I have already given an account of the breathtaking scenery that surrounded the castle, and here I feel compelled to give a description of the castle itself. It stands on the very summit of the mountain, on a small plateau. The castle walls closely follow the precipitous sides of the mountain, as if they were part of the mountain walls themselves. The walls of the castle are thus built on the plan of an irregular polygon, the shape of the plateau at its summit. Only on one side of the castle, at its entrance, does the plateau give way to form a dangerously narrow ledge along which the road, or rather a mere track, to Arefu circles down the mountainside.

From east to west, as I discovered, the actual courtyard, which is entirely encircled by the inner walls of the castle and between which the castle chambers are placed, measures a distance of one hundred feet. From north to south this distance is exceeded by twenty feet more. There are five towers at regular intervals around the castle walls; a donjon or strong central tower stands opposite the main entrance and then in each corner of the walls are four more towers, two of which are of classical cylindrical shape, and it is in the southwestern one of these towers that my bedchamber lies.

The whole castle combines all of the best features

of the grim Teutonic fortresses with the intricate and ornate design of Byzantium structures.

Between each of the towers, which are reserved for the reception rooms and living quarters of the household, run the stables, store rooms and quarters for the castle garrison. In the courtyard itself stands an entrance to the castle chapel and vault which stands at basement level. The castle is entered by one route only, which I failed to observe when I came across it at night. The great double wooden doors lead to a drawbridge which, when lowered, spans a chasm that drops nearly four hundred feet to the rocks below and then tumbles in leaps and bounds still further towards the valley of the Arges. A strange impregnable setting below which, as I was told, the *privnit* or cellar vaults have been tunnelled out of the very heart of the mountain.

I asked Vlad how many people inhabited the castle.

'In our father Dracula's time there were two hundred men-at-arms and two hundred more servants; but now we live frugally with Tirgsor as our *stolnic*—Tirgsor and a few other servants.'

I must confess that I had tried hard to recall memories of the first few years of my life at Castle Dracula, but such memories were few. I can recall the tall figure of my father standing before the fire, a sneer on his face, his voice raised in some accusation against my mother. I can recall the night I was awakened, wrapped in a warm blanket, and carried through long, dark corridors to a carriage, which must have been the night of my mother's dramatic flight from the castle. But apart from these, my remembrance of my life before arriving in Rome has all but faded; so my brothers were as total strangers and everything they showed me was new and alien.

Mihail proved the more expansive in conversation

and told me that the room in which I slept was the same chamber in which my mother had pushed me into this world, and that it had been my nursery room until the night of our flight. I asked him why he and Vlad had, in their letters to me, given the address of the castle as being at Poenari when in fact Arefu was the nearest village. Mihail led me by the arm to a window that overlooked the Arges valley and pointed to the far side. I saw some ruins, about a mile down the valley.

'That is Poenari,' he said. 'Poenari is well known, known better than Arefu, and thus messengers can more easily find their way there. Poenari is the site of the ancient Darcian fortress of Decidara, where the Romans first built their fortress to dominate this province. Upon that fortress a stronger castle was raised to resist the march of the Teutons in the thirteenth century, but it was almost levelled by the Turks and the Tartars.

'Our father, Dracula, maintained a garrison there, but Poenari was finally levelled by the Turks in 1462 when our father was driven into Transylvania.'

He paused and drew me back into the refectory room. A fire had been lit, for it was now early evening and the storm clouds had turned the day dark and chill.

This refectory room, which seemed the main living-room of the castle, was a large one, very lofty with long, narrow windows, shuttered on the outside. In fact, at no time during the day had I observed any servant remove the shutters from any of the castle windows. The ceiling of the room was vaulted with an abundance of black oak beams. At one end was the large carved stone fireplace. A long oak table dominated the centre of the room, while the rest of the furniture consisted of sideboards and chairs and gave a general atmosphere of comfortlessness. Dark tapestries and a few musical instruments, which lay about, failed to lighten the pervading gloom.

My brother Mihail continued in his discourse.

'This fortress of Arges, as we call Castle Dracula, was first built by our ancestor Basarab. It has a greater strategic position in the valley than that of Poenari, but the castle was ruined by the Tartars in the last century. It was our father, Dracula, who had it rebuilt when he became ruler of Wallachia, for he did not trust living in the towns, since the boyars were crafty and self-seeking. Indeed, they had murdered several of our blood. Do you know the story of our uncle Mircea, after whom you were named?'

I admitted such knowledge. We had seated ourselves before the fire and the silent Tirgsor had appeared with mulled wine.

'You know of the punishment our father meted out to the boyars of Tirgoviste,' Mihail continued, 'for the murder of his brother Mircea?'

'I have heard the story told,' I replied.

'Do you then know that after Dracula slew the assassins of Mircea, the five-hundred faithless boyars, their wives and children, he rounded up the remainder . . . three hundred boyars with their wives and children. It was Easter and he marched them to this very spot. Across the Arges were the ruins of Poenari, while on this side were the ruins of the fortress of Arges. Dracula told the boyars who had survived the march that he wanted an impregnable fortress raised on the ruins left by the Tartars. And so those faithless boyars, their wives and their children, were set to work like common serfs. They heaved the stone from the ruins of Poenari to the summit of this mountain, heaved the stone day by day, sweating and grunting like the pigs they were until, finally, Castle Dracula rose proud and strong and impregnable. Those boyars worked until the clothes dropped from their backs, and then they worked without clothes. Thus did Dracula build his castle and, with the same stroke, subdue his faithless boyar class and make them submit to unquestioning obedience to the house of Dracula.'

While Mihail recited this horrific tale, I noticed that his eyes had brightened considerably and that he was now leaning forward excitedly in his chair. His pale face was actually animated.

'Didn't the Turks try to destroy the castle when Dracula fled in 1462?' I asked.

'Of course,' Mihail replied, 'but the castle was well built. While our father was in exile, it was held by his governor, Gherghnia, who perished last year in the fight against the Turks.'

'And how did Dracula die?' I asked.

'As you know, our father married the sister of Mathias of Hungary. In so doing, he renounced the Orthodox faith and accepted the Church of Rome which is the faith of the Hungarian princes who are said to have their descent from St. Stephen. It was a political decision, for our father sought to return to his own, but the fools of the Orthodox religion made a great outcry, as if religion were important.'

I was surprised at the sneering tone of Mihail's voice; I had thought that my brothers would be strongly for the Orthodox faith.

'In spite of the outcry from the clerics,' Mihail went on, 'our father's third marriage was celebrated at Visegard. Soon after, in 1474, the princes of Hungary, Russia, Moldavia and Poland decided it was time to launch a crusade against the Turkish Sultan, Mohammed. The prince Radu, our father's weak brother who ruled Wallachia, was but a plaything of the Sultan, and so it was agreed to support Dracula in his claim to the throne.

'Radu died, however, and Basarab Laiota became ruler. At this, Dracula decided to invade from Transylvania. On 25th July, 1476, he and Prince Stephen Bathory held a council of war in Tirda, and during November Dracula entered Wallachia through the pass of Bran. Soon Tirgoviste fell, then Bucharest. At Curtea de Arges we saw Dracula come into his own again.'

'But how did he die?' I persisted.

Mihail was silent for some time.

'There was a battle near Bucharest,' he said finally. 'There are two tales about it. One, that the Turks were beginning to break and Dracula descended a hill to observe the position when he was mistaken for a Turk and cut down by his own men. Two, that the boyars, who remembered how he forced them to submit to his will, slew him.'

'So there *is* a mystery about the death?'

'There is no mystery,' Vlad interrupted with a certain fervour. 'His body was taken to the monastery of Snagov where it was interred.'

'Snagov?' I asked.

'It is an island in one of the lakes surrounding Bucharest in the heart of the Vlasie forest,' Mihail explained. 'Our grandfather, when he was voivode, endowed Snagov with more land than any other monastery in the realm.'

'So our father lies at Snagov?' I mused.

'And now our brother Mircea,' Mihail interrupted my thoughts, 'has returned to his proper place.'

'My proper place?' I smiled uneasily. 'I do not know. I was raised in Rome and I fear there is little Wallachian in me. I do not speak the language; nor do

I have knowledge of the history and customs of this land. In truth, I am a foreigner.'

'But in your blood runs that of Dracula,' Mihail said. 'An ancient red blood that has been shed many times for the furtherance of our honourable house. Blood cannot be denied.'

'I appreciate your acceptance of me, brothers, as one of the family, and yet I must confess to you that I feel a stranger in this castle.'

Mihail waved a dismissing hand.

'The strangeness will wear away,' he said. 'You are a Dracula and you are among your own people.'

'But being among them, what then?'

Vlad gave a strange, disturbing half laugh.

'We have plans, brother Mircea,' he said in a tone I did not like. 'Plans to restore the house of Dracula to its rightful place.'

'Its rightful place?' I inquired.

Mihail frowned and looked hard at Vlad, who turned away from my curious gaze.

'It is enough talk for one day, brother Mircea,' Mihail said. 'We will talk more of this tomorrow. But now, let us eat and offer you the hospitality of our wine cellar.'

I would have preferred to continue the conversation, for it seemed to me that my brothers had more in mind for my visit than merely fraternalism.

What plan could they have? I wondered. And where would I, their brother yet a stranger, enter into such a plan?

My uneasiness increased.

Tirgsor was summoned to lay the table and I noticed, with some confusion, that he laid only one place. When I questioned my brothers about this, they explained that they had eaten heartily at midday.

There was one strange thing I noticed about the meal—for I consider myself something of a *buongustaoi* or, as the French would say, a *gourmet*—and this was the total absence of spices such as salt and garlic. This absence I could not attribute to the poorness of the larder, so I wondered if Tirgsor, who seemed to do all the jobs in the castle, acted as cook as well. I made a mental note to go for a walk on the morrow to the village to collect some salt and garlic, after which I could explain to the sullen *stolnic* the art of cooking.

After the meal, and tiring of my brothers' endless questions about the world outside Wallachia, I made an excuse to retire to bed early. At this my brothers made no protest, but bid me sleep well and dream well.

Again, as with the night before, a fire had been lit in the hearth of my bed chamber and a warming-pan had heated the bed for my repose. Water had been placed for my toilet . . . and it was as I was washing that I heard a familiar noise at my door.

It was the unmistakable rustle of skirts.

Determined not to be made a fool of twice, I crept quietly to the door, gently turned the iron ring handle and threw it open as quickly as possible.

The girl who stood before the door started back, a cry on her lips, one hand raised to cover her mouth. She then froze before me.

As the light from my room fell upon the girl, I found it was my turn to be surprised. Indeed, I swear by the ancient gods of Rome that she was the prettiest thing I had laid eyes on since coming to Wallachia. She could not have been more than eighteen summers, and she had a fresh pale skin with touches of red on her cheeks which were coated so delicately with freckles that one would have sworn that an artist must have painted them there. Her hair was dark, and the blue eyes that stared at me were lovely, but wide with fright.

I immediately smiled in reassurance.

'And who might you be?' I asked, hoping she would understand my German.

'I am . . . Malvina, mein Herr."

'Ah,' I said, 'the daughter of Tirgsor.'

Silently I wondered how such a brute as Tirgsor could have sired such an exquisite creature.

'I am . . . Malvina, mein Herr.'

'And have you come to lead me another merry dance?' I said, warming to her blush and her radiant good looks.

'Mein Herr?'

A frown creased her well proportioned brow and her voice was clearly puzzled.

'Ah,' said I, 'you wish to forget this morning? Very well, your punishment in the cellar has erased the matter.'

Her lovely face was torn betwixt puzzlement and fright, and I swear that this seemed genuine. Then she suddenly darted a fearful glance at the stairway, raised a finger to her lips, and pushed me back into the room. She then followed me in and closed the door behind her, and stood for a few moments, listening intently, her head to one side.

'Mein Herr,' she said finally and with a certain fearful passion, 'you must leave Castle Dracula immediately.'

'Oh,' I said lightly. 'And why, pray?'

'Do not ask, mein Herr, just go. Go now! This very hour!'

Naturally I did not believe she was serious. Fearful though she looked I could not forget what had happened this morning and I even thought to compliment her on her acting ability.

'Malvina,' I said, smiling directly at her, 'I enjoy jokes greatly, but I am tired this night, especially after this morning's caprice.'

Again a frown of puzzlement crossed her brow.

'This morning, mein Herr? What happened?'

'Come now,' I said, 'admit it. Your father told me it was you.'

The girl shook her head slowly from side to side, blinked her eyes and looked even more bewildered.

'Mein Herr, tell me, what happened this morning?'

Overcome once more by an irrational unease, suddenly sensing that the girl was sincere, I explained. And, as I did so, I noticed the blood drain from those delicate features and saw her vainly trying to suppress her own trembling. When I had finished, she grasped me by the hand.

'Oh, mein Herr,' she cried, 'as sure as God watches us, believe me, it was not I who led you down to the cellars! Indeed, all this day I have been with my uncle Toma who keeps the inn at Arefu. I returned but an hour ago, and when I heard you were here I came immediately to warn you.'

'Warn me?' I said, now shaken by her intensity. 'Warn me of what?'

'To warn you to leave and leave now!' She held my hand tighter and her blue eyes were huge and fear-filled. 'Oh, mein Herr,' she almost sobbed, 'there is much evil here. Go! Go now, while you may!'

I started to press her further for an explanation, but she suddenly raised her hand and placed it over my mouth. We stood thus like statues for several minutes, she listening, with her head to one side. At last she looked back at me, and there was dread in her blue eyes.

'I must go, mein Herr, lest they miss me. Please,

mein Herr, for the sake of your unborn children . . . *leave the castle tonight!*'

Then she was gone, swiftly and silently, and, shaking slightly, I sat down on the bed to ponder the strangeness of it all.

Either she was a great natural actress or she was totally sincere. If it were the latter, then who was the woman in white? And why had Tirgsor and my brothers lied about Malvina?

There was one way to prove the truth of the matter. On the morrow I intended going to the village of Arefu to gather salt and garlic for my food. On the morrow, then, I would go to Arefu and ask the innkeeper, Toma, if his niece had been with him all day as she claimed. If the answer was positive, I could then demand an explanation from my brothers.

Thus resolved, and feeling none the easier for it, I completed my toilet and retired to bed.

It was dark when I started into wakefulness. I lay there awhile, still groggy from my sleep, trying to register what it was that had awakened me. Then, from my shuttered window, I heard a strange flapping noise. I listened more intently. Twice there was a soft thud, as if something was banging against the shutters. At this, I frowned. Outside the window was a drop of a thousand feet to the valley floor; how, then, could anything be banging at my window? Yet, as I listened, the noise came again, the strange flapping and the thudding, and then silence. I felt fear creeping through me.

Nervously, cautiously, I rose from the bed and walked slowly across the room to the window. First I had to unlatch the thick glass window and then, leaning forward, I opened the shutter.

At first I saw nothing. The night sky was clear and the moon, round and white, shone down cleanly. Emboldened by this, I leant as far out as I could and peered all around me, trying to trace the cause of my disturbed slumber.

Suddenly, with a start, I heard the flapping noise. I glanced up just as something struck me full in the face. I felt tiny pinpricks in my scalp and forehead, and something like a wet, chilly tissue covered my face.

Releasing a cry, I staggered back into the room, my hands flying up to claw at the thing on my face. I was blind. I felt revulsion. My heart pounded and my flesh crawled. It felt small, soft . . . nay, bloated like a bag filled with water, and . . . it had wings. I cried out again. I tore the thing away and feverishly hurled it from me . . . and, in the moonlight, I saw the black shape of a bat.

It lay stunned on the floor where I had thrown it, and I could see that it was a fairly large species. Its flapping wings must have been nearly eighteen inches long, and its body nearly six inches long. It had large ears, broad at the base but narrowing abruptly to sharp, recurved tips. It also had thick woolly fur extending on to its wing membranes, which appeared ash grey in colour.

It lay there for a moment and then, with a loud, high-pitched, penetrating squeak, rose with slow pulsating motions of its wings and commenced to hover at a height of five feet from the floor. At this distance I could observe, with something of a shudder, conspicuously large, white, canine teeth. But, above all, I suddenly became aware of tiny red eyes boring into me . . . red, malignant and hypnotizing.

I shook my head. I tried to recollect my senses. I

looked at the bat and saw the moonlight surrounding it and saw the great darkness beyond. The bat made no attempt to fly away. I had been given to understand that this was the habit with such creatures, so I grabbed my walking cane and moved forward, raising it at arm's length. To my surprise, the bat continued hovering, its tiny red eyes glinting in the moonlit room. Then, to my surprise, so much so that I stopped moving, it began to make a curious motion with its wings, swinging from side to side, slowly, rhythmically, as if in some strange, exotic dance. I stood still fascinated, the fear slipping away from me, an enormous drowsiness descending, seeing nothing but the moonlight, the slow sway of the wings, the red eyes, the night, the white teeth . . .

Suddenly, just as I would have fallen into a deep slumber, a high pitched shriek, like a demented scream of anger, jerked me fully awake. To my horror, I saw an even larger bat fly through the window, its huge black wings slicing through the air, its canine teeth gleaming white against a blood red mouth, before, still shrieking, it fell on the first bat and sank its teeth into its neck.

I felt myself recoil. My revulsion whipped me raw. I heard shrieking, snarling, saw a brief, shocking struggle; then, to my terror, the large bat swooped around the room, carrying the smaller bat in its jaws, and was swiftly gone back through the window, leaving me dazed.

The silence shook me awake. I blinked and saw the full moon. I rushed forward to draw the shutters and looked up in the direction that the large bat had taken. To my amazement, knowing that bats never fly in formation, I saw what must have been the large bat, now flying in the centre of a perfect, diamond-shaped formation of some twenty or so other bats, winging up towards the sky, black against the brightness of the full moon.

Shaken, shivering, I returned to my bedside, poured some water out of the jug, and bathed the tiny claw pricks in my head.

CHAPTER
12

The morning was bright and warm and, feeling no ill effects from my experience of the previous night, I decided to carry out my resolve to take a walk to the village.

I arose quite early, washed, dressed and made my way down into the courtyard. No one was about and I wondered at the lateness of the hours kept by my brothers and their servants. I have always had the disposition of rising early and find myself a little intolerant of others who do not do so. The castle doors were closed, but I found no difficulty in throwing open the bolts and opening the great wooden doors to a sufficient width to allow the passage of my body. Similarly, there was no difficulty to be encountered in working the well-oiled mechanism that lowered the wooden drawbridge over the chasm.

With the sun now beating hotly down, unusually hot for a November day, I made my way down the steep track. I paused frequently to drink in the clean air and the gorgeous fragrance of the surrounding woods, which seemed like nectar after the dank gloom of the castle. As I stood drinking in the air, I could observe the beauty of the landscape.

Dracula had, indeed, chosen well in making his home at this spot. The autumn flowers bloomed in many-hued abundance, and many of the trees were so overgrown that, in spite of the nearness of winter, it might well have been a summer's day.

I reached Aretu after a slow walk of an hour and a half. Here the sun suddenly deserted me, for the shadow of the mountain fell sharply across the houses that comprised the village.

At first glance it seemed that the village was deserted. Each house was boarded up, the shutters closed and the doors shut. Yet I had the strange feeling that I was being observed as I walked down the street to the building I supposed was the village inn. By the time I reached it, I was almost convinced in my belief that the place was deserted, for I passed the church whose yard was overgrown while the building itself was clearly in decay, its doors hanging open with goats and sheep huddling for warmth inside.

Each house, I noted, had a large black cross marked in some tar-like substance on the door, and at each door and window hung a garland of flowers. Indeed, even on the cow stalls, alongside the road, were hung numerous bunches of wild roses.

I came to the inn door and found it closed fast. The inhospitality annoyed me and I aimed a hearty blow with my fist at its heavy oak, crying to the innkeeper to open up.

A surly voice within urged the Mother of God to keep the inhabitants from harm. I threw back my head and exclaimed that it would take more than God's intercession to prevent harm coming to them if the door was not opened to a weary traveller.

Slowly came movements within. There was the rattle of chains, the creak of hinges, and gradually the door swung open. I strode in, almost pushing aside the portly man who stood holding a small figure of a Madonna in his hand. A woman stood at the foot of the stairs, a Bible in her hands, her face taut and white. I surveyed this pair with some amusement.

'Lord save us,' I said, 'but you are a superstitious people in this country!'

'Amen to the Lord saving us, mein Herr,' grunted the man, as he bolted the door after me. 'But it bodes no good to us if we do not have a care in these parts.'

The woman then asked me what I wanted; and her tone, I felt, was much too surly for an innkeeper's wife.

'If this is an inn, what should I want?' I replied, edging my tongue with sarcasm. 'I need to break my fast with a little ale and some bread, cheese and salami.'

Without another word the woman bustled away. The man put down his statue and knelt before the hearth, where it was obvious he had been laying a fire before my knock had disturbed him.

'And where are you from, mein Herr?" he said, trying to overcome the unfriendliness of his first welcome.

'From Rome,' I answered.

'What are you doing in this God forsaken country? There is nothing here, mein Herr. Where are you staying?'

The woman had brought me food and I sat down, eagerly biting into the soft warm bread.

'I am staying at the castle,' I said between mouthfuls. 'Castle Dracula.'

There was a crash of broken china. The woman stood before the resultant mess, her hands to her pale cheeks. The innkeeper had half risen and was crossing himself.

'Mein Herr,' he said, almost whispering, 'you are the guest who is staying at Castle Dracula?'

'Yes,' I snapped. 'What of it? Is it so strange?'

The man and woman exchanged a glance.

'Strange?' the man said. 'You have been in the castle and *you* ask if it is strange?'

I sighed and took a long pull at my ale. Had it not been for my own increasing uneasiness of late, I would have assumed that all the Wallachians were half wits.

'The castle is evil, mein Herr,' said the woman, whose frame was quite visibly trembling.

'Good God,' I said with as much authority as I could muster, 'does not your own niece, Malvina, work at the castle?'

At this the woman gave a pitiful cry, a cry of the most awesome anguish, and ran from the room.

'Forgive us, mein Herr,' said the innkeeper, Toma, now visibly trembling himself, 'but you are in a strange country and we do have strange ways. Indeed, our niece Malvina is forced to work at the castle.' Here he crossed himself and muttered, 'God between her and all evil!' He then paused a second before continuing: 'It is her stepfather, Tirgsor, who so ordains it. Many times have we tried to make her leave, but Tirgsor has a strange power over her.'

'And was Malvina at this inn yesterday?'

'Indeed, mein Herr. She spent two days with us, but returned to the castle yesterday evening. Why do you ask?'

I shook my head silently. I drank some more ale. Now I knew that Tirgsor and my brothers had lied to me, and I wondered why this could be so. The innkeeper, Toma, was still nervous.

'For the villagers of Arefu,' he said as I ate, 'Castle Dracula stands as a blight. Twenty years ago this was a happy village. Then the Voivode Dracula decided to rebuild the old castle and the unhappy boyars were driven here like cattle. Each day we saw them working, each day we saw them dying. Yes, mein Herr! Blood built Castle Dracula and blood will cause its downfall. The curse of the Dracula is sealed by blood; the whole mountainside is a citadel of blood. Young Herr, I beg you, leave this place.'

'It is not the first time I have been given such a warning. You Wallachians are not very welcoming.'

'Mein Herr, we Wallachians were once renowned for our hospitality; but here, at this time, in this place, we fear for strangers even more than we fear for ourselves, for there is a great evil at work here and strangers could spread it to the four corners of the earth. Then, indeed, all would be lost.'

I must confess that I thought the man to be rambling, but again the strange mysteries I had encountered in my journey forced me to listen further to him.

'Come, mein Herr,' he said. 'Let me show you something, as I see you are yet a sceptic.'

He motioned me to follow him up the stairs to a room whose large door he unlocked with a thick iron key. As he swung open the door, I heard a strange growling sound from within—a sound that was not quite the growl of a dog, nor quite like any sound I had heard before.

'Look inside, mein Herr,' Toma said. 'And please be prepared!'

I did as I was bid—and was revolted by what met my gaze.

Squatting on his haunches in a corner of the room was the hideous figure of what had once been a man. His clothes were now in rags and he was surrounded by his own excretia. His hair, streaked black and white, was matted and filthy, totally obscuring his face, except for his eyes which, in their fearful and nightmarish dementia, could well have made the demons of Hell shudder.

This thing was tearing at something in its hands. Stepping closer, a wave of nausea filled my stomach, as I observed that the creature was tearing at a raw piece of flesh, sucking the blood from the red meat with obvious relish.

I stopped my advance, and the creature raised its hideous eyes to mine. It dropped the meat from its mouth. It gazed at me intently. There was blood around its lips and the light in its eyes was a fearsome light. Then, letting out the most hideous shriek, it sprang at me.

I raised my arm to defend myself, but there was no need, for the thing was chained by its ankle to a corner of the room. Pulled back by this chain, it collapsed in the corner and clawed at the floor with its fingers and snarled like a beast. Feeling shocked and weak, I let Toma pull me from the room and relock the door. We then returned downstairs in silence and Toma poured me a glass of spirits which I hastily, and gratefully, drank down. Toma poured me another.

'By the living God, Toma,' I said, gasping and drying my lips, 'what sort of devilment is this?'

'Devilment is right, mein Herr,' he replied. 'That beast which was once a man, and a fine man at that, is my wife's young brother, Liviu. He is nineteen years old this Christmastide.'

'How can it be?' I said, for the thing I had seen possessed the appearance of one pitted for centuries against torment.

'Believe it, mein Herr,' Toma said. 'In this very room, only last June, we celebrated the wedding of Liviu to Gaia. They were young, handsome and very much in love. Then came word from the castle that Gaia was needed to work there and serve our lord.

'You may know that feudalism still exists in most parts of our unhappy land, but we, in this province, are *mosneni,* freemen who bow to no feudal lord. Dracula, who never observed the laws of man or God, was no longer Voivode; while he was alive he trampled on the rights of the *mosneni,* but he was dead and we had no feudal lord. Thus, Liviu laughed at the demand from the castle.

'Tirgsor, who serves as *stolnic* at the castle, had come to the inn with the demand, and Liviu just laughed at him. Ah, I well remember that day, mein Herr. Liviu, young, handsome, with a temper as hot as red iron, laughed at Tirgsor's anger and told him to crawl back to his masters, for Liviu himself had no master.

'Then, one night, we were awakened by an anguished cry. Gaia was gone. Demented with grief, Liviu strapped on a sword and rode up to Castle Dracula. We tried to stop him, mein Herr, but he rode away. We all could hear him crying for the blood of the Draculas, and then his voice was lost in the wind.

'When the village had finally gathered in his support, and collected sticks and stones and marched up to the grey walls of the castle, all was quiet. Liviu's horse stood grazing outside, abandoned. We milled around for a while, irresolute, not knowing what to do. Then a scream, such as I never wish to have offend my ears again, broke the silence of the night and sent us scurrying home like frightened rabbits.

'The next morning, when we ventured out, we found Liviu as you have just seen him. His eyes were inflamed, his hair was streaked white, and he snarled and grovelled like an animal. The one word remaining to him was "blood." That one word. And all he could digest was raw, freshly killed meat from which he would only suck the blood. All this happened but a few months ago. And, as for his wife, that poor innocent child, Gaia, no one has set eyes on her since.'

We sat for some time in silence. I was shocked, disbelieving, and finally outraged, and I boiled over with contradictory emotions which made my heart pound. Toma's voice seemed to come from far away and I listened in silence.

'That, mein Herr, is why Castle Dracula is evil. And that, mein Herr, is why you must leave if you fear for your immortal soul. I beg you, mein Herr, I beg you . . .'

'And what of Malvina?' I suddenly asked. 'Does she not live safely at the castle?'

Toma frowned.

'Tirgsor is her stepfather,' he answered, as if that explained all. 'He has some strange power over her,' he added. 'And perhaps he protects her.'

At that moment I felt both anger and shame: anger that my brothers should have deceived me in such a manner, and shame in the realization that I myself was a Dracula and in part shared their accursed guilt. Yet my shame went beyond this simple cause. I was ashamed of my own cowardice, of the fears that now pierced me, and I resolved to return to the castle and brave that which frightened me.

'Toma,' I said, laying a hand on his shoulder, 'there is a mystery at the castle and I am much intrigued by mysteries and I intend to clear this one up. Furthermore, if there is danger to Malvina, rest assured I shall return her to your safe keeping.'

So saying, I bought garlic and salt, strode from the inn, and took the path back to the castle.

CHAPTER 13

It was well into the afternoon when I reached the castle. Upon entering the donjon tower I was met by my brother Vlad who started to rebuke me in angry fashion for leaving the castle without permission. I replied hotly that I was not his servant, nor a *mosneni* of Arefu, whom he seemed to regard as his serfs. His eyes blazed in anger at this, and I feel blows would have been struck had not Mihail intervened, laying a pacifying hand on my arm and explaining soothingly that his brother and he had been motivated solely by concern for my welfare, since many wild animals prowled the woods, and also bands of *Szgany*, gypsies who would cut one's throat for the clothes on one's back. Somewhat mollified, I accepted Mihail's argument and again found myself in the refectory room, seated before the fire with my two brothers.

'Yesterday,' I said to Mihail, 'you spoke of some purpose that lay behind your invitation to me to come to this castle. Yesterday you said you would speak of such things today.'

Mihail nodded his head.

'First, brother Mircea, you must know what it means to be a Dracula. If you appreciate that, then you will understand our purpose.'

I settled myself before the smouldering logs of the recently lit fire and waited for Mihail to begin.

Mihail walked up and down the room as he spoke, swinging his arms and gesticulating to enforce and emphasize his statements. It was a strange diatribe, full of what I considered vainglorious nonsense, and yet, at the same time, quite thrilling. . . . a story that reviewed generations of forgotten history and set the blood tingling in my veins.

'Since the dawn of time,' began Mihail, 'this country of ours has been inhabited, both physically and spiritually, by man. The *munteni*, the mountain people, have lived and worked in these mountains even long before the tribe of Getae settled on the Wallachian plain, long before the Thracians, Soythians and Celts arrived, each group mingling its blood with the whole. The *munteni* have been in these mountains almost as long as the mountains themselves have been here. And always there has been a house of Dracula here.

'It was one of our house, called Burebista, who united the warring tribes into the centralized state of Darcia and made it secure from its enemies. It was a Dracula, Dicomes, who offered aid to Mark Antony at Actium. It was a Dracula, Decebalus, who strove to hold back the Roman conqueror Trajan and then spilt his own blood rather than submit to the eagles of Rome. Then, in 271, when the Roman Emperor Aurelianus ordered his legions to withdraw from Darcia, it was a Dracula who rebuilt the devastated country. It was a Dracula who repelled the Goths and when, in 375, the Huns from the Asiatic steppes came like a devouring fire, it was a Dracula who mingled his blood with Attila, and this seed reinforced our house.

'The Avars, Slavs, Persians, came and went like the wind. Charlemagne and his Franks tried to conquer and were blown like chaff from the wheat. The Bulgars of Khan Krum and, likewise, Arpad and the seven tribes of Hungary, aye, the Magyars too, the

Vlachs, Vzes, the Kumars, all went down into the melting pot. Only one house and one name survived out of all. It was *our* house and *our* name.

'We gave birth to the Szeklers who devoured the Carpathians and who, in 1213, swept down on the Wallachian plain to regain what was theirs. It was the Szeklers who halted the Magyars from their advance and then, in 1241, it was our house that threw back great Tartar invasions. Six years later, two of our house, Litovoi and Seneslau, established the right to be grand voivodes of Wallachia. Soon they had thrown off the suzereinty of the Hungarian rulers.

'The pride of our house is the pride of our name. Its glory is our glory, its fate is our fate.

'Out of this mingling of the races of Europe the house of Dracula springs unsullied, owing allegiance only to its heritage and to the ancient gods who made it. For countless generations our house has been the heart and brain of a million struggles, and always, while others went down into the pit, it has kept its noble crest aloft, challenging the infidels' gods to destroy it and knowing that they cannot.

'And you, brother Mircea, you, like us, are sprung from this noble seed. You are called by destiny, Mircea.'

He paused and looked eagerly at me, as if expecting me to spring up in a hymn of praise for my ancestry. Instead, I stretched indolently and looked bemused.

'Destiny?' I asked. 'What can destiny call me to?'

'Why, the house of Dracula must rise again; the fates decree it and it would be blasphemy to deny the course already charted in the heavens. It is our father Dracula's wish that we three brothers, the seed of his loins, may join and go forward into the world to seize what is rightfully ours. The world will supply the blood while we supply the brains and hearts, just as we have for a thousand generations before us. The world is but a bauble at our feet. We have only to reach out and it is ours.'

I sat back, trying to disguise my surprise. Were my brothers demented? Were they really trying to tell me that they planned to conquer the world? Or was my knowledge of our common language, German, so inadequate that I mistook their meaning?

'Do I understand correctly, Mihail,' I said. 'You talk of reaching out to grasp the whole world . . . by *conquest*?'

'Conquest?' Mihail said, smiling benignly. 'Yes, but not by military conquest. A conquest far more lasting, more immortal . . .'

He paused here and glanced quickly at Vlad who seemed to be signalling with his eyes, a slight, warning motion. I sat forward and pressed on with my questioning, now determined to clear this matter up.

'How then?' I asked. 'Even the throne of Wallachia has been given by Stefan of Moldavia to a Basarab not of your own house. How can you start a conquest of the world when you have not even a voice in your own country?'

'Pah!' Mihail exclaimed, his eyes flashing. 'Mortal symbol! I talk of something greater. Our father, Dracula, says . . .'

Vlad suddenly laid a hand on Mihail's arm and Mihail fell silent. It was an uneasy silence, and I looked from one to the other.

'Our brother was carried away,' Vlad said. 'Our father, Dracula, spoke long and often to us of establishing a dynasty that will last into eternity; a dynasty to whom the throne of Wallachia would be merely a plaything. We want to establish that dynasty and, as the seed of his loins, it is your right to join with us in that enterprise.'

'Yes,' I said, 'but how? And why? You leave me perplexed, brothers. Are you plotting some coup d'état to remove Basarab and put yourselves on the throne of Wallachia?'

'All will be explained shortly, brother Mircea,' said Mihail, 'that I promise. But as to your first steps, you shall know now. The day after tomorrow there arrives at Castle Dracula the Countess Irene Bathory, who is of the house of Prince Stefan Bathory who spilt blood for our house. The Countess is to marry Vlad and cement our two houses together, and thus will Vlad be made acceptable to the boyars when he sets out to claim the throne of Wallachia.'

My mind in turmoil, I took Vlad's limp, cold hand and pretended to congratulate him on the forthcoming nuptials. The idea of a liaison for political ends is not a new one, but nevertheless, when I encounter it, I am somewhat sickened by the idea of it. However, the whole philosophy of my brothers seemed horrific to me, and I was sure that the solitude of Castle Dracula had unhinged their minds.

And yet Wallachia had had a veritable plethora of rulers. Why was it mad for my brothers to stage some coup and continue the tradition laid down by the successive, and bloody, voivodes? No, it was their dream of world conquest that horrified me, for I am sure they were in deadly earnest. The pride and arrogance of their race (which, thank the saints, I had not inherited) made them capable of contemplating such conquest without a qualm. And was this Countess Irene Bathory privy to such mad dreams?

I confess to a slight malady of the head as I meditated on the strangeness of the many experiences I had encountered since I decided to accept my brothers' invitation. Now, I found any pretensions to fraternal feelings waning, if indeed there had been any in the first place. And yet there was some fascination, some morbid curiosity, that prevented me from laughing in their faces and leaving the castle forthwith ... some fearful fascination, some inexplicable desire, now conscious of a mystery, of a foul, murderous plotting, that I felt it was my duty to seek out and finally resolve.

Would to God that I had obeyed my instincts and fled the castle there and then.

CHAPTER
14

During my solitary supper that evening I had expected to see Malvina, but as usual it was the sullen Tirgsor who brought the meal and served it.

It was not until I started to eat that I remembered I had purchased some salt and garlic from Toma in Arefu to aid in Tirgsor's unseasoned cooking; but by then it was too late: my mind had been preoccupied with Mihail's monologue and I had forgotten to see Tirgsor about the addition of the salt and garlic to my food. This being so, I decided to leave the salt and garlic in my room until the following day.

Since coming to the mountains the chill had struck my chest several times, and the smell of garlic has a curious easing quality to chest ailments. Therefore it would do me little harm to spend a night inhaling the incense of my garlic, and indeed it would probably do me some good.

Having had an exhausting day, I again made my excuses to my brothers and started along the gallery to my bedchamber. Halfway along, however, I realized I had left my cloak behind and I therefore returned to the refectory door. I was just about to enter when I heard my brothers speaking.

'. . . less and less he behaves as a Dracula,' said Vlad.

'Nevertheless,' Mihail said, 'he will serve his purpose.'

'They are getting thirsty,' Vlad said. 'We cannot hold them off much longer.'

'They belong to me,' came a third voice, its harsh, chilling accent strangely familiar. 'I will make them obey me as I did last night. He will be kept until the nuptials. His presence will ease the mind of the female Bathory . . . then they can feast.'

A shiver ran down my spine. Who were 'they'? And surely it was I that was the subject of conversation. Squaring my shoulders, and trying to look more courageous than I felt, I pushed open the door.

My brothers were alone in the room.

A coldness seized me as I mumbled an excuse, quickly picked up my cloak and almost ran from the room.

The grim truth began to dawn on me that there was indeed something more than mere mystery here; that there was something evil, monstrous in this house of Dracula.

Once in my room, I bolted the door and made sure the shutters were secure. Then I sat before the fire, my head in my hands, and wondered what course I should pursue.

I could, perhaps, effect an escape, for by now I was beginning to suspect that it was only an accident which had let me out of the grim fortress that morning. But something within me rebelled at the idea of sneaking away like a thief in the night. In spite of their eccentricity, Mihail and Vlad were my brothers—and there was also Malvina, alone and unprotected, not to mention the unknown Countess Bathory who was to be duped into a marriage with Vlad. Surely I could not run from all this?

At that moment a gentle knocking on the door sent my fraying nerves jumping.

'Who's there?' I whispered.

'It is I, Malvina, mein Herr.'

Relieved, I unbolted the door and stood aside as the girl came into my room. I closed the door quickly behind her.

'Malvina, I was worried about you,' I said.

'Were you?' she said in a girlish way, placing a finger between her red lips and biting it gently. She then smiled coquettishly at me and walked to the end of the bed, where she sat down with her legs swinging to and fro. 'Why should you be worried about me, mein Herr?'

There was something slightly different about her manner, something about the way she carried herself, the way she spoke. At first I could not place just what it was, but then it came to me: I remembered her small, petite figure, her pale face and frightened manner; now she seemed self-assured, voluptuous, even seductive. Her figure was full, her face redder than before; and her lips, which previously had trembled with nervousness, now pouted in a lascivious smile. Indeed it was as if her whole being had changed, with a seductive grossness replacing her former fragility. Looking at her, I felt hot and cold; and then I felt almost desirous.

"And why should you worry, mein Herr?" she whispered in a low, sultry voice. 'Am I then that much in your thoughts?'

Her eyes glittered. They were bold and quite wicked. She ran her tongue along the crimson of her lips and her smile was a challenge.

'I saw your uncle Toma today,' I said.

She gave a brief, nasty laugh, throwing back her head, her body arched and her legs swinging freely.

'Him?' she said. 'Pah! He is an old woman. Why should we talk of the likes of him, mein Herr? Come here,' she added, now smiling and patting the bed. 'Sit beside me and tell me about yourself. You are the only decent man I have seen for a month. And I have been so lonely and neglected in this place . . .'

Ah, the proud vanity of man! As in a trance, bedazzled by her beauty and lewd, suggestive posing, my emotions stirred to the point where I was oblivious to danger, I crossed to the bed and sat beside the smiling, wanton creature. How long we sat there I do not know, for the room seemed to disappear, to vaporize around us, and I was conscious only of her lips, of the tongue that lightly licked them, of the white of her teeth and the pale beauty of her bosom and the scent of her breath in my face and the play of her fingers. What was said I do not know, but we murmured tender words, then we embraced and fell down on the bed and her warmth flooded through me. I felt her hot breath on my neck, felt her sharp little teeth tentatively explore my shoulder as I, in my turn, removed from reason and shame, began to pull the blouse from her body and smother her with kisses.

Suddenly she was seized by a paroxysm of coughing, and then, with a gasp, she jerked away from me.

'What is it?' I cried.

'There is an overpowering smell in here,' she hissed.

'Nonsense!' I said, my emotions now roused to fever pitch. 'It is the scent of garlic, that is all.'

I pressed her back down on the pillows and once more began to kiss her bared breasts, but even as I did so, a shocking, agonized scream was torn from her lips.

Aghast, I sprang back. She writhed furiously beneath me. Then I noticed that, as I had leant over her, my mother's crucifix, which I wore around my neck, had dropped on to her bosom. The girl was now making a ghastly hissing sound, and the sudden stench of burning flesh filled my nostrils. Then, as I drew back in horror, I saw that the image of the crucifix had burnt itself into Malvina's flesh.

Scarce able to believe this, I yet moved away from the voluptuous creature that now writhed so desperately beneath me. Her face, which before had been beautiful and wanton, was now distorted by pain and wild hatred. Her teeth, which somehow seemed longer than they had been, bit feverishly at her lips until the blood was trickling from them. And her eyes, which had been mischievous and infinitely seductive, were now wild and demented, hypnotized by the mark of the cross that was burnt on her bosom.

'Malvina!' I cried.

Then, with an angry and most peculiar howl, a howl which reminded me of the cry of a wolf and sent shivers coursing down my spine, she sprang from the bed.

Still howling like one demented, she ran from the room.

In a dream I raised my hand to my crucifix and gently touched its metal, half expecting to find that it was hot. But it was cold, and this made my thoughts spin. Trembling, in great fright, I walked across to the door, and slammed it shut and then bolted it. I then sat before the fire, trying to collect my scattered thoughts, shudder after shudder coursing through my body in uncontrolled spasms, while the black night threw its mantle about me and left me in terror.

CHAPTER 15

I sat there until dawn approached. Since I could no longer help Malvina, and since the dogma of my scholarship refused to let my mind believe what my eyes had witnessed, my resolve was to leave the castle immediately and return to the sanity of Italy.

As soon as the grey fingers of dawn crept through the shutters, I stood up, buckled on my sword, and threw my travelling cloak around my shoulders. Scarce daring to breathe, I left the room and managed to reach the castle courtyard without incident. As usual, no one was stirring and all the shutters remained firmly closed. But imagine my horror when I found that on drawing the bolts of the great gates, I still could not open them. Obviously someone had double-locked them.

There was no other way out of the castle except . . . except that my brothers, on admonishing me never to enter the castle vaults, had revealed that wild animals were sometimes found in the vaults. And, if wild animals could enter into the castle vaults, surely I could obtain my exit through them.

My mind did not rejoice at this idea, for I would far prefer to have scaled the impregnable mountain sides than venture through the ghostly vaults of Castle Dracula. However, I could not . . . so the subterranean horrors would have to be braved.

You may think me a coward for fleeing the castle, but this is not quite so. No, in my mind there had grown a plan more positive than mere flight. Fearful though I was, I had resolved to return to Tirgoviste and seek an audience with Basarab cel Tinar, the voivode, and reveal what I knew of my brother's plotting. In this way, perhaps, I could atone for the evil deeds of my family.

In the castle courtyard lay an entrance to a small chapel, which was sunk into the ground so that its main chamber was below the surface and its gloomy interior was lit by means of small ventilations. I had heard my brother Mihail remark that it was from this chapel and its vaults that a stairway led down into the very bowels of the mountain, and this connected with a tunnel in which had been found the animals. He had presumed that this tunnel emerged into a grotto on the banks of the River Arges.*

The iron gate creaked inward as I gently pushed it forward and started down the short flight of stone steps that led me into the chapel. On a narrow ledge to one side I found flint and tinder and several ready made torches. I had little trouble in lighting a torch, and with this I gave my surroundings a cursory examination. It was obvious that the chapel had not been used in many a year, for all the religious ornamentation had been removed and thick dust lay over the floor and discarded stonework. On the far side of the chapel an iron grating separated the chapel from the vault. I moved forward slowly, holding my torch high above my head.

There was the sound of scampering as the light shone through the grating into the vault. I felt the

* In fact that route can still be taken by the enthusiastic explorer even today. Van Helsing.

quickening of my heart when I saw several pairs of tiny bright eyes staring unblinkingly at me. I shuddered; but I knew that I must face the perils of the journey; and, indeed, the sooner I had started, the sooner I would finish. Thus convinced, I resolutely drew my sword and pushed open the protesting grating with my foot.

At once the sound of scampering came again to my ears and some of the tiny bright eyes disappeared. Some of the others remained, cold, unblinking and strangely malignant, sending a shiver down my spine.

I raised my torch and the light fell on a collection of animals, the like of which I had never encountered before. They were creatures a foot or so in length, with heads proportionately small and pointed; the eyes were predominant and the whole was covered in a fur which I could see was a grey-brown, with protruding, flesh-coloured feet. On some of them I could discern white teeth, and for a moment my will quailed; but, as I advanced more boldly than I felt, I took heart at the sight of those evil-looking creatures fleeing before me.*

I paused to observe my surroundings, and to my surprise found the vault as empty as the chapel. I pressed on to the narrow stairway which started to lead downwards to the mountain. It was extremely small and several times I was reduced to a sitting position, edging my way down the stairs on my nether

* Except that they are usually of a length of 8–10½ inches, it is an accurate description of *Rattus norvegicus* of the family *muridae*, or the common rat. They were certainly not known in western Europe until the first part of the eighteenth century, and it is fairly well substantiated that they did not reach Paris until 1753. It is reported, though I cannot vouch for accuracy, that they crossed the Volga in the wake of an earthquake in 1927. Van Helsing.

regions, which was both uncomfortable and cold, for the stairway was coated in ancient slime, and more than once I slipped and bruised myself. In fact, so small did my passageway become at one time that I had resolved to retrace my steps—but then it widened out again and I pressed onwards.

The mountain under the castle was a veritable honeycomb of passageways which must have led into other vaults or chambers, for several times, to my right and left, the passages opened up and seemed to invite me to explore their drier and more level ways. However, I knew that I must continue downwards, and so downwards I went.

After what seemed a great age the downward path stopped and I found myself in a wide tunnel which branched off both left and right with no indication of which way I should take. For a moment I nearly despaired, but by the science of logic, always uppermost in my mind, I recalled that the valley of Arges lay on the northern side of the castle and the direction of the stairway I had entered lay to the east. At no point could I recall the stairway changing its direction, and so the route must surely be to my left. I moved forward and found the tunnel sloping downwards.

I had begun to feel more confident in my journey and was trying to summon up a tune to my cold lips when an unearthly cry echoed along the tunnel. It shocked me into rigid stillness. Then it came again, and this time I recognized the howl of a wolf.

My heart began to pump at twice its normal rate. A choking sensation in my throat forced my to open my mouth and gasp for breath. Alone in a dark cave with a vicious wolf! The hand that grasped my sword suddenly seemed weak, and I could not feel the metal hilt in my palm. Indeed, it was as if all bone and muscle had been drained from my body. Then I found myself running blindly.

I ran down the tunnel, feeling an uncontrollable fear arise within me. Indeed, you, dear reader, may have experienced a similar nightmare, whereby you are running forward along some confined passageway and yet you seem to be standing still . . . and all the while you know that there is something, something terrible, something monstrous, just behind you . . . something about to reach out and lay a cold clammy hand on your shoulder . . . such a nightmare did I experience at that moment.

Then a stone caught the toe of my boot and I sprawled forward, my sword slipping from my hand and ringing on the stone floor of the tunnel, my torch flying from my other hand as I stumbled down on my hands and knees, and then hit the ground.

There was a momentary blackness. I know not how long it lasted, but after a while I sat up, flexed my bruised limbs to ensure I had broken nothing, and once more peered into the dank blackness. I could see nothing. Indeed, I might as well have been blind for all that I could encompass in my vision. Then, still on my hands and knees, I crawled forward in an effort to find the torch. After a while my groping hand encountered my sword, which made me feel a little better; but as to the torch, I had no luck at all, and a fearful panic began to seize me. At this point I realized that I had placed the flint and tinder in my pocket, and soon, with enormous relief, I had lit a piece of matchwood.

As the matchwood flared up, I could not suppress a cry of terror at the hideous sight that confronted me.

A pair of dead eyes were staring into mine.

When I managed to control myself, I saw that I was kneeling before a corpse which lay sprawled across the floor of the tunnel. The clothing had rotted from the body and the flesh was in an advanced state of decomposition. One of the eyes was hanging crazily down a cheek, yet it still contrived to look at me. And in the middle of the chest, a wooden stake had pierced the body to its backbone.

All of this I took in at a single glance, before I rose and fled again down the passageway.

In the haste of my journey my matchwood extinguished itself, but to my utter joy I found that I was no longer in total darkness. A faint white glow was emerging ahead, and I was certain that I could hear running water.

I hurried on and soon, to my eternal relief, found myself in a large cave which contained a sanded shore and a deep pool of water. On the far side of the cave I could see an opening into a grotto with a large entrance into the bright sunshine of day.

Pausing only to sheath my sword, I plunged head-first into the water and, after a few strokes, found myself in the swift current of the Arges. I am a fairly strong swimmer, so it was without too much effort that I swam to the river bank and gratefully hauled myself up.

I lay for some time, trying to recover my breath and drink in the bright rays of the sun; then, having dried my clothes to a fair degree of comfort, I began to walk along the river bank.

The tunnel had indeed emerged into the Arges valley, and looking up I could perceive the great granite walls of the mountain and the tiny black shape of Castle Dracula, perched on its top. About a mile along the valley, in the direction I was going, lay the village of Arefu, and I decided that my best course of action was to seek out Toma and see if he could provide me with a horse. By the time I reached the outskirts of the village, my clothes were completely dry, but I mistrusted the chill November air and made up my mind that my first comfort should be a glass of the local brandy.

It was while I was thus musing that I heard the sound of horses from the road which now lay but twenty yards away. Thinking of my safety, I hastened to a clump of bushes and flung myself down just as the black coach of the house of Dracula rounded a curve in the road. It was empty except for the tall figure of Tirgsor, sitting on the coachman's box, lashing at his team of horses and urging them to greater efforts as the whole vehicle, coach and horses, swung on its perilous descent along the mountain track.

I lay awhile after the coach had disappeared and found my conscience attacking me—for I knew that Tirgsor had gone to Citea de Arges where he was to meet the Countess Bathory and bring her back to Castle Dracula. Shame, my conscience said, for deserting this poor woman; though my rational self told me that I was not in fact deserting her, but effecting the best possible rescue by informing the Voivode Basarab of my brothers' evil plottings.

So engrossed in this rationalization was I that I was oblivious to any noise around me. Indeed, it was only when I heard a threatening growl right beside me that I came to my senses and looked up.

There, towering on his hind feet, forepaws waving in the air with claws extended, stood the tallest brown bear I had ever seen. And no dancing bear was this, but a wild and hungry denizen of the forest.

I turned to stone as it clawed at the air and advanced upon me.

CHAPTER 16

I had closed my eyes and commended myself to God's keeping when the bear let out a grunt of pain. Opening my eyes I could not suppress an exclamation of astonishment as I beheld an arrow protruding from one of the bear's eyes. The animal was threshing about in its agony, and I quickly rolled away from its blind grasp I then heard the twang of a bowstring and a second arrow embedded itself in the creature's chest. It crashed down to the ground, its limbs kicked for a moment, and then, eventually, it lay dead.

With a prayer of thanksgiving, I turned and beheld my strange saviour. A short, stocky man in the habit of a Catholic monk was returning a third arrow to his quiver and smiling broadly at me. He then said something in a guttural language that I did not recognize, and I decided to answer him in Latin, this being the language of the universal church, which indeed he understood immediately.

'The bear will be tough eating,' the monk repeated in Latin, 'but it is better than going hungry, and you are welcome at my camp fire.'

He motioned behind him to where a small fire was sparking merrily. He then drew a knife and hacked two generous steaks from the carcass of my late antagonist and, with me following, went and sat down by the fire. He methodically attended to the steaks and, since I had said nothing, looked up at me and grinned quizzically.

'You can understand my poor command of Latin, I trust?' he said.

'Yes,' I said, smiling. 'It is just that I am unused to monks armed with the accoutrements of war, for indeed, sir, I notice that you carry not only a bow and arrows, but a short strong sword as well.'

The monk laughed. He had wide blue eyes which twinkled in a fleshy and ruddy face which was surmounted by a shock of sandy hair.

'I am a Dominican and thus the matter may be explained,' he said. 'I am but recently returned from a pilgrimage to the Holy Land, and there, and indeed here in this country, a Catholic brother has to be prepared to defend himself, both physically as well as spiritually.' Here he patted his sword and grinned mischievously, adding: 'It serves me better than prayers.'

I was surprised by his frankness and humour, and, I confess, found it refreshing in a religious. I introduced myself as the Baron Michelino of Rome and he in turn told me that he was Brother John of the Dominican Order from Glasney Priory in Cornwall. I asked him where this was, for I confess I had not heard of it, and he told me that if I saw a map of England it would resemble a boot and that I should look into the toe of that boot and there find Cornwall.

'So you are English?' I asked, perplexed.

'No, young friend,' he replied. 'We Cornish are an ancient Celtic people who lived in Britain long before the English came, and we were the disciples of Christ long before the English turned from their worship of Woden and Thunor.'

I sat with this strange monk as he roasted the bear

steaks over his fire and learnt that he had been away from England for seven years on his pilgrimage. His priory, the Collegiate Church of Glasney, stands near a town called Falmouth, and he informed me that it was the centre of learning and literature in his native land. The language of Cornwall differs vastly to that of England, and although English was much influencing his people since they were conquered some centuries before, the monks of Glasney were given to writing religious plays in the language.

Gradually our talk turned to what I was doing in Wallachia. It is strange that sometimes one can meet a person and within a few minutes feel they have known them all their lives. Such was the feeling I had for the English monk (his Cornish ancestors will forgive me, for I have grown to think of him as such) and therefore it seemed natural to pour out my story, from my birth to my journey to Wallachia and then to the events at Castle Dracula and my subsequent escape. He listened for the most part in silence, save for a question here and there to clarify a point, and only when I had finished did he speak.

'Friend Michelino,' he said quietly, leaning forward with his blue eyes very bright, 'there is a force at work here that is more evil and terrifying than you have ever imagined. I fear, my friend, that unless it is fought and destroyed it will spread itself over the world and obliterate any hope of salvation for human kind.'

I was surprised at the intensity of his reaction and I sat back a little.

'What do you mean?' I asked.

'You are a learned man, my friend,' said Brother John, 'and I fear that in your knowledge you may reject the old knowledge which is in the lives and experiences of the ancients. I fear that you will ridicule what I have come to suspect about the strange occurrences you witnessed at Castle Dracula.'

'Brother John,' I said, 'I confess I am not a religious man. I accept the teachings of the church, but I care more for my living body than I do for the thought of life after death. However, I believe, as you do, that something strange and evil is being plotted by my two brothers.'

'More than that,' Brother John said. 'Much more than that. And I believe it is imperative, my friend, for the sake of the immortal souls of all human kind, that you return to Castle Dracula with me to fight this evil. Will you do it? I ask you in the name of all that is beloved by you.'

So intense and sincere was he that all my previous fears vanished.

'I will,' I said.

He grasped my hand tightly and we sat for some minutes, not speaking, each meditating on our decision. Then eventually the monk woke me, as if from a dream, by laughing ruefully.

'Our steaks seem all but burnt,' he said. 'Now let us eat. And once fed, we shall go up to the castle.'

'Would it not be better,' I ventured, observing that he had apparently closed the subject in order to give his full attention to the bear steaks, 'if you told me what evil threatens us? You say I might ridicule your idea, but I have seen enough to know there is something inexplicably strange up at the castle.'

He laid a hand on my shoulder and gave a small smile.

'So strange, my friend,' he said, 'that I do not think you would give it credence if I told you. No, rather you must place your trust in me until I observe the situation; and when I have observed it, and when I have confirmed my suspicions, I shall tell you what the evil is. I pray God that I may be wrong, but I fear it will not be so. Do you trust me enough, my friend, to place yourself in my hands until I can tell you what I suspect?'

I nodded. I felt no qualms in placing my trust in this stocky, humourist monk who could wield a sword as readily as his rosary beads, who had wit as well as knowledge to back his philosophies, and who was a religious but did not fear being a man as well. This confidence he inspired in a simple conversation while cooking meat over a camp fire.

Thus, when we had finished our meal, we journeyed back to the castle.

It was just after midday when we reached our destination. I was surprised to see that the drawbridge spanned the chasm and the great gates stood wide open. Evidently Tirgsor had not thought to close them when he set off for Arges. Brother John and I entered with a certain trepidation and I conducted him directly to the donjon tower.

The refectory room lay as it had done on every occasion that I had seen it. The fire was in the hearth, the table laid for a meal—but this time I was more than a little startled to see that the table had been laid for two. Of my brothers there was no sign, but a note was lying on the table. Wonderingly, I picked it up and read it.

Brother—We regret not being able to join you this day, but urgent business dictates our absence. The castle is your home—use it as such. You and your guest are welcome. Your loving brothers, Vlad and Mihail.

'You and your guest are welcome,' I repeated aloud as Brother John scanned the same note. 'How did they know?'

The monk smiled.

'The road is visible to the castle all the way down to Arefu,' he said. 'It requires little powers of foresight to see two men climbing the road.'

'But where are they gone?' I said. 'I swear Tirgsor was alone in the coach.'

'We will see,' Brother John answered. 'But first let us explore the castle and see whether we can begin to fit the pieces of our mystery together. Come, show me first your room and we will make that our starting point.'

My room was as I had left it hurriedly that morning, and I found it odd that the fire had been allowed to die out and nothing attended to, as if no one had entered the room since I left it. This I found odd because always the room had been cleaned and the fire relit by the unseen hands of a servant. I remarked on this fact to Brother John, who peered closely around the room and then seized upon the garlic and bag of salt which still lay beside my bed.

'This may explain the matter,' he said enigmatically.

'Explain what?' I said, agitated by my ignorance.

'Trust me,' the monk said in answer to my query. 'All will be explained soon. But it is excellent that you have these things here.'

I conducted him back to the refectory room again and tried to open the door to the vaults. As on the previous occasion, the door was locked. Unconcerned, I went to the main door, explaining that there was a second mainway to the cellars, but on trying to open that door I found it also barred.

I began to get a strange feeling of panic, of being trapped, and I rushed to each door and each window in vain . . . even the door by which we had just come from the castle courtyard was barred and locked . . . only the gallery between my bedchamber and the refectory room stood open, and it was only between these rooms that we could traverse. I turned and looked fearfully at Brother John.

'We are prisoners!' I cried. 'All the doors and windows are barred against us. We are incarcerated! What are we to do?'

Brother John bowed his head and crossed himself.

'God between us and all evil!' he whispered fervently.

CHAPTER 17

In the first two days of our confinement we saw no one during the daylight hours, and at dusk Brother John insisted that we retire to my bedchamber. Here, much to my surprise, the monk took the garlic and hung little bunches of it at the door, the window, and above the chimney breast. Around the bed he laid a full circle of salt and then, and only then, did he resign himself to sleep. At no time did he cross this salt circle. When he wished to move out of it, he brushed a little of it aside as if making a door in it.

Nothing untoward occurred during our first night of imprisonment and, indeed, I passed the night in deep, refreshing sleep. The next day food had been placed in the refectory with another note exhorting us to use the castle as our home.

It was late in the afternoon of the second day that I heard the sound of horses clattering into the courtyard, accompanied by the rumbling of a coach.

Both Brother John and I raced to the window of the refectory room and peered down through a gap in the shutters, for the windows were barred and it was impossible to open them. We were in time to see the black coach of the house of Dracula, with Tirgsor driving, come to a halt below.

Tirgsor dismounted and stood respectfully when he opened the carriage door to help out his passenger. A small figure, muffled in a sweeping blue travelling cloak with a hood that shielded most of the face, emerged and paused a moment on the step of the coach so that for a brief second, just before she had alighted, I caught a glimpse of a determined chin and red lips against a lovely fair skin. It was obviously the Countess Irene Bathory.

In agitation I cried aloud and banged on the window, but the girl had already vanished. Only the malign face of Tirgsor glanced up at the shuttered window, and, for the first time, a gloating smile spread across the sullen lips of the steward.

Brother John was as agitated as I was.

'The girl is in deadly danger,' he said. 'We must seek a way of reaching her immediately.'

He turned back to the window and pointed at the red orb of the sun, now hanging in the mountains.

'Too late! Too late!' he cried. 'She must now pass this night unprotected. But tomorrow, my friend, we must act!'

I asked him to explain, but again he refused, shaking his head and saying that I must have patience.

'My head tells me I am still unsure,' he said, 'though I feel in my heart that I am right. When I know for certain, I will explain all. Please be patient till then.'

That night we retired to my bedchamber again, but this time, try as I might, I found slumber elusive. There was a fierce wind howling around the castle; and somewhere, far away, I heard a door banging to and fro. These sounds, which made the castle seem alive, kept me wide awake, my thoughts in turmoil, remembering my brothers, the mysterious third voice, the metamorphosis of Malvina, the malign face of Tirgsor, the ghostly lady in the cellar, the bats and the howling of the wolves and all the tales of dark horror. I twisted and turned. The wind groaned beyond the room. Then, just as I thought I might sleep, I heard a woman's voice outside the door.

I sprang from the bed, but before I could move further, Brother John had clasped my arm in a vice-like grip.

'*No!*' he hissed. '*Not for your soul!*'

I froze where I stood, but looked quizzically at the monk, who was now lighting a candle and peering around at the garlic and salt.

'What is it?' I asked.

'All will be well,' he said, 'so long as we do not leave the circle of salt.'

'But this is madness!' I exclaimed, my fear mixed with frustration. 'You must explain!'

'Later,' he said.

Just then there was another sound at the door. A woman's voice called out to me, a whisper of a voice, soft, appealing and helpless.

'*Mein Herr, mein Freiherr! Verstehen Sie mich, mein Herr? Würden Sie mir helfen?*'

I cast an anxious look at Brother John who stood in the flickering candlelight, his stocky frame hurling huge shadows on the walls. I heard the wind howling outside.

'It is a girl asking me to help her,' I whispered.

The voice came again, disembodied, almost ethereal, a soft and most seductive sound that yet gave me the shivers.

'*Ich fühle mich nicht wohl. Ich bin verletzt.*'

'Listen, Brother John,' I said, not quite believing my own words. 'She is ill. The poor girl has been injured.'

Brother John took hold of me again and his grip was unyielding. Then he called out in a loud voice to whoever was behind the barred door.

'*Fraulein!*' he called. 'Do you hear me?'

'Oh, Master, I do!' came the purring reply. 'Please hurry, mein Herr! I am ill!'

'Fraulein, do you acknowledge the Lord Jesus Christ as your Saviour?'

The seconds ticked by. Fingers scratched at the door. The wind howled and shadows leapt on the walls and I felt my heart beating. Then came a most plaintive wail:

'Mein Herr, I am ill!'

'Fraulein!' Brother John shouted, even louder than before. 'Do you acknowledge the Lord Jesus Christ?'

Again there was silence, but for the howling of the wind and the strange, mice-like scratching at the door.

'Fundementa ejus in mortibus sanctis!' Brother John suddenly cried out in a loud, almost terrifying voice. 'Creature of salt, I adjure thee in the name of the Living God!'

From behind the door came a hideous scream of anger, echoing up and down the halls, blotting out the howling wind, a cry of rage and anguish and hatred that made me turn cold. Then it died away. We stood a long time in silence. The shadows danced on the walls and the wind howled and nothing else moved. Finally, after what seemed an eternity, Brother John spoke.

'We will have to be on our guard, my friend,' he said. 'I fear they realize that we recognize them for what they are. Yes, we are ranged against the forces of evil, my friend, and tomorrow our greatest trial will come. So rest now, Michelino. For the moment, at least, we are safe.'

I lay back on the bed, both fearful and intrigued, too bemused to ask yet again for a full explanation. I now knew he would tell me in his own time.

* * *

The sun awoke me. I rolled from the bed to find Brother John had already washed and was fully dressed, and was now looking thoughtfully out of the window. I dressed quickly and joined him.

'We must go climbing today,' he said by way of greeting, pointing to the sheer drop from the window. 'It is our only avenue of escape.'

'That is a thousand feet into the valley,' I said. 'Exactly how are we to accomplish this miracle?'

He took my arm and pointed downwards.

'Twenty feet below is an open window. We will simply tie the bed linen together and you shall lower me down. I will climb through the window and then retrace my way to the refectory room and unbolt the door, providing our hosts have had the goodness to leave the key in the lock on the other side of the door.'

I peered out of the window. By some oversight, it would seem, a window had indeed been left open below us.

'It has possibilities,' I said, 'but I am lighter than you are, so I am the one who should be lowered.'

We wasted little time in breakfasting, and before long I was climbing through the window, a sheet tied around my waist, attached to strips of sheet that Brother John had tied to the bed frame to prevent my sudden plunge into the gorge. Brother John then payed out his makeshift rope and soon I was descending dizzily into space. There was little hold I could take of the castle wall, and I suffered a thousand cuts and bruises as I swung to and fro, bumping against the hard granite blocks. When I tried to steady myself by placing a foot against the wall, it only caused me to swing out further, and my heart beat faster as I felt the knots of the sheet slipping. It seemed an age before I finally found myself opposite the window and, thanks be to God, saw that the window stood wide open so that all I had to do was carefully swing my way through and prevent myself swinging outwards again while I untied my lifeline.

The room gave an impression of greyness and smelt strangely musty. Yet I saw it was a bedchamber and noticed that the curtains of a large four-poster bed were drawn. The fire had been allowed to go out and there was an air of chill about the room. With a twinge of horror I suddenly realized that it might be the bedchamber of one of my brothers, or even that of Tirgsor, and I slowly unsheathed my sword and crept up to the curtains. Then, gently, and with hardly a sound, I drew back the curtains and let the sun's rays fall upon the still figure that lay on the bed.

My breath caught in my throat.

It was a girl. She was beautiful. There was no doubt that it was she whom I had seen from the window the night before: the Countess Irene Bathory. She lay like some exquisite marble statue, so pale, so still that I thought for a moment she must be dead. Then I saw the gentle rise and fall of her bosom. Her fair, gold-brown hair was coiled around her pale face, and there was a touch of blue on her lips.

I tried to rouse her with a gentle shake, but there was no response. Then, as I gave her shoulder another gentle shake, I noticed that there were tiny drops of blood on the pillow and across the sheet. The girl was evidently seriously ill, so I raced back across the room and cried out through the window to Brother John. His voice had a calming effect on me, and he told me to hurry quickly to release him.

Sword in hand, wary of meeting either my brothers or Tirgsor, I sped from the countess's bedchamber and along the gallery, which passed underneath the one which led from my own bedchamber to the refectory room. Then I went up the stairs and found myself outside the refectory room door. It was not locked, but merely bolted, and it took merely a second to throw the bolts and open it. Brother John was waiting impatiently in the room and bade me lead him quickly to the countess's side.

The young girl lay as I had left her, a disturbing, almost death-like pale. The bones of her beautifully shaped head stood out, and seemed to disfigure her lovely face. Yet her breathing was now different, more marked and painful, and I was sure that she was close to Death's door.

Brother John stooped over her, holding a hand to her forehead, and then he placed a finger on her wrists and checked the beat of her pulse. When this was done, he peered at her face again, bending his head close to hers. Then he turned her head to one side and studied her neck.

"*Sancta simplicitas!*" he gasped, crossing himself. 'It is as I thought! It is as I suspected! There is a great evil here, my friend. And this young lady is in very great danger.'

I leaned forward to peer at the thing that had brought forth this ejaculation. Just over the pale blue mark of the jugular vein, which now stood so prominently from the transluscent flesh, there were two small punctures, red marks with white around the edges, not pleasant to look at.

'What is it?' I demanded, somewhat mystified. 'It looks like the bite of an animal.'

'Animal indeed!' Brother John exclaimed. 'But quickly, my friend! I will explain afterwards! For now, we have work to do to save her. Go to your room and bring the garlic flowers and my bag.'

Hardly had he given the order than I was flying to our room, the sight of that beautiful face on the bloodstained pillow lending me strength and resolution. Upon returning with the garlic and Brother John's bag, I found that the monk had lit a fire in the room, that his sleeves were rolled up, and that he was busy boiling water in a pot. He took the bag from my hands and smiled anxiously.

'Pray that the spirit of the ancient healers Hippocrates and Theophrastus and Pliny look down upon us.'

He took from his bag some phials and herbs and, being interested in the practice of alchemy and medicine, I inquired what he was doing.

'The young woman suffers from a loss of blood,' he said, 'from anaemia, and we must restore her blood to her and prevent further loss. Here,' he continued, picking up a phial, 'is the herb Bloodroot, from which the juice has been extracted, and this red juice will pour down her throat. It will purge uncleanliness from her body and will relax her so that she may sleep naturally. Next we apply an infusion of hyssop, which will cleanse again, calming the nerves and regulating the flow of blood from her poor heart. This is all we can do for the moment, except to ring her bed with these garlic flowers whose aroma will cause her to sleep peacefully and be protected. Should she wake, we will allow her to drink only the juice of the dandelion leaves and lady's mantle in order that her blood might flow naturally again.'*

---

* These seem to be the same symptoms as were shown by poor Lucy Westenra for which treatment I immediately prescribed a blood transfusion. In Brother John's day such a transfusion was unimaginable. It was not until 1818 that Dr James Blundell of London attempted a transfusion of human blood from which the patient died. The theory had been put forward, however, as early as 1665 when Sir Christopher Wren suggested to the Cornishman Dr Richard Lower that blood might be passed from one animal to another. I can boast that I was one of the pioneers of blood transfusion. Van Helsing.

He paused from his activity and looked at me sharply.

'And now, my friend,' he said, 'we must leave this evil place and take her down to the village where she will be safer.'

I nodded my agreement. Certainly the sooner we left Castle Dracula the happier I would feel.

'I shall look for the best way out,' I said, 'and check if our path is clear.'

The stairway to the bottom of the tower I found barred by a large wooden door. Curious, I pushed it open . . . and the sight that met my eyes caused a cry to be wrested from my lips and brought Brother John scurrying down the stairs to my rescue.

He, too, froze, open-mouthed.

We stood on the threshold of the room and gazed about us in wonder. Then, breathing deeply, Brother John crossed himself and stepped inside.

'It is incredible,' he said. 'Incredible! For some years I have been gathering information on sorcery and witchcraft for a learned treatise which two brothers of my order hope to publish as a guide to the justiciary of all Catholic countries—but never in my researches have I come across such a place as this.'*

'What is it?' I asked, stepping inside.

'It is the devil's own temple,' Brother John replied.

The room was hung in black drapes and lined with the most curious symbols I have ever seen. At one end stood an altar-like table, also covered in black, while benches, on which were many ancient manuscripts,

---

*This comment is interesting inasmuch that a few years after the events described, Brother John's order, the highly learned Dominicans, published *Malleus Maleficarum*, or *The Hammer of the Witches*. This was in 1486. It became the minatory text of the Inquisition. Van Helsing.

stood around the room. Above the black altar, on the wall, was hung a wooden board, and the letters were burnt into the board as if with an iron poker. I recall the shape of those letters very well, and have reproduced them as I recall them.

ᚺᚱᚨᛏᛁᛚᚾ

Brother John informed me that it was writing in Runic, the language of the ancients, and that translated it stood for Dracula. In the meantime, he hurried to and fro among the ancient books and manuscripts, exclaiming all the while that never in his life had he encountered the like, saving one time when he saw a few such books in a Dominican library, which works had been confiscated from Pietro de Abano, an Italian philosopher who had studied medicine in Paris and then returned to Padua to practise as a physician. He had written some highly respected medical books, but it was believed that he practised witchcraft; and later, when he wrote a work called *Heptameron*, or *Magical Elements*, he was tried by the Inquisition. Although acquitted, he was rearrested and died while awaiting trial. All this did Brother John tell me as he walked from one object to another, all the while talking as if to himself, for I am sure that I understood little of his excited mutterings.

'Siddhi,' he suddenly said, peering at an old manuscript which contained such strange letters that they looked more like a child's jottings than a language. He then explained that this was the ancient hieroglyphic language of the Pharaohs of Egypt. 'It is a book that explains the ways of evoking *Siddhi*, the magical power of *Om*, the root of creation.'

'*Siddhi*,' I said, a little impatient. '*Om* . . . I know not these words.'

'They are ancient Sanskrit words,' Brother John said, 'a language that must go back to the dawn of time. They evoke the ancient power. Look, my friend!' He pointed to a manuscript written on rolls of strange paper. 'This is a copy of the Book of the Dead, the religious scrolls of Egypt's Eighteenth dynasty . . . it must be nearly three thousand years old.'

'What does all this mean?' I asked.

Brother John looked into my eyes—a grim glance that bespoke serious resolution.

'My friend,' he said slowly, 'we stand in the house of the Undead!'

'The Undead?'

'Aye, my friend. You were born of this flesh, but it has pleased God to remove you all these years from the source of a vile damnation. So have no thought that this is the house of your family. It is the house of the Undead.'

'You will have to explain further,' I said, feeling ignorant, 'for I cannot understand what you say.'

'Do you know what a vampire is, my friend?'

I looked stupidly at him for a moment. 'Do you mean . . . ?' I could not bring myself to finish the question.

'Friend, in every country in the world, from Asia to Ireland, each culture has its tales of vampires—stories of reanimated corpses which cannot lie still in their graves, but must go out between sunset and sunrise to suck blood from the living, whereby they live in a state of Undead. On the warm blood of the living they maintain their ghastly semblance of life.'

'But this is a superstition of peasants,' I said, not daring to believe he was in earnest.

'No, my friend,' he said, 'it is the truth. In your native Italy there are few tales of the vampire—although your notorious vendetta is based on the belief that murdered people cannot rest in their tombs until the blood of the assassin or his kin is spilt. But elsewhere, the Undead is known and feared—even in my own country. During the last century the stories of the Undead of England were chronicled by the Augustinian Canon William of Newburgh in his *Historia Rerum Anglicarum*; and Walter Map wrote *De Nugis Curialium* to warn us of the Undead and their ways.'

'And you believe in all this?' I asked incredulously.

Brother John paused and shook his head sadly.

'Ah, my young friend,' he said. 'Scholars of today scoff at the mysteries which the ancients knew and understood well. We think our forebears were primitive and superstitious, yet all the while they had more knowledge of the natural and of the lost arts than we can conceive. Euripides and Aristophanes knew the Undead as *Iamiae*, while the great poet Ovid warned of the *striges*, or *mormos*, that assumed the shape of the great bats which flew at night, sucking the blood of the living. Do we scoff at the knowledge of such men? Do we jeer at the very founding fathers of the church? The blessed St. Clemens wrote of the Undead, and explained their need to devour the blood of the living.'

I raised my hands to my head and shuddered.

'Can such a thing be true?' I said. 'God, I pray it is not, and yet, Brother John, you say it is and you are vastly more learned than I. And, too, I have seen with my own eyes such strange manifestations that I have no explanation to credit them . . . Brother John, my logic tells me such things cannot be true, but that same logic cannot explain the things that I have witnessed since I came to this God forsaken country. I must place my trust in you, good brother. Now tell me: what are we to do?'

'My friend,' he said, taking both my hands in his, 'we have to destroy this evil before it bursts like a plague over the earth.'

'How can this evil spread?' I asked.

'The vampire gains immortality, but immortality carries with it a curse: they cannot die, but must go on forever multiplying their kind, for all that die from their kisses become as they: *Undead!*'

Suddenly my blood ran cold.

'And the countess . . . ?' I began.

'No,' he said promptly, 'she can recover. The vampire took but little of her blood.'

The extent of my relief was such that I knew I now believed all that he told me. And, with the acceptance of this belief, came a deep and abiding fear.

'But what can we do against such supernatural powers?' I asked. 'Is there no way we can destroy the vampire?'

'Indeed there is, my friend,' he replied to my surprise, 'but first let me tell you the nature of the Undead. He casts no shadow, casts no reflection in a mirror; he has the strength of many and can transform his shape into a bat or wolf, or can swirl in a mist, or come on moonlit rays as elemental dust. He can see in the dark.

'But though he is not of nature, he has to obey nature's laws. His power ceases at sunrise, and from sunrise to sunset he must return to lay helpless on his native soil—the soil wherein he was buried. Nor can he pass running water, except at the slack and flood of the tide.

'The symbols of good he abominates—such as the crucifix, which protects the living from the Undead. He can be destroyed by the driving of a wooden stake through his heart, or by cutting off his head and stuffing garlic in his mouth.

'Yes, my friend, he can be destroyed—and we have three powerful weapons to fight him with. First, there is iron. Iron from time immemorial has symbolized purity and protection from evil. Even the great philosopher Pliny says, in his *Natural History*, that iron nails above the threshold of a house give protection from devils.

'Then there is salt. Salt, likewise, incorruptible, medicinal and preservative in nature, is symbolic from the land of Persia to the land of the Finns. Did not the ancient Greeks say, "Trespass not against salt and board"?

'The third weapon is garlic, one of the oldest medicinal herbs in the world. The ancients of Babylon used it over four thousand years ago. Aristophanes used it for virility, Dioscordes, the official physician to the Roman army, recommended it for internal disorders, and Galin used it as an antidote to poison. From time immemorial it has been used to keep the devil and witches at bay.

'Thus we are armed, my friend.'

'But, Brother John,' I exclaimed, 'if what you say is true, and I know you say it in all sincerity, there occurs to me a thought which is puzzling. I have seen and talked to my brothers Vlad and Mihail, and also Tirgsor and his daughter Malvina, when the sun has been up and they have come and gone about the castle with ease. How can you then say, as you previously did, that the power of the Undead ceases at sunrise?'

'This is true,' he replied without pause, 'and I well

understand your confusion. But regarding those you mention, it simply means that they have not yet joined the ranks of the Undead. Indeed, because of the restrictions placed upon him, it is necessary for the Undead to have slaves or servants that will protect him during the daylight hours. Yet to be such a slave one has to be in a state of semi-Undead.

'Do you recall how you told me that Tirgsor was so insistent upon travelling on St. Andrew's Eve, a night when the power of evil is at its height? And the next day, in daylight, you said he was pale and wan, but as night drew on he became stronger and more healthy. You said that you also noticed the same phenomenon with your brothers who were pale and wan in the daylight but grew more animated towards dusk. Is that not so?'

I nodded slowly, feeling dread coil within me, not wanting to face up to what his words were revealing yet enslaved by a horrified curiosity, seduced by my nightmares.

'Yes, that is so,' I said.

'Then we are agreed,' Brother John said, and the words that he uttered scourged my soul. 'While they are not yet Undead, which in this case they are not, they are limited in their powers also. Perhaps, as time progresses, their strength is gradually drawn from them, so that they can move in the daylight less and less. And if such be the case, then they too must finally become Undead.'

'But if they are the slaves of the Undead,' I said, 'who then is this Undead you speak of? Who is their master?'

Brother John leant towards me. I saw the blazing of his eyes. They were fierce and they held a great compassion and a welter of pain.

'Why, my friend,' he said, seizing my arm, 'who else

by your own father whom you thought dead? Who else, indeed, but *Dracula?*'

My senses reeled. I fell against him and wept. I let the anguish and the horror flare up and die away, and then, when I recovered, and Brother John had dried my eyes, we returned to attend to the sleeping countess, secure in our mutual faith and trust.

BOOK THREE

THE UNDEAD

CHAPTER 18

It was in the late afternoon that Brother John and I, carrying the unconscious countess between us, made our way down into the village of Arefu and raised the innkeeper, Toma, from his shuttered inn. We prevailed upon him to give us a room, and I do believe it was only the priestly vocation of Brother John that persuaded him to do that much for us.

Our prime concern was for the health of the countess, and it was agreed that one or both of us should sit with her through the night. Although garlic flowers and crucifixes were hung in abundance in the inn, Brother John insisted on reinforcing these precautions in the bedchamber. We ate a less than hearty supper and retired early, and took up positions in two chairs on either side of the young girl's bed. A blazing fire made the room warm and induced drowsiness, so to keep from sleeping we engaged in a whispered conversation across the sleeping form of the countess.

'When I was born my father was as we are,' I said. 'Of that I am sure from my mother. How then could he now be as you say . . . Undead?'

'There are many ways, my friend,' Brother John replied. 'A suicide may become a vampire, or an unbaptized child, or, indeed, a seventh son* or a man with a

---

* This is an interesting point, for in Romania and surrounding countries a seventh son is a bad omen, perhaps to do with the caul or membrane covering his head at birth. Also those who have eaten the flesh of a sheep killed by a wolf, those over whose dead body a cat has passed, those who have been murdered and have remained unavenged, and those who have dabbled in sorcery and led evil lives. Also those who have been kissed by the vampire. Such, my friend, are the ways in which this disease may spread itself.'

'But my father hardly fitted any of these descriptions. True, it is said he lived a life of evil; but others were just as evil and did not become Undead like he.'

Brother John nodded.

'There are three ways that Dracula may have become Undead. First, he may have fallen prey to the disease; he may have been a victim of a vampire—though that is not likely from the manner of his dying in battle and in the strength of character he had. Second, he did change his religion from the Orthodox Church to the Catholic Church, and the peasants hereabouts believe that a person who so changes his religion becomes without a soul, and thus becomes a prey to the vampire. As a priest of Rome I must discount this belief as nonsense. But third, those who dabble in sorcery and conjure the devil, and seek immortality from the dark powers, can achieve such immortality by becoming Undead.

'You saw the great room wherein were all the ancient books of lore on sorcery and symbols of the ancients. I say that Dracula, by means of sorcery, sold his soul for immortality and his reward was to become Undead—for what purpose I know not.'

---

fact that offerings to the dead have to be seven in number or in multiples of seven. It is only in Ireland, and subsequently in England, that a seventh son is believed to be a symbol of good luck. Van Helsing.

We fell into silent contemplation, enslaved by our own thoughts. I knew, now, the evil of my own family and was forced to accept this vile truth. Yet I also knew, with a fresh, clear conviction, that in braving the full horror of what had been unveiled I had somehow discovered new strengths in myself. The truth was a nightmare. The nightmare was my inheritance. Yet by facing this darkness, and by braving that which I feared, I was strengthening my own childish spirit and emerging to manhood. Yes, I was pitted against my very own flesh and blood, but I knew that good would come from this incestuous war. Of this I was confident.

As midnight approached the countess grew more and more restless in her slumber and, as if in sympathy, the wind began to rise and beat about the inn, howling almost mournfully down the chimneys. The draught sent the sparks flying and the candles flickering, and it put a fierce chill in the air.

Brother John sat with his rosary in his hands, calmly telling his beads, while I kept my gaze upon the small, helpless face of the countess, now beating restlessly from side to side on the pillow. Her breathing was somewhat stertorous and her mouth was wide open, as if to take in bigger mouthfuls of air. I could see her pale gums and the pinkness of her tongue; and although, perhaps, it was a trick of the light, her white teeth seemed unusually sharp and long.

In her sleep she made futile attempts to push away the garlic flowers, and I called Brother John's attention to the fact, wondering whether the fumes were too much for her tortured lungs. However, Brother John forbade me to touch or remove them.

The wind increased in ferocity, and suddenly, as if from the next room, came the long drawn out howl of a wolf.

Brother John sprang from his chair.

'What in God's name was that?' he cried.

I was wondering myself until I remembered the poor madman Liviu, chained like an animal in what indeed must have been the next room. I briefly explained this to Brother John, and we listened together and could hear, beneath the breathless fury of the wind, the dragging of a chain on the wooden floor, and a scratching upon the wall, as if a beast of prey were seeking entrance. Another horrific howl came from the next room, and a ghastly human voice cried out:

'It comes! It comes! Blood is life! Blood is life!'

Just then there was such a violent gust of wind that it roared down the chimney and in one mighty blast turned the wooden logs into an explosion of flying embers and extinguished all the candles in the room.

We stood for a moment, unnerved by the sudden darkness, and a tingle of cold apprehension shivered down my spine when I realized that the wind had now ceased . . . ceased so abruptly that there was not another sound to be heard. Indeed, so quiet was it that I could almost hear the growing of the grass, the decaying of the inn, even feel the rotation of the earth itself.

'Blood is life!' came the scream of the poor lunatic next door.

Then, horrified, we heard the sound of flapping wings, a scrabbling and scratching in the chimney, and before we could move a monstrous bat flew out of the hearth and hovered malignantly before us.

The stench of corruption filled the room.

'Don't look at its eyes!' Brother John cried. 'In the name of God don't look at its eyes!'

But I had already focused on the tiny red eyes that

seemed to grow larger and larger. The room was dark, but the bat was even darker, a shadow upon the shadows, swaying sluggishly back and forth, the eyes cold and blood-red and burning out of the blackness like hot coals in the deepest pits of Hell. It was drawing me in. It was bending me to its will. I felt myself succumbing, vaporizing, floating out of myself. Then Brother John stepped forward. This movement jerked me awake. I remembered the bat in Castle Dracula, its power to enslave, and I hastily forced my gaze to the floor and refused to look up.

The flapping wings moved towards me.

Suddenly Brother John ran in front of and threw his rosary at the beast. With a screech, as if in rage, the bat flew swiftly sideways and attempted to swoop down upon the countess. Recovering his crucifix, Brother John again ran towards the bat, which, screeching like a soul in the fires of damnation, suddenly flew back up the chimney and disappeared.

Brother John immediately hung the rosary before the chimney piece.

'It will not enter this way again,' he said.

Instantly, once more, the howl of the madman riveted us both to the spot. It was a scream of hatred, of infinite frustration, and it was followed by the sound of plaster being torn from the wall, and then by the smashing of glass.

'By the Gods!' I cried. 'The poor thing that was Liviu has freed itself and leapt through the window!'

As I turned automatically towards the door, Brother John laid a restraining hand on my arm.

'No!' he said. 'We must not leave this room tonight! You have just seen the powers of the Undead!'

Accepting this wisdom, I nodded at Brother John, but made my way to the window and looked out.

The moon was high and the scene was brightly lit, though this light cast shadows which created a plethora of weird figures which appeared to dash this way and that. For a while I had difficulty in focusing my eyes, but eventually I saw the movement of a man . . . No, surely not a human, but a beast, something that seemed to crawl on all its limbs, something wretched, obscene . . . Then it cried out in a voice not quite human: the cry of a soul in hideous torment.

'Dracula!'

The thing had crawled from the shadows and raised its pale, ravaged face to the full moon. It was Liviu: the poor, insane beast that a few months ago had been a handsome youth enjoying his wedding night. Now, Liviu was gone. Only that tormented beast remained. And the broken chain dangled from the iron around its neck and I wondered at the strength needed to sever it.

'Dracula!' Again the tormented cry broke from his lips. 'Great Voivode, I am here!'

The cry was in the language of the Wallachians, but by now I had acquired enough of that speech to understand some simple meanings.

'Dracula! Great Voivode! Give me life, Master! Life is blood! Blood is life!'

I stared down in pity at this poor unhappy creature which gestured so feebly towards the moon. My soul cried out that his trembling, demented form might have some peace. Then a cold shiver shot through me. I found myself looking skywards. There were no stars to accompany the white disc of the moon, but again I heard the flapping noise of wing beats, the wings of many creatures, and the breath caught in my throat when I saw them. I gasped and cried out. I could not believe my eyes. Brother John rushed to my side and he followed my gaze and we both saw a multitude of bats They were flying in perfect formation. They were led by a monstrous creature. They sped upwards and raced across the face of the moon, then suddenly turned and plummeted earthwards.

I cried out a warning.

Liviu looked up and saw death racing towards him. He saw death and as he looked he suddenly stood tall and strong, and held his arms high and wide, and threw back his head and laughed crazily. Then they were upon him, a black mass all over him, and he struggled and fell down, and was clawing them off, and then exploded into blood and rent flesh, and was suddenly still.

The silence was hideous. It emphasized their thirsty drinking The black form was crumpled up and the black mass shifted over it and I thought of cats lapping up their milk. I could not suppress a shudder. It passed through me and left me frozen. I wiped sweat from my forehead and looked again, and my blood turned to stone.

The bats were still there. They were a black mass on the body. But behind them stood a tall man, a pale, ghastly spectre, covered from head to foot in a black cloak.

He raised his white face to mine. His eyes were crimson and luminous. There was blood on his chin and his lips were curled back in a mocking smile.

I knew that face. It floated back from my childhood. It was now a hellish face, but its features were unmistakable; and I gazed out of terror and despair at the face of my father.

Indeed, it was Dracula!

Slowly he raised his cloak, like a huge pair of black

wings and then, as if he had never been, he quite simply vanished.

I blinked my eyes. I felt that I were dreaming. I saw a long line of bats, led by a larger bat, flying in perfect formation towards the full moon.

Then I passed out.

CHAPTER
19

We were woken in the morning to great cries of lamentation from below. For a moment I was startled, suddenly remembering, as I did, the terrifying events of the previous night, and confusing these lamentations with the tormented cries of Liviu, I jerked awake drenched in fear. It was a moment or two before I fully comprehended that I was actually awake, that Liviu was dead, and the lamentations from below were doubtless related to these facts.

I glanced across to the other side of the countess's bed, where Brother John was just wakening, blinking his eyes and looking down at the chair in which he had slept all night. Then my gaze fell on the sleeping figure of the countess.

She lay amidst the garlic flowers and her breathing now seemed more normal, deep and rhythmic, than her tortured gasping of the night-time. Indeed, there was even a touch of colour on her pale cheeks, and I was reminded of the legend of the sleeping princess who would only wake when the right man kissed her.

Again we heard the lamentations rising up from below our room, and Brother John heaved himself from his chair.

'What is it?' he asked.

'I believe they have found Liviu's body,' I said.

He lowered his head and frowned.

'Then let us go down,' he said quietly.

When I hesitated, looking towards the countess, for whom I now felt a more than common regard, he smiled and added:

'Have no fear. She is safe until sunset.'

We went down into the parlour of the inn and found Toma trying to comfort his wailing wife. Through the window I could see two men of the village bearing away something on a sheet. Toma looked at me through anguished, red-rimmed eyes and then, almost pleadingly, at Brother John.

'We have no priest here,' he said bitterly. 'It is my wife's wish that her brother Liviu be buried as a Christian.'

Brother John nodded and laid a hand on the sobbing woman's shoulder.

'You understand what has to be done first?' he said.

Toma and his wife exchanged a glance, and then the woman nodded, before sinking her head to her breast in a renewed paroxysm of weeping.

'We understand, Father,' Toma said.

'Very well. Where will you bury him?'

'In a corner of our churchyard, Father.'

'Let us go there then. Do you have the necessary things?'

Toma nodded, and Brother John turned to me.

'It is best if you stayed here and took a glass of my medicinal mixture to the countess,' he said. 'It is dandelion and lady's mantle. She must drink it in order that her blood may flow freely and uncontaminated.'

I did as I was bid, and I must confess that I was glad to escape the grim ceremony of burial. Brother John was to tell me afterwards of the task he had to perform in order to give eternal rest to the victim of the Undead, and avoiding this was something I therefore did not regret.

Firstly, he hammered a wooden stake through the heart of what remained of Liviu's body. Then he hammered an iron nail through the head. Then garlic flowers were spread across the body which was laid face downwards in the makeshift wooden box that passes with these simple folk as a coffin. All this was done to the accompaniment of prayers, and I could hear Brother John's sonorous tones coming from the churchyard that lay opposite the inn.

I stood by the window in the countess's bedchamber, the window from which I had seen Liviu die, and found myself taking comfort from the stalwart figure of Brother John as he stood with raised arms over the grave, defying all the dark powers. The ceremony ended with Toma planting a rose bush on the grave, which belief, as I understand it, arises from the idea that if the occupant of a vampire grave tried to rise from it, the thorn bush would prevent the vampire from so doing. Brother John finished by raising his hands above his head and crying out loudly, in a tone so clear and ringing that I could clearly hear it even from the bedchamber:

'*Gott Väter, Du Schopfer von Himmel und Erd! Beschirm unsern Ring, behüt unsern Herd!*'

'What is it?' said a bewildered and very feminine voice from the bed. 'What is happening?'

I turned to see the countess propped up on one elbow, a perplexed frown on her lovely face, and I took a hesitant step in her direction.

'It is nothing,' I said. 'It is a burial. Do you feel well?'

She looked at me in bewilderment, her hair tumbling around her face, her eyes large and beautiful.

'I . . . I feel weak. I . . . Oh, my Lord!'

A hand went to her mouth and her eyes went even larger as memories of the past days flooded into her tortured mind. I stepped forward immediately and held her hand.

'Have no fear,' I said. 'You are safe now.'

'Horrible!' she exclaimed, clutching at me like a drowning child, her voice rising dangerously near to hysteria. 'Horrible! It was horrible!'

Involuntarily my hand went up to stroke her soft hair, and I found myself pressing her nearer to my breast, not only to comfort her, but because of a growing emotion in myself.

'You are safe now,' I repeated, feeling an onrush of warmth, a pain and an ecstasy combined, a blind, overpowering need. 'Please be calm. It is all right.'

She lay some time against my breast, quiet but quivering, her breath warm and quickened by fear. Then, abruptly, she pulled herself away from my arms with a bright blush tinging her cheeks.

'Who are you?' she demanded, surprised rather than angry, and perhaps just a little embarrassed. 'Who are you?' she repeated. 'You say I am safe, and yet I recall being in Hell. Was it a dream? No, it could not be so.' She blinked and glanced around her and I noticed that her eyes, now open for the first time, were like pools of amber, bright and intoxicating. 'You say I am safe,' she continued, 'and curiously I believe and trust you. Please, who are you?'

I told her my story as briefly as I could, sparing her the more gruesome details. When I had finished, she turned pale and lay back on her pillows, a little fear and much puzzlement in her lovely eyes.

'You say you are a Dracula,' she said. 'The son of the evil one?'

I nodded, but not with great pleasure.

'Yet you are not as they,' she said. 'I feel safe here,

and your eyes tell me I can trust you with my safety. Truly, it is very strange . . .'

'Yet not so strange, my lady!' Brother John cried, entering the room and smiling broadly. He then introduced himself with a stiff, awkward bow and fell to performing his physician's duties. 'Indeed you have been sick, my lady, but you now appear much better. Our medicines did you no harm and so you must continue to take them for your health's sake.' He pressed his herbal concoction into her unprotesting hand. 'Drink this down now, and then let us hear your story, for I believe that friend Michelino has told you ours.'

She drank the mixture and lay back on the pillows. Her sweet face was relaxed, and it seemed that the terrors of the night had fled.

'My story is simple, dear friends . . .'

Dear friends! How ridiculous that my heart leapt at the words and bathed in the radiance of her smile. Indeed, on this instant, I was enslaved by her.

'I am, as you know, the Countess Irene Bathory. The Bathory family is an ancient one, as old as the Carpathian mountains that suckled them and shelters their castles. We have long been of the first noble house of Transylvania. But there is a tragic side to our house, for there are two branches of the Bathory family: one is called the Ecsed branch and the other the Somlyo. I am descended from the Somlyo branch, but the branch of Ecsed is tainted by madness, epilepsy and cruel aberrations in character . . . and yet, yet it is the Ecsed branch that rules our house. Stefan Bathory, a morbid man who is my cousin and would be voivode of all Transylvania, is the head of the Bathory house. It was he who rode alongside Vlad Dracula last year in a bid to restore him as ruler of Wallachia.

'Alas, I am but nineteen, my parents are dead, and therefore I am ward to Stefan Bathory and have to obey him. Some weeks ago he sent for me and told me I was to marry with Vlad, son of Vlad Dracula. I knew him not, save that I had heard of the stories of the cruelty of the house of Dracula. Yet I came willingly enough to the Citadel of Arges, where I was told a coach of the house of Dracula would wait for me. I reasoned that my own house was cruel enough, so what harm to go to another and perhaps gain my freedom?

'At Arges I waited. My maid Kata became suddenly ill and died on the very day Tirgsor arrived. Therefore it was alone that I went to Castle Dracula, and once inside things became a nightmare ... an evil dream ...'

She shuddered and caught her breath.

'Go on!' Brother John whispered.

'I cannot recount the horrors ... I recall that I awoke in the night ... a bat ... the red eyes boring into my own with basilisk horror.'

She raised both her hands to her face and cried out in the dread of her remembrance. I sprang to the bed immediately and rested a protective arm around her shoulders.

'Do not fear, dear countess,' I exclaimed. 'We will do all that is within our power to protect you.'

She raised her large, tear-stained eyes to mine.

'But where am I to go?' she said. 'What am I to do? The Bathorys will only return me to Castle Dracula!'

I shook my head vigorously.

'No,' I said. 'Brother John and I will take you from this God forsaken country, do not fear. I have a modest income which will suffice to protect you from the evils of life until you decide on your own future.' I paused, embarrassed by the vehemence of my declaration and wondering if I had gone too far in my boldness. 'That is,' I added, 'if you so wish it.'

The countess smiled, bathing me in her radiance, and raised my hand and pressed her lips to it.

'Brave sir,' she said softly, 'I cannot thank you and Brother John here for the services you have rendered me. My thanks would appear an insult to the nobility of your good deeds.'

Brother John cleared his throat.

'Yes, my dear child,' he said, 'but first we have to earn that thanks, for while we have thwarted the will of the Undead for a while, we are far from winning the conflict.'

'What must we do, Brother John?' I cried, determined to do battle with all the furies of Hell itself for another look of gratitude from the fair countess.

'Why, friend Michelino, we must track down the resting place of the great Undead and there end his existence. We must find Dracula's resting place and drive a stake through his heart.'

I felt the countess shudder against my arm.

'And what of Lady Irene?' I said. 'We cannot leave her unprotected.'

Brother John turned and took a hand of the countess.

'We must leave her alone one night,' he said kindly. 'Perhaps more. But we will not leave you unprotected, and we will get Toma and his wife to sit with you. We will leave you surrounded by all the protection available to us. Will you be brave and endure it?'

The girl silently bit her lip.

'I shall be afraid,' she finally said. 'But you are the ones who will be going into a great danger, and therefore I will be brave for your sakes.'

Brother John pressed her hand and I felt a surge of pride at her courage—a pride tinged with love, for indeed, at that moment, it was such I felt, and in a manner I had never felt before.

'Where shall we begin our search?' I inquired. 'At the castle?'

Brother John shook his head.

'You must tell me of the spot where Dracula rests, for you recall that a vampire must lay in his own grave from sunrise to sundown. Between those hours he has to lay helpless in his natural earth—in the earth in which he was buried.'

'If that is so,' I said, 'then he would lie where he was buried and many saw him buried.'

'And where was that?'

'The story is that he was killed in a battle outside Bucharest.'

Brother John shook his head.

'It cannot be,' he said, 'for a man killed in honourable battle does not become an Undead such as he.'

'So goes the story, which I only repeat,' I said. 'It may be false. But of one thing I am sure: his body was taken to the monastery of Snagov, near Bucharest, and there, in the presence of many, he was laid to rest.'

'I know the place,' Brother John said. 'It is an Orthodox monastery that stands on an island in one of the lakes surrounding Bucharest. It is one of the three largest and most important monasteries in all Wallachia.'

'I know it, too,' the countess said, grasping my hand and filling me with warmth. 'It is a fearful place and I fear you going.'

'We must,' I said, absurdly pleased that she should fear for my safety.

'It is a place where the princes and boyars of Wallachia hid in times of peril,' she said. 'It is a grim place which serves as a prison as well as a monastery, for the buildings are heavily fortified and guarded by boyars as well as monks. How can you hope to get in, accomplish your purpose, and escape the wrath of the monks?'

'Nevertheless, my lady,' said Brother John determinedly, 'we must do it, for many may depend on us.'

I nodded my agreement.

'We will be well protected,' I said. 'Never fear.'

'And now,' Brother John said with an air of impatience, 'we have delayed enough. We must get horses from Toma and depart at once. It is fifty miles to Snagov and a hard ride. I will go and make the arrangements.'

I sat in silence for some time, with the countess's hand in mine, too embarrassed by the depth of my desire for her to offer a word. And she, too, obviously aware of my feelings, was quiet and could not look at my eyes, though a blush tinged her cheeks. Finally, after what seemed an eternity, I said that I must go.

'I wish it were not so,' she replied. 'I feel safe with your presence, and I will not feel happy till your return.'

At this lightly veiled confession I felt my heart leap, and I wanted to rush forward and embrace her.

'I am happy it should be so,' I said, smiling yet making no move, 'but we will be safer when our task is complete.'

Impulsively she leant forward and kissed me on the cheek. Her lips were cool and yet they seemed to burn through me.

'Go then,' she said softly. 'God ride with you and protect you and hurry you safely back.'

I kissed her hand and left her. As Brother John and I spurred our horses away from Arefu on our grim mission I saw her slim figure at the window of the inn, waving after us.

CHAPTER 20

Of our ride to Snagov, I can recount but little. I recall that on that long ride we exchanged few words, each being sunk into his own thoughts. Villages, hamlets, forests, streams and rivers went by all unnoticed until, by the late afternoon, we halted our tired horses on the shores of a lake in the heart of the Vlasie Forest, which is near the city of Bucharest.

On an island in the lake, its grey stone walls towering to the sky, stood the great monastery of Snagov ... Snagov, where Dracula lay.

The monastery was a large fortified complex, more secure than most castles. The island was about a mile wide and a mile and a half long, the outer walls of the monastery following closely the shore line. In addition to the various chapels, cloisters and guest houses, there were farm houses and outbuildings by which the monastic population retained a degree of self-sufficiency from the outside world.

I knew little about Snagov except that my grandfather, old Vlad Dracul, had endowed it with more land than any other monastery in his realm so that it was now one of the three largest and most important monastic establishments in Wallachia. Radu cel Frumos, my uncle, also endowed it with land, and I have heard it said that a mistress of my father became a nun here.

BLOODRIGHT

The great monastery walls surrounded the island on all sides, coming right down to the water's edge, and a ferry was the only means of entrance or exit.

Brother John and I sat a time contemplating this forbidding building and discussing the best means of ingress. As it was an Orthodox monastery, Brother John felt it would be useless to try to gain an entrance openly and honestly, and certainly futile to convince the abbot of the necessity of defacing a tomb and mutilating a corpse . . . and the corpse of a prince to boot. The situation was indeed difficult.

I suggested that perhaps we could gain entrance as ordinary travellers seeking refuge, and then wait an opportunity to enter the tomb of Dracula to destroy him. Brother John wordlessly pointed to the sun now low on the distant hilltops. There would be little time to succeed before Dracula was able to move freely once again. However, when all was said and done, my suggestion seemed the only feasible one.

Brother John removed his habit and ornamentation, for there is sometimes great hostility to Catholic monks from those of the Orthodox persuasion. Securing them in his saddle bag, he then mounted his horse and we rode down to the jetty, where a fat and indolent boatman, grumbling his protestations, rowed us across for a silver *aspi*, which I felt was more than adequate for his services.

A brother greeted us at the great wooden gates of the monastery and demanded to know our business.

'We are travellers in your country,' Brother John replied, 'seeking hospitality for the night.'

'You are foreigners?' the monk inquired, regarding us in suspicion, though there was no strangeness in this since, at this time, Turk and Christian rode across the country bringing bloodshed and disease wherever they spread their sleeping blankets.

'We are,' Brother John replied.

'Enter then,' the monk said. 'Come in peace, go in peace and leave something of the happiness you bring.'

The monk took us to a cell-like room, sparsely furnished, but with two strong wooden cots on which were two blankets. There was also a small table with a bowl and a jug of cold water for a toilet, and a Bible of Byzantium decoration for the salvation of our souls.

'When you have refreshed yourselves,' the monk said, taking his leave of us, 'you will be expected to join the brothers in the refectory.'

'What now?' I asked Brother John when the monk had departed.

'As he says,' Brother John replied. 'There is little we can do until we find out exactly where Dracula rests.'

The immense rectory hall to which we were summoned was filled with many monks attending their one meal of the day. On a long table at the far end of the hall sat several of the hierarchy of the monastery and a monk came forward to conduct us to this table where we were introduced to a tall, grizzle-haired man who was the abbot.

As Brother John had originally stated such, so we pretended to be foreign merchants travelling through the country, and soon we were exchanging gossip on the political events of the world. We congratulated the monks on the defeat of the Turks, and then Brother John managed to pass a comment on the death of Dracula.

'Ah, yes,' smiled the abbot. 'He was once a great defender of this monastery and of Christendom against the Turkish incursions.'

One of the monks leaned forward. He was lean and very pale and there was something strangely familiar about his face. The abbot waved a hand in his direction.

'Our brother Vlad here,' he said, 'is the brother of Dracula.'*

I gave an involuntary start. I had heard of this brother who had, in fact, been the half brother of my father, the third and youngest son of the old dragon. He hated and despised my father, but it was a hatred born of envy. I did not like this Vlad's face: it was mean and envious. It seemed strange that he and I were of the same blood, and yet he did not sense any relationship between us. I thanked God that I favoured my mother more than my father.

'The Voivode, my brother,' said Vlad the monk, 'was buried here.'

'Indeed?' said Brother John, and I could not help but marvel at his acting, for it seemed he had never heard of the fact before, so well did he feign his surprise.

'Yes,' Vlad the monk said. 'After the battle of Bucharest, the Voivode's servants brought his body here and it was entombed in our southern chapel.'

Brother John started to talk casually about the Turkish army and their expansion, as if he were not interested in the burial of Dracula, and for some hours we feasted and talked generally with the monks. But later, in the privacy of our cell, Brother John whispered:

'At first light we will go to the southern chapel and destroy him!'

---

* This must have been Vlad Calugarul, or Vlad the Monk, half brother of Dracula, who later became abbot of Snagov but was then defrocked. He claimed the throne of Wallachia in 1481 and ruled until 1482, during which time he betrayed the country to the Turks. He died in 1492. Van Helsing.

'Why not now?' I asked.

'It is two hours since sunset. He will not be there. We must wait until he returns to rest here at sunrise.'

'What now?' I asked.

'Now?' he said, smiling. 'Well, friend Michelino, we must try to get as much rest as we can. I'll wake you before first light.'

With that, we both lay down and slept.

We approached the small chapel as the first rays of the coming dawn began to shine through the slit windows of the great monastery walls.

The chapel stood in a small corner of the monastery's main courtyard, and we crossed to its small but heavy carved oak door without encountering any of the monks, who must now be rising to the hollow tolling of the great bell. We pushed open the door and found ourselves in a small vault-like chapel, scarce twenty feet long and ten feet wide. The stone floor was cold and damp, and there was an altar at one end on which two candles spluttered, giving forth an eerie light.

Before the altar stood a smaller, slightly raised altar piece.

Brother John pointed silently. There was some writing in the old Slavic script which even I could interpret.

DRACULA

Without a further word we bent to our task of removing the weighty stone slab from the top of the altar grave. The sweat glistened on our faces as we pulled and tugged with all our might. Slowly, grating, stone against stone, the slab swung to one side. With our combined strengths we pushed it over and then peered into the silent sarcophagus to confront the great evil which plagued Wallachia.

It was empty.

Brother John and I looked blandly at one another.

'What does it mean?' I whispered. 'I thought you said . . .'

Then, remembering, I indicated the brightening sky, and Brother John nodded grimly.

'He should have returned,' Brother John said, 'unless . . .'

'Unless what?'

'Unless he has found another resting place.'

We stood irresolute a moment, crushed and confused, and then Brother John shook himself.

'We must find him,' he said. 'Quickly! Let us push back the slab!' He threw his crucifix into the tomb. 'That will ensure he cannot return here.'

Together we exerted all our strength and slowly swung the stone slab back into position.

'What are you doing here?' a sharp voice barked.

Startled, we looked up. The tall figure of the abbot was framed in the door, while behind him I could see the lean, stooped figure of Vlad the Monk.

'Why,' Brother John said, quickly recovering his wits, 'we were so enthralled about your conversation last night concerning the Voivode Dracula that we came to view his tomb.'

'To view?' Vlad the Monk's voice was suspicious.

'I was merely looking closely at the inscription,' Brother John said, 'to ensure that there was no mistake.'

The abbot looked at us closely.

'And?' he said.

'It seems that this is indeed Dracula's tomb,' Brother John said smoothly, 'and we are honoured at being able to see the last resting place of the great Voivode.'

'Not so honoured,' said the abbot, obviously convinced of our sincerity. 'While it is true that the Voivode Dracula was buried here after the battle of Bucharest, a few months ago his sons sought permission of the Metropolitan to have the body exhumed and reburied in the family crypt at Castle Dracula. The tomb you see is thus empty.'

The abbot turned to leave, and I could see Brother John's face turn ashen, signalling that something, I knew not what, was wrong.

'My lord abbot,' Brother John said, visibly trying to control his shaking voice, 'before we leave on our journey, tell me, was Dracula reburied at the castle with great pomp?'

The abbot glanced back questioningly.

'That is a strange question,' he said.

'It is merely, my lord abbot, that most people think the prince is buried here, and I wondered why this is so.'

'There is no mystery,' the abbot explained. 'Dracula's body was exhumed during the reign of the late lamented Basarab the Old, who was the arch enemy of Dracula. It was therefore not prudent to reveal such things to the general public. But it was the sons of Dracula who also insisted on privacy—pious sons both. Why, they even had some earth and materials taken from our tomb to Castle Dracula in order that their father's sleep might remain undisturbed. A great Christian symbolism. Such piety!'

'Well, we will take our leave, lord abbot,' Brother John said, now trying to disguise his agitation. 'We thank you for your hospitality.'

The abbot nodded absently and was gone. Reluctantly, Vlad the Monk, with suspicion still in his eyes, followed.

'Come!' Brother John cried, when they were out of earshot. 'We must ride like the wind for Castle Dracula!'

'I do not understand,' I said. 'I thought you explained that the Undead must return to their grave between sunrise and sunset, and that an Undead could only lay in the ground wherein he was buried?'

'But did you not hear what the abbot said?' Brother John said, with an uncommon snort of impatience. 'Do you know what it means?'

I shook my head dumbly.

'It means that your brothers, Vlad and Mihail, have removed the body of Dracula to Castle Dracula, bearing with them the earth from Snagov in which he was buried. It means that Dracula lies with impunity at Castle Dracula!'

'Merciful God!' I cried, once more stricken with fear, but this time not for myself. 'What of the Countess Bathory? If he can get past the protection we left her . . .'

I left the sentence unfinished. I could not bear to think of it. I was shaking and my heart started pounding and my thoughts were in turmoil. There was dread all around me.

'Let us ride!' Brother John urged. 'Let us ride for our immortal souls and hers! And may God give us aid!'

The journey to Arefu went quickly and fearfully, while our heads spun with mysteries and questions. Indeed, so hastily did we ride that at one point I rode my horse into the ground, after which the poor beast lay there, unable to get up, blood and foam dribbling from its nostrils. There was nothing to do but leave the unfortunate beast and mount double behind Brother John. This I did and we rode off again. Then his horse, too, fell exhausted to the ground, and another night was upon us before we managed to purchase fresh mounts and ride on as if the furies of Hell were pursuing us.

We came to Arefu at dawn, our horses wheezing beneath us, their muzzles flecked with foam and blood to show that we had ridden them too hard.

The inn was as before, silent and shuttered, wreathed in the cold mists of the morn. Hardly bothering to pull rein, I leapt from my mount and hurled myself against the inn door. To my surprise, it swung open and I rushed into the room, glanced wildly around me, and then, thinking only of the countess, my new love, bounded with all haste up the stairs.

The bedroom was empty.

The despair flooded over me. It swept away my senses. I felt anguish and a cold, demented rage that first burned me, then numbed me. A sob escaped my lips. I hammered my fists against the wall. Then, feeling murderous, beyond reason or logic, I suddenly left the room, brushed aside Brother John, and shouted for all my might down the stairs.

'Toma!' I shouted. 'Toma! *Where are you?*'

There was movement below and then I saw the innkeeper, standing at the bottom of the stairs, his face drawn and haggard.

'What in God's name happened?' I cried. 'Where is the countess?'

'Young Herr, young Herr. . . .' He raisd his hands, palms outward, and shrugged. 'We know not, young Herr. Yesterday morning we found her room empty. That is all we know. We fear that . . .'

He raised his shoulders again and then let them fall

resignedly. His red-rimmed eyes gazed at mine for a second and then fell away.

Brother John stepped up to me. He held out the gold crucifix. It was the one we had left with the countess.

'Someone has emptied the room of the garlic flowers,' he said. 'I found this lying in the corner.'

A coldness seized me. This ice pierced my heart. I felt I could not breathe and the walls seemed to spin all around me.

'Who removed the flowers?' I cried out to Toma.

'As God is my witness,' he replied, 'I do not know, mein Herr.'

Not pausing to think, no longer dwelling on reason, impelled only by anguish and my love, I rushed down the stairs.

'Where are you going, Michelino?' Brother John called out.

'Where?' I cried without stopping. 'Why, to the castle, of course! We have rescued her once and I shall do so again! Farewell, my old friend!'

'I am with you, Michelino!' the brave monk cried out. 'Pray she is still of the world! Hold! Let me be by your side! Let us go there together!'

And so saying, he bounded down the stairs after me, and together we ventured back to Castle Dracula.

CHAPTER
21

The castle stood silent and seemingly deserted as we wound our way up the mountain track. Our entrance was gained easily and no one disputed our passage as we wandered from room to room in the grey light, searching vainly for the countess.

'Brother John,' I said, as we encountered empty chamber after empty chamber, 'there is one thing that puzzles me. You say that my brothers Vlad and Mihail, and indeed Tirgsor, are not Undead and this is proved by the fact that they are able to move in daylight?'

Brother John nodded.

'They act as servants to Dracula,' he said. 'The Undead are helpless during the hours of sunrise to sunset, and therefore it is a great aid to have someone who is faithful to them and who can move in daylight to protect them.'

'And yet,' I interposed, 'I initially saw them during the hours of daylight and now we never encounter them at all during these hours. How can this be?'

'Can you cast your mind back to when Tirgsor brought you here? When you saw him on the Eve of the Feast of St. Andrew he appeared strong and healthy, but the next day he was weak and sickly until the sun set, and then he became strong once again.

You noticed the same phenomenon with your brothers.'

'Yes,' I said. 'This is true.'

'It is my belief, friend Michelino, that the Undead control them. But the Undead can only exercise full power after sunset, so that during the day this strength is diminished. Perhaps the weakness during the daytime gets progressive as the Undead drains more and more of their energies: each night the Undead must prey on them so that, little by little, their life's blood is sapped and they weaken until they, too, become Undead. I believe that your brothers and their servant are finding it increasingly difficult to move about in daylight and that is why we have the freedom of the castle now.'

Horrific though it was, this explanation seemed logical. Certainly there was no sign of my brothers, of Tirgsor or his daughter Malvina, nor was there any sign of my beloved countess. And, at the thought of the countess, I was immediately overcome with a great sense of grief and an anger that fuelled my courage.

We had entered the large refectory room again, and I was about to suggest to brother John that we start a search of the vaults when something suddenly flashed by my head. Then there was a thud, and a quivering knife embedded itself in the door not a foot from me.

For a brief second I stood looking at it in disbelief.

'*Look out!*' Brother John cried.

The cry stirred me from my stupor and I turned around quickly, sliding my sword from its sheath.

Two men were moving across the room towards us. One was holding a duplicate of the knife now wedged in the door behind me, and the other was brandishing a cudgel. They were evil looking fellows, dirty and dressed in rags, and their snarling features displayed yellow, decaying teeth.

'Szganyl!' Brother John hissed, also unsheathing his sword. 'Gypsies!'

The two men approached cautiously. They were crouched low and they were grinning. I flicked my blade towards their faces, but while they maintained a respectful distance, they displayed no fear at all.

'*Mandi maur!*' one cried suddenly and tried to leap under my guard.

He nearly succeeded and might have crippled me with a blow from his cudgel had not Brother John, who displayed remarkable skill as a swordsman, given him a slash across the arm which caused him to cry out in pain and retreat a step or two.

The other man poured forth a volume of sounds which even to an unknowledgeable ear was obviously cursing. I swung towards him, trying to gain an advantage, but the man backed hurriedly away, seized a candelabra and threw it at me. I tried to knock it aside with my sword, but the man followed so closely that he was upon me before I had disengaged from the candelabra and was able to meet his attack. I had only time to grasp the wrist of his descending knife hand, and we fell to the floor in a struggling mass of arms and legs.

There was the sound of someone shouting and instantly I became aware that the man on top of me had ceased his struggle and was now climbing off me. I came to my feet, ready for action, but the sight that met my gaze sent my heart sinking to my boots.

Half a dozen men had crowded into the room, all heavily armed, and all the same breed as our attackers.

I edged nearer Brother John.

A man, short and stocky with a shock of black hair,

his skin dark and his eyes humorous, shining alertly from an angular face which had a hooked nose and high cheekbones, stepped forward and shot a number of rapid questions at our two attackers. The two men, offering monosyllabic replies, stood before him like disobedient children. The stocky man then turned to us and smiled. He said something which neither of us understood and to which we both shook our heads. Brother John then spoke to him in German.

'Who are you?' Brother John asked.

'I understand,' the man said, smiling broadly. 'I speak. Me Putzina. Me *Kako*, chief of tribe.' He waved a hand at those behind him. 'Szgany tribe. All Szgany. What you do here? Here is *doosh* place, evil place.'

He suddenly broke into his own gypsy language in which there was much repetition of the word *doosh* (evil) and *Bang* (Devil) and *choovikin*, which was their word for witch.

Brother John explained carefully that he was a priest and I was his friend, and, when the man Putzina repeated this in his own language, a great muttering broke out amongst his men. Our two assailants looked uncomfortable, and one or two of the gypsies near them jostled them in a threatening manner. Putzina then snapped something to his fellows and the two men were seized and marched out.

'Forgive, Father,' he said with a mischievous smile. 'They punished. They be tried by *Kriss*, elder council of tribe. But what you do in evil place?'

Brother John told him we were searching for a young girl who was ill and who had been kidnapped by the wicked owner of the castle. Putzina's angular face was all smiles.

'Look for *rakli*?' he asked. 'Look for girl?'

'Yes,' I said. 'Have you seen her?'

His bright eyes searched my face. A broad smile split his lips. I found myself blushing and then Putzina broke out in a laugh.

'*Kom rakli?*' he said. 'You love girl?'

I nodded, blushing even more furiously, but determined not to deny what my beating heart told me.

'Good!' He laughed again. 'Girl safe at my camp. Found on mountain road by my *meero romni*. You understand? My wife. Girl found. She ill, but Szgany cure.'

I could not express the relief that flooded through me. Indeed, this whole experience was one of contrasting emotions, from anger to fear, from the urge to kill to the need to love, and it seemed to me that whatever the outcome might be, I would never be quite the same afterwards. As for the moment, I felt only relief and joy.

'Your camp,' I said to Putzani. 'Where—?'

'No worry,' he interrupted, holding up one hand, a broad smile lighting up his face. 'Night before last *rakli* found walking towards castle. She walk as if in sleep. Szgany take her to camp. Look after her. Szgany cure.'

He waved us to follow him and we did so, leaving the castle and quickly entering the forest on the mountainside. It was a walk of several minutes before we entered a large clearing where several tents were pitched by a small stream. Two or three donkeys and a horse were tethered nearby to a tree while a lot of men and women sat round a large smoking fire, preparing to eat some delicious smelling concoction which was simmering in a large pot over the burning wood.

'Putzina's people,' said our mischievous looking guide. 'Putzina *Kako* of tribe.'

I understand that *Kako* meant chief although, literally, it means 'uncle.' In each tribe, it seems, there is one elder who is accepted by general agreement as chief, but it is not a hereditary title, for the wisdom of the gypsies is great. They prefer to elect a man for his wisdom, strength of character and feeling for justice. The *Kako* governs with a council of elders called the *Kriss*, and these elders hold enormous influence over the people. Obedience is not based on fear, however, but on an awareness that within the tribe discipline is the only way for survival.

Putzina pointed to an old woman, whose face seemed obliterated by a mass of snow white hair which hung in profusion almost to her waist.

'*Phui Dai*,' he said. 'Wise woman of the tribe. She cure *rakli*. Your woman get better.'

The old woman smiled at me, brushing some hair from a weather-beaten face in which twinkled a pair of bright blue eyes. She then inclined her head and said: 'Come.'

The woman, Oraga, for such was her name, led us into a tent and there, the saints be blessed, lay my fair countess. She was pale, but alive, her breath coming out in the deep, heavy rhythms of sleep.

'*Rakli* get well if taken away from the evil place,' the old woman said, peering narrowly at Brother John. '*Dadus* knows of herbs that heal?'

Brother John nodded.

'*Dadus* listen,' the old woman said. 'Me purify blood of *rakli* with tea of centaury, and mugwort causes her sleep. The evil that drinks of her blood has twice drank so . . .' She paused, turning her gaze on me, her eyes bright and piercing. 'You destroy evil,' she said, 'but first take her to safe place. She get better.'

Words were little enough with which to thank this

wise old woman; nevertheless I offered them and Brother John echoed me. The old woman, Oraga, shrugged.

'Luck be with you, boy,' she said. 'And with you, Father.'

Putzina entered and took us both by the arms, smiling broadly.

'No go before guest,' he said, pointing to those seated around the fire. 'Look! *Holomus*! Feast! Drink and eat, yes?'

Protesting, but quietly grateful for the sustenance, we sat down with the Szgany and enjoyed a simple meal. The food consisted of a meat and vegetable soup ladled from a cauldron. This soup was mopped up with bread and washed down with either a beer called *libena* or a wine called *mol*. Both were delicious.

Over the meal we learnt more of their finding of my beloved countess. It seemed that they had been moving across country from Transylvania and had been journeying several days. They did not know this part of the country at all, but had made camp and, seeing the castle, gone to '*mong, loor, nash*', which is a phrase they use, meaning to 'beg, steal or borrow.'

It had been nearly dawn on the previous day when they had encountered the princess walking towards the castle; there was blood on her clothes, and strangely she was attired for the night. She walked like one in a sleep and they could not rouse her. Instead they brought her to the *Phui Dai* who told them the castle was an evil place.

Putzina had ordered his tribe to shun the place, but this morning they found that two of the tribe had disobeyed orders and gone to the castle. Putzina and his men had followed, and thus it was that they found

Brother John and myself being attacked by their miscreant fellows.

Putzina now jabbed a thumb towards the castle towers.

'When wind high, move tent to other side of hedge.'

I understood this to be a Szgany proverb meaning when all is not well it is time to move on. I wanted to do something more to show my gratitude to Oraga, the wise woman, so I left the encampment and started to pick some flowers to give to her. Putzina, however, stopped me from doing this.

'What you do?' he demanded.

'I am thanking Oraga by giving her some flowers,' I said. 'A small token of . . .'

'Flowers picked, symbol of death coming. Flowers should grow like life. Gypsy say picked flowers unlucky.'

His face was so stern that I dropped the flowers immediately.

'Then take this,' I said, tossing him a silver *aspi*.

He raised it to his mouth, bit it, spat on it and then pocketed it, now grinning mischievously.

'Listen, *gorgio*,' he said, using the term by which the Szgany call all foreigners. 'Cloudy morning often change to fine day. Behind bad luck comes good.' He raised his right hand. '*Kooshko-bok!*'

After this we left Putzina's encampment, I carrying the unconscious countess in my arms. Oraga had promised me that the unconscious state would last but a few hours more, after which the countess would awaken naturally. Once out of sight of the camp, Brother John made me lay the countess on the ground while he examined her.

'It is not that I have no trust in the Szgany, but I want to be sure,' he said. 'However, it seems they are right. She is in a deep and natural sleep and that is good. Her blood, though she has lost much, flows well. It is her young heart that comes to her aid in this, and, given care, she will recover . . . if she is not exposed to this evil again.'

'What about those?' I said, pointing to the tiny wounds on her neck, which seemed to be more marked than before.

'They will disappear in time,' he said. 'But I think you should return to the inn. Tell Toma he must protect her with his life, and then return to me.'

'What will you do?' I asked, puzzled.

'I shall return to the castle and continue the search to find the Undead and destroy it.'

'Do you think it wise?' I asked, concerned for his safety.

'I have all the protection I need and there are still six hours to sunset. If she awakens, try to find out all you can from her . . . it may help us in our fight.'

With a wave of his hand he started up the mountain towards the castle, and I stood looking after him for some moments. In my heart I silently saluted a brave man.

Then, gathering the sleeping countess once more in my arms, I turned and set out for Arefu.

CHAPTER 22

Toma greeted me as if I were the very prodigal returning home. Indeed, I doubt that the returning prodigal was made more welcome than I. A fire had been lit in the countess's room and I noticed that the garlic flowers had been carefully replaced and some religious icons had been placed around the room. Toma's wife put the countess to bed while I prepared a brew of the juice of hyssop, dandelion leaves and lady's mantle, as Brother John had instructed me.

'The countess must drink a small glass of this every hour,' I told Toma and his wife. 'I shall go up to her room now and stay a short while, but then I must leave for the castle before the sun sets.'

At this Toma seemed much perturbed.

'Must you go, young Herr? It is dangerous.'

'Yes,' I said, 'I must go. Brother John needs my help.'

At this Toma hung his head and mumbled a prayer. I pressed his arm and told him to be of good cheer, for we were not yet dead.

'Some things are worse than death,' he whispered.

I smiled and left him and ventured up to the countess's bedchamber. She lay pale and still, but her face was calm and relaxed in slumber. I poured Brother John's mixture between her lips, but even though she swallowed most of it, she slept on. My heart went out to her, for she lay so small and helpless, and all my protective instincts were raised. I watched and waited some time, hoping she would awaken, and just when I was about to give up, my vigil was rewarded.

She stirred and gave a sigh. I saw a redness tinge her cheeks, saw her eyelids flutter open and then go wide. I quickly leaned across and touched her arm.

'Do not fear,' I whispered. 'You are safe again.'

'Michelino!'

It was the first time she had used my name and my heart leapt at the sound of it. Then she raised her head from the pillows and laid it gently against my shoulder.

'Oh, Michelino,' she murmured.

'There,' I said, thanking God for Brother John's herbal knowledge. 'There, all is well now.'

After a moment or two, when she had choked back her tears of relief and taken a drink of the herbal brew, the countess lay back on the pillows, both hands gripping mine.

'Now, poor child,' I said, 'I must know exactly what happened. God knows, I do not wish to cause you more pain by the remembrance of that which can only be hurtful, but Brother John is even now at the castle, the day is drawing to a close, and we must know how you came to be taken to the castle when we left you so well protected.'

The poor girl shivered, but her hand gripped mine firmly, and she offered me a look of resolution. There was a pause while she ordered her confused thoughts, then she began:

'After you left me and night drew on, I found it impossible to sleep. Indeed the many horrible fantasies that crowded my mind—blood and pain and death and living corpses—seemed to preclude all hope of sleep. Then, after a time, I began to doze. It was a fretful, half waking sleep, filled with dreams and recollections, and the aroma of the garlic flowers seemed to oppress me; they gave me a strange choking sensation in my throat and chest, and I felt my lungs would burst. Finally, unable to do anything else, oblivious to the possible danger, I pushed the garlic away from me.

'Later, I became aware of a thin white mist in the room. At first, in my half sleeping state, I thought it was a night mist which had come in through the window. The window! It was then I sprang fully awake—for I noticed that the window was open. Do not press me how it happened. I know not. All I know is that in my struggle to breathe, to escape the oppressive atmosphere of the garlic flowers, I must have risen from the bed, taken the flowers and deposited them out of the window.'

She gave a groan and held a hand to her head.

'How could I have done this after promising you and the good monk that I would not tamper with them?'

'It was not your fault, dearest countess,' I said, squeezing her hand in sympathy. 'The evil we fight has such powers of hypnotism at its command that it was but the thought implanted in your mind that caused you to act so. You did not do this of your own free will.'

She gave a small, brave smile, held my hands more tightly and, gazing downward, shivering slightly in recollection, continued:

'Horrible! Horrible! As I started awake, staring in terror at the open window, I suddenly became aware of a tall, thin figure in a long black cloak. Indeed, he seemed to step from the mist, and my heart lurched in dread. He made no step towards me, but simply stood there, his two hideous red eyes glaring malevolently at me from a waxen face. Oh, Michelino! Michelino! I would have screamed in terror had not his gaze turned me to stone, paralyzing me.'

She raised a hand to massage her slim, peach-coloured neck, as if remembering vividly the sensation. Then, when her fingers touched the wounds of her throat, she shuddered violently.

'I was paralysed. I could not make a move. He stood blackly before me and hissed: "Remove those baubles of a debased superstition." Again, the malevolent red eyes bored into mine and, as if I had no control over my own hands, I felt them rise, take off the crucifix and fling it from me. At this he laughed, so sneering and horrible, and then he moved quickly towards me. Oh, my God! My God!'

Sobs shook her frail body and she pressed herself tighter to me.

'What am I to do?' she cried. 'How can I tell you more?'

'You must,' I urged. 'You must tell me all, for all our sakes.'

She withdrew from my embrace and lay back on the pillows, sighing and gazing forlornly above her. Her breathing was heavy. She licked at her lips. She was seized by a spasm of shuddering and then it subsided. Her voice was a whisper.

'His eyes, those malevolent eyes, bored into mine until I began to feel him inside my very mind. Then I began to feel . . . excited, to feel I wanted him, the pain and the pleasure, an ecstasy . . . I craved it, I needed it, I could scarce control my own breathing, and . . . he approached me and I lay back, closing my eyes, helpless, wanting him, burning, as he bent over me . . .'

At this point she paused. Her face was inflamed. There was shame and confusion in her eyes and my heart went out to her. She touched the wounds on her neck once again.

'He was breathing all over me . . . his breath was warm and reeking . . . I felt his lips, moist, heavy, on my . . . skin. Then, a sharp bite . . . sharp and thin, like a needle, and . . . such pain, such ecstasy, such shame and wantonness . . . I felt my strength being sapped and I lay back in a half swoon, delirious, ecstatic, beyond shame or caring, as if . . . as if he had made love to me.'

Again she burst into sobs, now ashamed and bewildered, and once more cursing the foul house of Dracula, I drew her into my arms and stroked her hair. Eventually she calmed down and continued:

'I know not how long I lay there with him on top of me, sucking out my very life, but soon he rose, his sneering mouth dripping with my blood. And even . . . Oh, God, the shame! The shame! Even as he rose, I cried out that he must not stop, that he must take more from me, that I would die if he did not allow me to achieve the climax of my shameful desires . . . He merely smiled at me. It was a smile of pure contempt. He said: "You are now flesh of my flesh, blood of my blood. I will take no more of you for now, for you will be mine as long as I desire and I take from you only as I wish to." I swear, Michelino, that this he said to me, and I, in my debased need, accepted it.'

She paused again, and I saw tears on her cheeks, and the shame and despair in her face now filled me with rage—rage against Dracula and his accursed house. So thinking, I leaned forward and kissed her burning brow, and she suddenly seized me with both hands.

'Oh, Michelino! Michelino!' she cried. 'I fear for your life, for indeed he knows you. That same night he said to me, "My son Mircea thought to protect you, fool that he is. My son! He is no son of mine, but the son of his mother, for he would shun me. Yes, he thinks to pit his puny wits against mine, thinks to thwart me—I, who commanded armies when he was but an ache in my loins! But he shall soon know what it is to cross my path." Then he turned to me and said: "To seal our bond, my beautiful vine, we shall drink from each other and become one." And, so saying, he opened his shirt and, with long sharp nails, opened a vein in his breast. Horrible! Horrible! The blood, so rich, so red, so vile, began to spurt out, pumping in time to his black heart. Then, with one vice-like hand, he seized the hair on my head and dragged my mouth forward that I might suckle like a baby at the wound. And, God forgive me, I did it, I did it willingly, in some strange dream of ecstasy and despair, after which he turned away and vanished, leaving me spent.'

She cried out and fell into my arms and her whole body shuddered. I stroked her hair. I kissed her eyes and her lips. I felt my love and my anger flowing out around us both, and in the violence of these clashing emotions lay my hope of salvation.

'We shall destroy this beast,' I said. 'Have no fear of that, my love. And then we shall cleanse you of this evil.'

She sobbed pitifully.

'Oh, Michelino, would that it were true! But I am tainted, tainted like a leper, and for that there can be no cure. Who will touch me now? Who will take me to them after I have mated with such a fiend? Michelino, my love, my heart breaks from this!'

I raised her tear-stained face to mine.

'My heart is full of love for you,' I declared passionately, 'and I care naught for what has happened to you.'

'Do not pity me, Michelino,' she murmured, her fingers scratching like mice at my spine. 'Please God, do not pity me.'

Pity her I did not, but rather loved her with all my heart, and proved it by smothering her with kisses, first gently, then more fiercely, my lips to her lips, our limbs intertwining, until, our desires overcoming us, we sank back on the bed and became lost in those passions for which adequate words have yet to be created. Ah, but it was wondrous! It left us spent and it exhilarated us. It cleansed us of fear and opened the gates to the future, and it passed without shame or regret, and it filled us with fresh hope.

Only later, when I had recovered from my ardours, did I remember that I had left Brother John alone in the castle. At this I rose from the bed and hastily dressed myself, resolved to venture forth and aid my brave friend.

'You will remain here,' I told my beloved. 'Toma and his wife will spend the night in the room with you, and you must at all times keep the protective objects around you. Fight off all urges to sleep, and should you feel any attempt of outside influences on your mind, you must resist them with all your powers.'

'Very well, my love,' she said, stretching up from the bed and pulling my head down for another fiery kiss that sent my blood coursing.

'Now,' I said, disengaging from her embrace, 'if Brother John or I should not return by sun-up tomorrow, I shall give Toma instructions that you are to be driven into Tirgoviste. I shall leave you enough money to continue your journey to wherever you decide to go. Tonight we must attempt to defeat this evil, but you must assume, if we do not return at daylight, that we have failed, that we have become as they are.

Should this be so, and I pray that it will not, you must find someone to convince of the truth of our story, someone who will be able to release us from this curse. God be with you, my love.'

We kissed and parted. On the way out I paused only long enough to explain matters to Toma the innkeeper, and then I rode hard for Castle Dracula. The sky was quickening and storm clouds were gathering, and I knew I would be lucky to reach the castle before nightfall.

CHAPTER
23

It was nearly dusk when I drew rein before the castle. The storm clouds were now boiling in the sky, low and ominous, and I heard the distant rumble of thunder and then the rain fell.

I threw myself from my mount and raced into the castle. There was no one in sight. All seemed deserted. Shadows fell all around me from the towering grey walls, and beyond them the thunder was now roaring. Several times I called out for Brother John, but received no answer. All was as before, silent, desolate, though fires blazed in the hearths and the crackling and spitting offered proof that life still went on here.

The thunder roared. Lightning flashed across the window. I saw whiteness and shifting black shadow, and my footsteps were echoing.

Again I called out for Brother John, and again I received no reply.

I raced to the refectory room, then along the gallery to my former bedchamber. Both were deserted. Tentatively I tried the door to the vaults. It opened and I started to descend the stairway, treading carefully lest I stumble in the gloom.

A sudden sound made me whirl around. There was no one there, but I could clearly hear the patter of feet in the room I had just left. Immediately I retraced my steps but, to my surprise, I found the room still empty.

Then, having a sudden idea, I made my way to the tower where we had originally found the countess. The room was dank and cold, but again all was as we had left it.

The noise of someone moving came again . . . this time from below . . . from that profane temple of sorcery.

I turned around. The thunder roared and the lightning flashed. The darkness of the room exploded into glaring whiteness and then the darkness swooped in again. I shivered. It was cold. The room was damp and claustrophobic. Then, sword in hand, I started down the stairs.

'Brother John!' I cried out upon reaching the temple door. 'Are you in there?'

There was no reply. I could hear my own heart pounding. From above me came the roar of the thunder. I pushed open the door.

Kneeling on the floor, his back turned towards me, was a bulky figure in a monk's habit.

'Brother John!' I cried out in relief, sheathing my sword and quickly starting forward.

He rose and turned towards me, pushing back the cowl of the habit from his face.

I stepped back and gasped.

It was, indeed, Brother John, but the change in his appearance now froze my blood. His face was a waxy pallor, haggard and death-like, and his eyes stared at me without emotion. Also, his lips were unnaturally red; they were parted and I could see two rows of white, sharp teeth, very pointed, and with two canines longer than the rest.

'Brother John!' I cried out, horrified, in despair,

feeling fear and frustration all at once. 'Oh, God! Not you!'

'Welcome, friend Michelino,' he said, his voice rasping, hollow, and unreal. 'I knew and prayed you would return.'

My hand went to my sword. I started backing towards the door. His cold and lifeless eyes stared into mine, and then he raised both his hands.

'No,' he rasped. 'Do not fear me for the moment. As yet I can still control myself, but . . .' The alien eyes stared up at the darkening skies. '. . . not for long. And, before I succumb, you must set me free.'

I stopped moving backwards and studied him carefully, in anguish for my lost friend, yet wary that he might now be enslaved by the Undead and seducing me for his own accursed ends. He made no move towards me. I sensed a plea behind the cold eyes. I kept my gaze from the hideous mask of his face and, in that moment, bound by love and affection, I knew that my old friend spoke the truth.

'God have mercy, Brother John,' I said softly. 'How did it happen?'

'When you left,' he rasped, his voice hollow, disembodied, 'I foolishly set out to explore the vaults. I believed that the Undead must rest from sunset to sunrise wherever they were. I now know that even in daylight the Undead can move if they be sufficiently deep underground where the atmosphere of day cannot penetrate. Stupidly I went into the vaults and was seized by two of Dracula's handmaidens—she that was called Gaia, the wife of Liviu, and she that was called Malvina. They drank long and deeply from my blood until I, as Brother John, died and took on the semblance of the Undead.'

'But if Brother John is dead, how . . . ?'

He raised a hand to silence me.

'I have studied long hours,' he said. 'My mind is now so attuned to occult conflict that I still retain domination until the sun finally sets on another day. How I prayed you would return before that moment . . . that moment which is nearly come.'

He glanced stonily towards the blackening window. The thunder roared and for a brief moment the window was illuminated in white light before turning dark and bleak again.

'We must hurry, my friend,' he said. 'I will tell you what you must do, and you will do it without question or hesitation. And, when you have performed this task for me, you must then perform it on the other Undead so that they, too, may obtain the peace of the grave.'

'No!' I cried out, tears springing to my eyes, an anguish much deeper than death lancing through to my torn heart. 'Is there no way other than death for you?'

'No!' he exclaimed hoarsely. 'Quickly now! In that bag you will find some wooden stakes and a hammer. I will lay here and you must drive the stake through my heart.'

'No!' I cried in horror.

'You must! You must! If you value my soul, it is the only way!'

We looked at one another. The thunder roared beyond the walls. I saw the shadows of the walls fall about me and I felt I was dreaming. Nay, it was a nightmare, and it filled my whole being, filled me with a pain and despair such as no one should know. And yet, in that moment, through my dread and helpless fury, I sensed that I was changing, that all innocence had finally fled, and that I stood on the brink of a renewal and was becoming a man. I looked at Brother John. His eyes were alien and cold. I found courage and I took the stake and hammer from the bag, and with tears in my eyes walked towards him.

'Hurry!' he gasped. 'The sky is dark! I can feel my self-control ebbing! There is no time to lose!' He stretched himself out on the table that served as an altar. 'Strike swiftly, my friend,' he said. 'I will watch over you from the next world. *Strike now!*'

As I stared down at the prostrate form of my friend, over whose heart I held the sharp, pointed end of the stake, I suddenly saw the eyes change. A look of hatred came into them and, as the final shadow passed across the window, as the thunder receded and the rain ceased to fall, the look of hatred turned into vindictive triumph. It was then that I understood that the creature beneath my wood stake was no longer my friend, Brother John; rather, it was a nightmare parody of him. Indeed, the pointed teeth were set in a cruel voluptuous mouth, smiling a vicious smile, and it was clear to me now that Brother John had gone, that this thing, what he would call *nosferatu*, the Undead, had taken his place. All this passed through my mind in a second and strengthened my resolution.

Even as the trembling departed from my hands, the thing started to rise, its hands clawing up towards me, and I brought the hammer down, heavy and true, pounding the stake into its heart. I heard a shriek. It reverberated around the temple. It exploded in my mind and blotted out all thought, but still I did not cease from my travails. Again and again I struck with all my might, instinctively muttering a prayer as I did so. The thing's shrieks were blood-curdling. It writhed beneath the trembling stake. Its sharp white teeth champed until the lips were torn and bloody, and it shrieked and it heaved and the blood splashed upon it, and still I continue to strike. Then the writhing thing was still and I was done.

I leant against a wall, bathed in sweat and wanting to vomit. My breath came in great gulps and gasps, and again I was weeping. Then, as I gazed down, the thing started to change, its foulness seemed to disappear, the malignancy, the brute hatred, and there, in its place, lying serene and undefiled, no longer a slave to the great Undead, lay my friend, Brother John.

I thanked God for His mercy.

And now, with determined resolution, I realized that I must carry out the wishes of Brother John, that it was now up to me to track down the resting place of the Undead and release them from this vile corruption. Night had come. They would be stirring soon, if not already. I picked up the hammer and the bag of wooden stakes and quickly started towards the door. Once there, I glanced back at Brother John.

'Sleep in peace,' I said. 'Sleep in peace, my old friend, for I shall soon avenge your death.'

And so saying, I left him.

I went back towards the refectory room. I resolved that I must go down into the vaults and destroy the things that lurked there. It was now night, and I prayed to the spirit of my dead friend to give me the knowledge and protection I needed for my task.

As I came to the door of the refectory room, I caught the sound of furtive movement. I paused before the door and unsheathed my sword, then I gently pushed it open. No one stood before me, so I slowly edged into the room, holding my sword at the ready.

Suddenly a hand seized my sword wrist in a vice-like grip and my brother Vlad sprang from behind the door. I tried to free myself, but Mihail also appeared, and between them they managed to overcome me and bind me to a chair. Their eyes were filled with malevolence.

'Well met again, brother Mircea,' Vlad sneered.

'I am no brother of yours!' I cried hotly, though a fear gripped my heart.

'That has been arranged,' Mihail said in vindictive triumph. 'You have thwarted our designs too long. Now our father awaits you.'

'Brothers!' I cried desperately, hoping to make them see reason, for indeed they were not yet Undead. 'Come back to the true god and be saved! Renounce your false god!'

'False god?' Mihail laughed. 'It's your god who is false. Where is He to save you now?'

'Dare you reject God's truth?' I challenged.

'God's truth?' Mihail sneered. 'Truth in your Christian prattling? Dear brother, Catholic and Orthodox have fought long over our souls, each proclaiming his own truth. I have my truth already, brother, and that truth is immortality on earth.'

'We waste too much time, Mihail,' Vlad interrupted. 'Let us take him to the vaults where he will confront the one truth.' Vlad smiled like the devil and patted my shoulder. 'Fear not, little brother, you will soon come to love and serve the master, and our blood will be reconciled.'

With that Vlad and Mihail released me from the chair and, with my wrists bound before me, led me down the spiral stairway to the great vault and bound me to a pillar by passing a rope several times around my middle. Mihail smiled as they turned to leave.

'Fret not, brother Mircea,' he said. 'You will not have long to wait for some company. The sun is well down and soon they will come, for they are always thirsty . . . *very* thirsty.'

He laughed, a horrible, mocking laugh, then he followed Vlad back up the stairs and left me alone.

The great vault was gloomy. The flickering torches

cast queer shadows. There was silence and it seemed to be alive with a voice of its own. I struggled against my bonds. They were tight and I was well held. I glanced about me and the shadows danced and writhed and the silence was chilling. I was sure that my end had come.

At that moment I heard a scraping noise. It seemed like stone being slid against stone. The hairs on the nape of my neck stood up as I realized that I was listening to the stone sepulchres opening.

Then came the chilling tinkle of soft laughter and, in the gloom, I could see something white moving towards me. I held my breath. I tried not to succumb to panic. The creature was moving stealthily and it was dressed all in white and then it suddenly took on a definite shape.

At that moment I recognized the burn mark on her bared shoulder: the burn mark of a crucifix.

'Malvina!' I gasped.

She stopped in her tracks. Bloodshot eyes stared at me. Her features were distorted by evil and her smile was sharp-toothed.

'Mein Herr, mein Herr,' she whispered voluptuously. 'Dear, beautiful Herr. I knew you would come. I knew you would be mine. My lips have longed for the warmth of your flesh, the sweet wine of your young blood. Ah, mein Herr, gently. Do not struggle so. Just one kiss and I swear you will cry out for more. Come, my love!'

She raised her arms. She moved closer to me. The white dress fell around her and I saw her bosom heave and I felt her reeking breath in my face. Suddenly I shuddered. I could not control myself. She had opened her mouth and I saw the pointed teeth and my innards were torn by revulsion.

Her fingertips touched me. Her hands travelled up

and down me. I felt dread and then I felt languor and a helpless desire. Her crimson eyes were bright. They were wanton and corrupt. They grew larger and they filled my whole being and my body was burning. I tried to close my eyes. Her very presence held them open. Her red lips stretched back across her white pointed teeth, and then I felt her hot breath at my neck and I wanted to swoon.

Her lips were at my skin. I felt the darting of her tongue. She pressed her body against me and she was writhing and groaning, and then, as her mouth sucked at my throat, a harsh voice rang out:

'He is mine!'

Malvina snarled with rage. She whirled around with her face distorted. A tall man in a black cloak emerged from the shadows, and one hand shot out to grasp Malvina by the neck and hurl her across the floor of the vault.

'I say he is mine!'

My heart pounded furiously. I heard Malvina hiss. I saw the man's ghastly face and his red, piercing eyes, and I knew that at last, and probably too late, I faced the hellish creature that lurked within the body of my father.

I was in the presence of Dracula.

CHAPTER 24

He towered before me, encased from neck to ankle in a long, black cloak that made him appear taller than he was. Immediately, childhood memories of my father came flooding back to me, for indeed this ghastly figure was familiar.

The face was strong, aquiline, with a thin, high-bridged nose and arched nostrils below a lofty, domed forehead. The mouth, which could just be seen under a heavy moustache, was thin, fixed and extremely cruel. The chin was broad and heavy, the cheeks firm yet thin. Around the temples the hair was scanty, but it grew thickly towards the back of the head. The eyebrows were massive and almost met across the nose; and the eyes themselves were a piercing crimson void beyond which was nothing but the charnel house.

Protruding over his lower lip were peculiar, unusually long, sharp white teeth.

The extraordinary pallor of his face emphasised the livid aspect of his hideous eyes, and not until the day I die shall I be able to eradicate the memory of his frightful face as it leaned towards me, the mouth curling back from the sharp, demanding teeth, until even the gums showed, in a revolting smirk.

'Well met at last, Mircea, my son,' he said.

I looked on in helpless horror as he drew nearer, the

parody of a smile on his evil countenance and his eyes filled with hunger and contempt.

'At last you have come to join me,' he said. 'At last you have come to take your rightful place in the house of Dracula.'

I tried to avert my eyes from his, in a futile attempt to free myself from the hypnotic spell he was casting over me. He laughed long and loudly, a sound most horrible, until the hairs on the nape of my neck stood out.

'You thought I was a mere earthly tyrant, my son? Hah! I wish to talk to you, to explain the truth to you, before I finally take you as my own. Earthly power, my son, is but the power of a flea compared to that which is now mine. For years I have pursued the path to knowledge, for indeed in knowledge is power. And, just as knowledge is the pursuit of power, so death is the very inspiration of all philosophy—for it is death that prompts us to consider our brief earthly span and, in so doing, makes us dream and hope of conquering death itself.

'In my life I have contemplated philosophy, alchemy, theology and law in my quest to wrest Nature's secrets from her. The ancients in the days of the early Pharaohs knew her secret and thus believed in material existence after death. They believed we had another body, which they called *ka* or *sekhem*, which had all the characteristics of its original being, which was the real body of man, and which, through subordination to the physical body, could separate and move freely from place to place, reuniting itself at will.

'Only in death could *sekhem* really come into its own, and thus were offerings made in the ancient pyramids to sustain *sekhem* in the after life. The ancients of Egypt pursued their knowledge to its rightful conclusion: the method by which *sekhem* could be released to immortality in this world.

'Years ago those ancients succeeded in attaining this immortality, and those who did so were lauded in the land of the Pharaohs. Indeed this movement came to be called the flowering of the Draconian Cult, for its members worshipped Draco, the fire-breathing beast of the Great Deep, and Setek Ab Ra was the chief of priests in the order of the immortality seekers.

'Our family is old, older than the oldest pyramids, and even our name Dracula still links us with our ancient origins by the Nile—for were we not the spawn of Draco himself? Indeed, our history might have been different had it not been for that puny weakling, Amentotep the Fourth, who tried to destroy the ancient gods and set up a worship to Aton, the sun god. Because of this the Draconians were killed or driven underground; but their ancient lore scrolls were passed on to their descendents of which the Dracula house were foremost.

'While others pursued the new religions, we of the Dracula blood upheld the old. Your friend, the priest, he who was Brother John, said we worshipped the devil. What devil? I know of no such being. I, and my ancestors, from time immemorial, have worshipped the god of the south whose star is Sothis—Set, the Lord of the infernal region of Amenta, epitome of all subconscious atavisms and of the true will and hidden knowledge.'

His demoniac eyes flashed at me and a sneer circled his gross, blood-red lips.

'I have studied long,' he said, 'until, by my own diligence, I have become a Shamblu in the service of Set.'

'God forgive you!' I cried out.

'Forgive?' He laughed harshly. 'Why, your own

Christianity applauds my actions and accepts, in the words of the book of Deuteronomy, that blood is life. Yes, even the gospel of St. John quotes your Jesus as saying: "Except ye eat the flesh of the son of Man and drink his blood, ye have no life in you. Whoso eateth my flesh and drinketh my blood hath eternal life: and I will raise him up at the Last Day. For my flesh is meat indeed and my blood is drink indeed. He that eateth my flesh and drinketh my blood dwelleth in me." Ah,' Dracula sneered, 'why should I dispute what your own Christ tells his Christians to do?'

He paused. He studied me. His eyes blazed with chilling mockery. The torches cast writhing shadows and these black shapes fell upon him and emphasised the starkness of his features. I heard his harsh, hungry breathing.

'But then what do you know of Shamblu,' he sneered, 'the Horn of Plenty, the title of Shiva, our Lord Set? You know of nothing outside your Christ! For years I applied myself to gaining the knowledge that would free my earthly body for all time and enable me to walk this earth forever. Doubtless you call it a pact with the devil; perhaps, in your terms, it is. But to me it was the supreme achievement of the thirst for knowledge—the ultimate goal of man—immortality. And in this, of course, as it is with nature, the strong must dominate the weak. I, therefore, the conqueror of life, am supplied with eternal life through the blood of lesser beings, and in turn I can grant them immortality.

'So, my son, Mircea, you are of my blood and that blood will be my sweetest drink. Then, and willingly, you will join your brothers and I in spreading the will of Dracula over the earth.'

Dracula smiled. He held his hands upwards. The black cloak hung from his arms and he looked like some monstrous, rapacious bat. Then, in a voice that almost stopped my heart beating, in a strange and hypnotic Egyptian tongue, he threw his head back and cried out:

'*Shanti! Shakti! Shamblu!*'

Dracula, the lord of evil, was about to drink.

My soul plunged into despair. I tried to tear myself free. The ropes bit into my flesh and my heart was pounding madly and I felt the blood beat at my temples and the room seemed to spin. Then Dracula bent towards me. His eyes blazed into mine. They were a furnace and the fire drew me in and made me surrender. He placed his hands upon my shoulders. My resistance fell away. He was hissing and his eyes were hypnotic and filled me with rapture. I had no shame. I was his to command. Then, just as he lowered his lips to my throat, Malvina rushed under his arms like some wild, vicious beast.

'No!' she hissed. 'He is mine! You shall not cheat me of him!'

Dracula's fiendish eyes left mine, and thus released me from his hypnotic gaze. He glared at Malvina, who ducked aside and lunged at me. She gasped and then her teeth closed on my wrists and I felt the cord loosen as her sharp canines severed some of its strands.

Suddenly, Malvina's head jerked back.

With a terrible scream of rage Dracula had seized her by the hair and he now flung her violently across the vault. Shrieking, teeth gnashing, she leapt to her feet and desperately hurled herself back upon me. I heard myself cry out. I tried to pull the ropes apart. I saw Malvina rushing at me, and then I saw Dracula's back, as he swiftly placed himself between us both, guarding his prize.

'He is mine!' Dracula roared, seizing her by the

throat and, with astonishing strength, throwing her back to the floor.

Malvina hissed at him. She was on her hands and knees. Her mouth reddened with blood and she started to crawl towards him, her lips drawn over her gums, her teeth gleaming in the torchlight, sharp and pointed, with two hideous canines. Then she stood up.

Dracula's right hand shot out. His fingers were outspread. His eyes gleamed and stared directly at Malvina and she suddenly froze.

'No!' Dracula said. 'You cannot disobey me! I am your master and lord, and my will is your will.'

Oh, hideous sight to behold! Malvina's eyes widened, her spine arched and her lips opened; and then Dracula embraced her with a harsh and bestial snarl, his cloak billowing like gigantic wings behind him. Then, revoltingly, his mouth fastened on her neck, and the two rapacious creatures, first struggling, now silent, were bound together in their perverted devil's rite. He drank of her blood. She gasped and begged for more. He opened his shirt and opened a vein in his breast, and then he took hold of her head and pressed her lips to the wound and she kissed it and hungrily drank of it. Dracula's eyes gleamed. They gleamed down upon her head. Then he cried out and wrapped his cloak around her in a vile consummation.

I forced my eyes away from this blasphemous sight and then, with a strength born of fear and desperation, pulled my hands apart and snapped my bonds.

Without another glance, I fled up the stairway, knowing not where I was heading, intent only on flight from this nightmare. As I neared the top of the stairway, which led into the refectory room, I heard a terrible shriek from below.

'After him, my children!' Dracula screamed. 'Find him or you shall all be accursed!'

I bolted into the refectory room, slammed the door behind me, and looked desperately around me.

My brother Vlad was standing by the table.

'Fool!' he snarled. 'There is no escape!'

His lips curled in a condescending sneer as he started to move towards me. I began to back away, not knowing what to do, then I saw my sword lying where I had dropped it.

The sword had been blessed by the Pope, and I saw my salvation.

I launched myself across the room and seized the sword. Once in my grip I suddenly became aware that it had more defensive properties than that of a normal weapon. Indeed, at that moment, I could feel the power flow through it, the power of our blessed Lord and creator. I held it up. My spirit seemed to flow through it. I felt strong and my fears fell away and I knew I could face them.

Even as I raised the sword and waved it before me the unholy ones passed into the room. I say 'passed' for they did not enter through the door, but rather through a crack in the wood. I stared in horrified disbelief as, through an interstice where only a knife blade could go, Dracula and his two disciples emerged. Suddenly, as if from nowhere, they were standing before me with corporeal bodies as real as my own.

They walked slowly towards me and I held up the sword, and, as I did so, felt some Almighty power vibrate along my arm, and then saw a light, from where I know not, flash on the blade of my weapon. At this the hell fiends immediately recoiled, hissing and snarling, their faces distorted with such expressions of hatred and rage that words could not adequately describe them. Then I saw Dracula staring at me. He was trying to hypnotize me. I held the sword before my eyes and a snarl came to his lips; and his teeth, which were dripping with the blood of Malvina, gleamed in a gory, malign smile.

'Vlad!' he said sharply.

My brother sprang to the fireplace where two swords hung below an ornate shield. He took command of one and advanced upon me.

'There is no escape, brother Mircea,' he said. 'Why not simply join us?'

Then he was at me, swinging his blade viciously, leaping forward and moving very fast and displaying great skill. I backed towards the door. I parried his initial strokes expertly. Yet the Undead held sway over him and his strength was therefore tenfold, and I knew that I must end the contest quickly lest my stamina betray me.

He came in swinging his blade again. I then leapt to the offensive. I feinted at his head, but he parried it with ease, darting away and returning on his guard. We moved across the room. Our swords clashed. I saw Dracula and his wide-eyed acolytes, all of whom were just watching. I cut at Vlad's side. Again he blocked the stroke. My eyes fixed on his forehead and I deliberately raised my sword, and, as I expected, he raised his own blade to counter, and I suddenly leapt forward and pierced his heart.

Vlad straightened up and gasped. I withdrew my blade. He glanced down at the blood pumping out of his chest and then he fell forward to the floor.

Immediately Gaia and Malvina, or the creatures in their bodies, leapt upon him, snarling and pushing, struggling like wolves to get at his fresh, flowing blood.

Only Dracula had not moved.

I backed away towards the door. Dracula watched me with a smile. I held the sword before my eyes and the light flashed upon it, and I knew that this was keeping him at bay. Then I reached the door. I heard the females at their gory feast. I heard the door opening and I turned to find myself facing Tirgsor.

He had a sword in his hand.

'Only disarm him, Tirgsor,' Dracula said. 'This one is mine.'

'Very well, great Voivode,' Tirgsor replied.

He moved in and in the opening moments of our engagement I realized that he had great knowledge of the art of swordplay. A few strokes were enough for me to realize that I had met with a master, and had it not been for Dracula's insistence that Tirgsor merely disarm me, I do not doubt that I would have died with Tirgsor's blade in my heart.

For a long while I fought solely to hang on to my sword. The sweat began to pour off me and I knew that I was tiring before Tirgsor's onslaught. Tirgsor knew it, too, for he smiled and redoubled his efforts.

Then the inevitable happened.

A sudden cut from Tirgsor's sword sent my blade flying across the room. Fear of the consequences lent added strength to my failing limbs and I sprang after it as Dracula turned on me. Even as I did so I knew I could not reach the blade in time; instead I seized a heavy candelabrum and flung it full in the face of the great Undead. Then, without hesitating a moment, I once more grasped the comforting hilt of my sword.

As I turned, I found Tirgsor almost upon me with upraised blade. God had been good to me, but it was nothing short of a miracle that, at the moment Tirgsor poised to make his final strike, the foot of the *stolnic* slid on the blood of Vlad, which lay wet and slippery on the floor. Thus, with a frustrated cry, Tirgsor fell forward and my blade ran into his stomach.

He coughed blood, his eyes rolled back, and then he fell heavily to the floor. I stepped back and glanced quickly around me.

The candelabrum which had halted Dracula had also struck a hanging tapestry and, as if the room were merely dried tinder, a blaze had started and spread rapidly across the wood panelling of the room. The dark smoke was thickening and, peering through it, I could see the Undead creatures backing away before a bright wall of fierce, yellow flame. I promptly made towards the door and, on going through it, turned to glance back into the room.

The creatures were backing towards the cellar door, snarling and shrieking, and I could observe that they were entirely surrounded by blazing beams and falling tapestries, both of which were spreading the flames even further.

However, the malevolent figure of Dracula still towered above the inferno, and even through the billowing smoke, and across the rising flames, I could see his eyes boring into mine.

'You think to escape me?' he called through the smoke and flame. 'You think to thwart me? You who are sprung from the seed of my loins would dare to turn on his own blood? You fool! You puny mortal! You will find that I am not thwarted yet, that I cannot be so easily destroyed! You will learn that my revenge has yet to begin, that I can spread it with impunity across the centuries! Time is my friend as it is your enemy, and soon you will be a Dracula, soon you will be my slave, to do my bidding, to obey without question, to be one with my will. Remember, my son Mircea! One day soon . . .'

The rest of his tirade ceased abruptly as a blazing beam detached itself from the roof and fell with a great shower of sparks and roaring flames, crashing into the floor and sending up clouds of smoke that obliterated them completely from my view.

The crash had the effect of making me realize the perilousness of my situation, and I retreated through the door, down the stairway and out into the courtyard.

The flames spread up the old tower, leaping and crackling, and the woodwork was ablaze within seconds. I barely had time to get to the courtyard door before the fire ate its way across the wooden floor and stairway. As I passed out, coughing and choking, I saw my brother Mihail, his face a deathly white, running straight towards the inferno.

'Dracula!' he cried out. 'Dracula!'

I threw myself into his path. In retrospect I know not what madness it was that seized me and urged me to save him. Had he not been in league with the devil himself? Had he not tried to steal my very soul? Yet try to save him I did, perhaps because he was my brother, no matter how corrupt and beyond redemption. Indeed, I threw myself at him, clutching him by the shoulders, and tried to prevent him from his suicidal flight.

'No!' I cried out. 'It is useless, Mihail! They have all perished!'

He gave a scream, long and drawn out, and his eyes flashed with terror.

'*No!*' he screamed.

He threw off my clutching hands as if he had the strength of ten, and I fell against a stone wall and lay there, winded and dazed. Then I glanced up. I saw Mihail run forward. His hands were before him and he cried out for Dracula and then, as if oblivious, he threw himself into the blazing inferno.

I rose unsteadily to my feet and staggered after

him, but the heat of the flames was now so intense that it stayed me at the door. Through the flame and smoke I could see the distorted figure of Mihail, his clothes all aflame, lurching across the hall and up the blazing stairway to the refectory room. I could hear his voice growing fainter and fainter between violent paroxysms of coughing: 'Dracula! Mihail, will save you! Dracula! Drac . . . ul . . . la . . .' His voice disappeared and then the intense heat drove me backward into the courtyard. There I stood for a moment, silent and strangely stricken, cowed by the flames which shot up and gave light to the dark sky.

The sound of frightened horses revived me. The flames were now leaping all over the castle, and I turned and raced for the stables. They were filled with smoke, but as yet there was no sign of any flames. I ran quickly through the stables, undoing the stalls and sending the horses galloping down the mountain road. When I came to the last stall, I threw a saddle over the beast within and mounted. I urged it forward out of the stable, across the smokey courtyard, and finally, heaving a huge sigh of relief, headed down the mountain road, into cold, pure night air, away from the funeral pyre of the voivodes of Wallachia.

It seemed but a moment before I was leaping from the beast in front of the inn at Arefu.

'God save you, mein Herr!' Toma cried, rushing out of the inn and grasping my hand.

'Is the countess all right, Toma?' I asked immediately.

'A few moments ago, mein Herr, she woke as if from a troubled sleep. The colour seemed to flood back into her face as she saw the flames. She is well, mein Herr.'

'Thank God,' I said, and dismounted.

Slowly, one by one, the doors of the houses in Arefu were opening. In ones, twos and threes, silent bands of villagers came out into the street and stood looking up the mountainside. They stood silently. They hardly seemed to move. The flaming pyre on top of the mountain cast its red light on their faces, faces graven with lines of suffering and spiritual torment. But wondrously, with each crackle and explosion of falling wood and masonry, the lines started leaving their faces, the light of relief passing across them, and the spark of gratitude seeming to flicker in their dim eyes.

They stood in silence, as I did, looking to the mountain top until the sun's rays bathed them in a golden glow and Castle Dracula was revealed as a heap of grey-black, smouldering ruins. Only then did the villagers return to their homes, and then, for the first time, at least in my experience, they took down the shutters, removed the blinds, and let in the bright light of life.

Toma smiled and laid his rough hand on my shoulder.

'It is over, mein Herr,' he said. 'Now we can live again.'

I smiled and went into the inn and went up to the bedchamber. My beloved, more beautiful than I had ever imagined her, rose up from the bed and with arms outstretched ran into my encircling embrace.

We left Arefu that same day. Arefu: nestling under the shadow of the charred ruins of the citadel of the Voivode Dracula—Dracula, whose dream of revenge, conquest and immortality had led him into a diabolical tryst with Lucifer himself. Yet the shadows had finally been blown away from Arefu, and we therefore left it happy, the peasants dancing and celebrating, for the first time in years, in the clear, sharp air of a brilliant December day.

* * *

There is little left for me to recount. In Tirgoviste the Countess Irene Bathory married Barone Michelino of Rome and, by easy stages, we returned to my adopted country, Italy. I closed down my palazzo near Piazza Venezia in Rome and bought an estate in the prolific wine producing country of Apulia in the south where I now raise vines in the wild, rugged countryside where the fierce sun and the heavy, though poor, soil makes the coarse wines that I produce admirably suitable for blending. I swear that I now produce the finest full red wine in Italy.

And so I watch the vines grow, and soon, so I have been told, I shall be watching my children grow strong and healthy. I pray God that they will never know the curse of Dracula.

I have long debated whether I should reveal that Dracula's blood flows in my veins. But what matters now? The curse has passed away for all time, and so, safe in that knowledge, I have set pen to paper in the hope that some day my children and future generations may know of the evil that nearly shattered the world and give thanks that it was not so.

Deus vobiscum, 1480 A.D.

Peter Tremayne

Van Helsing's Final Note

ALAS, as Horace wrote, *Nec scire fas est omnia*—it is not permitted to know all things—for Mircea, or Michelino as he preferred to be called, seems to have remained in happy ignorance.

Castle Dracula was not completely destroyed that night, for its edifice still dominates the village of Arefu even to this day, and I have stood in the shadow of its walls. One may even view it in a painting executed by the Swiss Hensie Trenk in 1865, which is a work of excellent quality.

In spite of that last vision of Mihail rushing into the inferno of the castle, by which Michelino thought his brother had perished together with the Undead thing that had been his father, Dracula, Mihail lived on. He managed to save the greater part of the castle from destruction—how, I know not. But this I do know: Mihail lived on to become ruler of Wallachia, known as Mihail cel Rau, or Mihail the Bad. From April 1508 until October 1509 he held Wallachia in thrall, until the people rose to destroy him. Even then he fathered a son called Mircea who gave birth to a line of Wallachian princes, the last of which was one Mihail Radu who was driven out of Wallachia into Transylvania and exile. This Mihail Radu settled in the Borgo Pass in the Carpathians, and it was to this

Castle Dracula that friend Jonathan Harker journeyed to see Count Dracula—for above all, Mihail saved his father, Dracula, from the flames of the castle and, as the world knows to its cost, Dracula survived another four hundred years to spread evil and horror across the face of the earth.

THE END

Dell Bestsellers

- [ ] TO LOVE AGAIN by Danielle Steel $2.50 (18631-5)
- [ ] SECOND GENERATION by Howard Fast $2.75 (17892-4)
- [ ] EVERGREEN by Belva Plain $2.75 (13294-0)
- [ ] AMERICAN CAESAR by William Manchester ... $3.50 (10413-0)
- [ ] THERE SHOULD HAVE BEEN CASTLES
  by Herman Raucher $2.75 (18500-9)
- [ ] THE FAR ARENA by Richard Ben Sapir $2.75 (12671-1)
- [ ] THE SAVIOR by Marvin Werlin and Mark Werlin . $2.75 (17748-0)
- [ ] SUMMER'S END by Danielle Steel $2.50 (18418-5)
- [ ] SHARKY'S MACHINE by William Diehl $2.50 (18292-1)
- [ ] DOWNRIVER by Peter Collier $2.75 (11830-1)
- [ ] CRY FOR THE STRANGERS by John Saul $2.50 (11869-7)
- [ ] BITTER EDEN by Sharon Salvato $2.75 (10771-7)
- [ ] WILD TIMES by Brian Garfield $2.50 (19457-1)
- [ ] 1407 BROADWAY by Joel Gross $2.50 (12819-6)
- [ ] A SPARROW FALLS by Wilbur Smith $2.75 (17707-3)
- [ ] FOR LOVE AND HONOR by Antonia Van-Loon .. $2.50 (12574-X)
- [ ] COLD IS THE SEA by Edward L. Beach $2.50 (11045-9)
- [ ] TROCADERO by Leslie Waller $2.50 (18613-7)
- [ ] THE BURNING LAND by Emma Drummond $2.50 (10274-X)
- [ ] HOUSE OF GOD by Samuel Shem, M.D. $2.50 (13371-8)
- [ ] SMALL TOWN by Sloan Wilson $2.50 (17474-0)

At your local bookstore or use this handy coupon for ordering:

**Dell DELL BOOKS
P.O. BOX 1000, PINEBROOK, N.J. 07058**

Please send me the books I have checked above. I am enclosing $ _____
(please add 75¢ per copy to cover postage and handling). Send check or money order—no cash or C.O.D.'s. Please allow up to 8 weeks for shipment.

Mr/Mrs/Miss _____

Address _____

City _____ State/Zip _____

THE SUPERCHILLER THAT GOES BEYOND THE SHOCKING, SHEER TERROR OF *THE BOYS FROM BRAZIL*

THE AXMANN AGENDA

MIKE PETTIT

1944: Lebensborn—a sinister scheme and a dread arm of the SS that stormed across Europe killing, raping, destroying and stealing the children.
NOW: Victory—a small, mysteriously wealthy organization of simple, hard-working Americans—is linked to a sudden rush of deaths.

Behind the grass-roots patriotism of Victory does the evil of Lebensborn live on? Is there a link between Victory and the Odessa fortune—the largest and most lethal economic weapon the world has ever known? *The Axmann Agenda*—it may be unstoppable!

A Dell Book $2.50 (10152-2)

At your local bookstore or use this handy coupon for ordering:

| Dell | **DELL BOOKS** THE AXMANN AGENDA $2.50 (10152-2)
P.O. BOX 1000, PINEBROOK, N.J. 07058 |

Please send me the above title. I am enclosing $_____
(please add 75¢ per copy to cover postage and handling). Send check or money order—no cash or C.O.D.'s. Please allow up to 8 weeks for shipment.

Mr/Mrs/Miss_____

Address_____

City_____ State/Zip_____

BY REASON OF INSANITY

Shane Stevens
author of *Rat Pack* and *Go Down Dead*

"Sensational."—*New York Post*

Thomas Bishop—born of a mindless rape—escapes from an institution for the criminally insane to deluge a nation in blood and horror. Not even Bishop himself knows where—and in what chilling horror—it will end.

"This is Shane Stevens' masterpiece. The most suspenseful novel in years."—Curt Gentry, co-author of *Helter Skelter*

"A masterful suspense thriller steeped in blood, guts and sex."—*The Cincinnati Enquirer*

A Dell Book $2.75   (11028-9)

At your local bookstore or use this handy coupon for ordering:

| **Dell** | **DELL BOOKS** BY REASON OF INSANITY $2.75 (11028-9)
P.O. BOX 1000, PINEBROOK, N.J. 07058 |

Please send me the above title. I am enclosing $_____
(please add 75¢ per copy to cover postage and handling). Send check or money order—no cash or C.O.D.'s. Please allow up to 8 weeks for shipment.

Mr/Mrs/Miss _____

Address _____

City _____ State/Zip _____

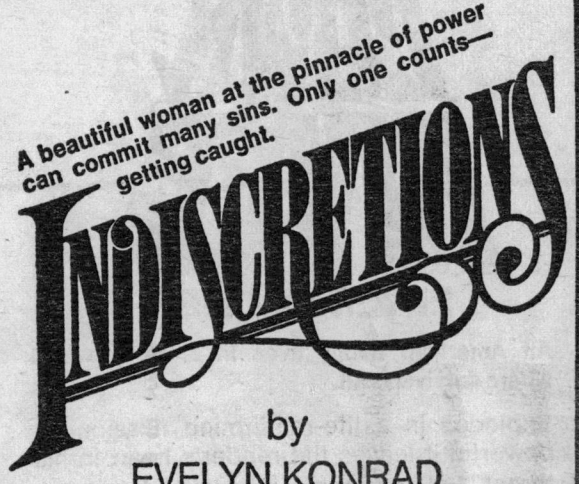

A beautiful woman at the pinnacle of power can commit many sins. Only one counts— getting caught.

INDISCRETIONS

by
EVELYN KONRAD

"Sizzling."—*Columbus Dispatch-Journal*

"The Street" is Wall Street—where brains and bodies are tradeable commodities and power brokers play big politics against bigger business. At stake is a $500 million deal, the careers of three men sworn to destroy each other, the future of an oil-rich desert kingdom—and the survival of beautiful Francesca Currey, a brilliant woman in a man's world of finance and power, whose only mistakes are her *Indiscretions*.

A Dell Book   **$2.50**   **(14079-X)**

At your local bookstore or use this handy coupon for ordering:

| **Dell** | **DELL BOOKS**
 P.O. BOX 1000, PINEBROOK, N.J. 07058 | INDISCRETIONS $2.50   (14079-X) |

Please send me the above title. I am enclosing $_____
(please add 75¢ per copy to cover postage and handling). Send check or money order—no cash or C.O.D.'s. Please allow up to 8 weeks for shipment.

Mr/Mrs/Miss_____

Address_____

City_____ State/Zip_____

DOWN RIVER

PETER COLLIER

An American family lives in a brutal world where survival is all.

"Explodes in a life-reaffirming mission so powerful it leaves the reader's heart in his throat."—*San Francisco Herald Examiner.*

"Brilliantly conceived, beautifully written. Nothing less than superb."—*New York Times.*

"A skillful blend of William Faulkner and James Dickey, author of *Deliverance*. Gripping, moving. A very contemporary tale."—*The Houston Post.*

"A book primarily about family, about continuity, about belonging. A true lyrical touch."—*Newsweek.*

A Dell Book $2.75 (11830-1)

At your local bookstore or use this handy coupon for ordering:

| Dell | **DELL BOOKS**
P.O. BOX 1000, PINEBROOK, N.J. 07058 | Downriver $2.75 (11830-1) |

Please send me the above title. I am enclosing $_____
(please add 75¢ per copy to cover postage and handling). Send check or money order—no cash or C.O.D.'s. Please allow up to 8 weeks for shipment.

Mr/Mrs/Miss_____

Address_____

City_____State/Zip_____